exasperating

exasperating

AN
ELITE
PROTECTION
SERVICES
NOVEL

ONLEY JAMES

EXASPERATING
Elite Protection Services Book 3

Copyright © 2020 Onley James
WWW.ONLEYJAMES.COM

All rights reserved. No part of this publication may be reproduced, stored in a retrieval system, or transmitted, in any form or by any means (electronic, mechanical, photocopying, recording, or otherwise), without the prior written permission of the publisher.

This book is a work of fiction and does not represent any individual living or dead. Names, characters, places, and incidents either are products of the author's imagination or are used fictitiously.

ISBN: 979-8-6194-7435-0

TRIGGER WARNING

This book references past childhood abuse.

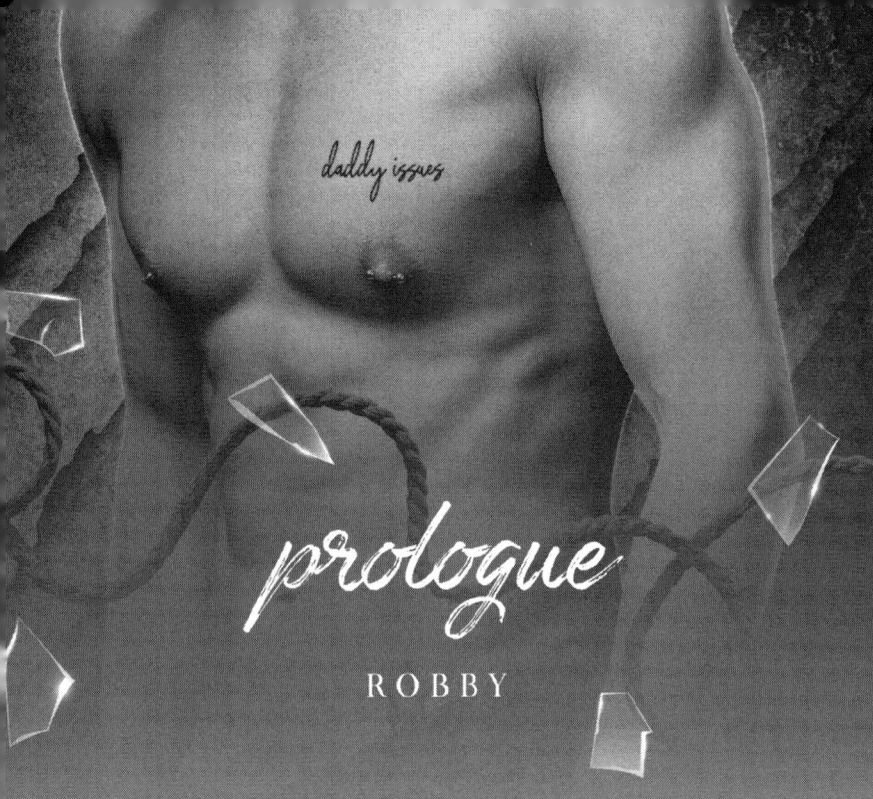

prologue

ROBBY

THIS WAS THE WORST PART OF HIS DAY. THE CHAPEL. Obi didn't know why they called it a chapel when it was really a barn. It smelled like sweat and manure and moldy straw, and there weren't even any animals. It was always dark, even in the daytime, like now. The only light came from the sun shining between the wooden boards that made up the walls and the spots where the black paint had peeled away from the windows.

He pushed his brown hair from his eyes with grimy hands, his fingers cracked and bleeding from digging up rocks the day before. The overalls he wore were too big and rolled up at the ankles. The soft blue shirt

exasperating

he wore with the white plastic buttons was also too big, but his mother had tacked the sleeves up over his elbows so he wouldn't have to keep pushing them up while he worked. He'd started off the morning in his brother's old work boots, but he'd wiggled them off the moment the storm clouds had blotted out the sun.

At the front of the church, his mother stood in a dress the same gray blue as the overcast sky outside. The wind was kicking up a fuss, whistling through the gaps in the planks and causing the rickety building to groan. None of the grown-ups seemed worried about the safety of the building, but Obi had his doubts.

He wasn't sure what was worse, staying outside digging up rocks all day or kneeling on the concrete floor reciting bible verses. Maybe they were equally bad. The adults of the congregation were already in place, on their knees with hands raised as they whispered hissed prayers that made Obi think of a thousand vipers. He didn't understand any of it. His older sister Sarah said it wasn't for him to understand. They just needed to have faith. Faith in what, Obi didn't know. God? He was only twelve, but he was pretty sure God wasn't out here in the middle of nowhere Kentucky watching his mother pour uncooked rice on the cement floor.

All the children of the congregation stood with him

in a line from oldest to youngest. Seven of the thirteen kids were his siblings; his brother Daniel was the youngest at just four years old. The pastor, Samuel, stood in a pair of black pants and an untucked black shirt, his long brownish-blond hair falling to his shoulders. He watched as Obi's mother drew a line with the rice all the way down the row of children. When she finished, Samuel stepped forward, starting with the oldest in the line, his seventeen-year-old sister, Rebecca.

"How are you, sweet Rebecca?" Samuel asked, kissing her knuckles.

His sister giggled. "Well, Brother Samuel. And you?"

He laughed. "I am also well. Even though it is dark skies outside, the light of the lord shines down on all of us, does it not?"

"Yes, Brother Samuel."

"Now, sweet Rebecca, please recite Leviticus 19:15."

Rebecca closed her eyes and squinted. "'You shall do no injustice in court. You shall not be partial to the poor or defer to the great, but in righteousness shall you judge your neighbor.'"

"Excellent, child. Excellent. Please go kneel with the rest of the congregation."

Rebecca pivoted, a smug smile on her face, her

exasperating

white dress twirling around her, one strand of her long brown hair escaping its bun.

Down the line Samuel went. Obi's sixteen-year-old brother, Abel, his fifteen-year-old sister, Sarah, and his fourteen-year-old brother, Jacob, all recited their verses without incident. When he got to thirteen-year-old Ruth, his demeanor changed. Samuel's brown eyes narrowed and his mouth flattened as he stared at the freckle-faced girl with her frizzy ginger hair and her white dress that looked dingy gray from wear.

"Ruth. Your mother says she found you playing in the sunflower fields again. You know we never go past the fence line. You are a stubborn and ornery child. You are confined to your room for the next three days. Now, recite Romans 13:4."

Ruth's eyes grew round and welled with tears. "'For he is God's servant for good… But…'"

Obi's insides slithered at the barest hint of a smile on the old man's face. He didn't understand why Rebecca thought he was nice. There was something so…wrong about him. He ordered people around, made them work all day, while he did nothing. Rebecca wasn't the only one. Both his parents always went out of their way to please Samuel in all things. They said he was a servant of God and his word was God's word, but that didn't make sense to Obi. Wasn't God's word,

God's word? They had a whole book about what Jesus wanted, why couldn't they all just read that?

"Perhaps if you spent less time trespassing and being disobedient and more time studying your verses you wouldn't be struggling now."

Tears streamed down her dirty face. "'For he is God's servant for good. But if you…if you…'"

"That's enough. Kneel."

The girl looked down at the row of uncooked rice. "On that?" she asked, voice wavering.

"'For he is God's servant for your good. But if you do wrong, be afraid, for he does not bear the sword in vain. For he is the servant of God, an avenger who carries out God's wrath on the wrongdoer,'" Obi recited before dropping to his knees on the rice, hissing as the hard grains dug into the tender skin. "I'll take her punishment."

A hand gripped his upper arm, hauling him to his feet and brushing off his knees. "You'll do no such thing, Obidiah Shaw," his mother snapped. "Ruth must answer for her own sins."

"What sin? She couldn't remember a stupid verse. The bible says we're supposed to love one another. Matthew 5:44. 'But I tell you, love your enemies and pray for those who persecute you.'"

His head jerked as his mother slapped him across

exasperating

the mouth hard enough to feel like his eyeball had exploded and his cheek had caught fire, but that didn't stop him. He was right. Jesus taught about love and being good. He didn't want them to punish one another. "Matthew 6:14. 'For if you forgive other people when they sin against you, your Heavenly father will also forgive you.'" His mother began to drag him down the makeshift aisle. "John 13:34. 'A new command I give you. Love one another. As I have loved you, so you must love one another.' John 15:13. 'Greater love has no one than this: to lay down one's life for one's friends,'" Obi continued shouting so that he could be heard over the chatter of the congregation.

Before he could go on, his mother slammed the door of the barn, all but dragging him across the dusty dirt field. Overhead, thunder rumbled and clouds swirled in shades of smoke and ash. He stumbled, his bare feet catching on chunks of rock and weeds. He yelped as his mother yanked him up by his arm. "What is wrong with you?" she shouted. "I don't understand why you're like this. You could be one of his chosen ones."

She hauled him into the small white cabin that his family called home. She tossed him down on the thin mattress that he shared with Daniel before dropping herself into a small wooden chair and putting her face in her hands. "You work hard, you know your bible by heart, but you insist on sticking your nose where it doesn't belong. You can't help everybody."

"That's not fair. What he did wasn't fair. She's just a little kid."

"*You're* a little kid, Obi. Younger than her, and yet, you study hard and you work hard. You cannot keep trying to save people who don't deserve to be saved."

Obi's eyes filled with tears. "That's not what the bible says."

She looked at him with exasperation. "God helps those who help themselves, Obidiah."

"No," he said, his heart racing. That wasn't right. "Jesus helps those who cannot help themselves."

His mother just shook her head. Obi didn't understand why she couldn't see the truth in his words. All of these people read the bible for hours every single day, but they didn't see what he saw. It didn't make any sense. Before he could say anything further, the door crashed open. His father stood there, his expression stormier than the sky outside, his belt in his hand.

"Get up. Now."

Obi did as he was told. He'd take his punishment. He'd take whatever punishment they wanted to give him. He was right. He was right and they were wrong, and he'd let them flay the skin from his body before he

exasperating

betrayed what he knew was the right thing to do.

As his father's belt fell across his back and his bottom, he prayed in silence. He prayed that they would see the truth in his words. He prayed that they would someday understand they were meant to help people, and if that didn't work, he prayed that someday, he'd finally be free from Magnus Dei and free from Brother Samuel, even if it meant letting them kill him.

one

ROBBY

ROBBY SHAW CRACKED OPEN ONE RAW, SWOLLEN EYE, trying to make sense of the images swimming into view around him. Everything was a swirl of lights that made him want to hurl. Also, somebody wouldn't stop screaming. It was relentless. His arms and legs were leaden. He tried to move, but everything hurt. His exposed skin stuck to the vinyl beneath him. It smelled like vomit, or maybe he did. Why did his throat feel like he'd gargled razor blades? Where was he?

He forced himself to focus. He was in a car. He could feel the vibrations of the tires over the road, and his whole body jumped with every imperfection in

exasperating

the asphalt. He was on his stomach, one leg smooshed up against the door, the other on the floorboard. A black grate separated him from a shadowy figure in the driver's seat. Was he in a cab? It smelled like a cab. Another wave of nausea rolled over him, and he shivered as he forced himself not to throw up.

"Let me out," he mumbled over the screaming. "I'll walk home."

"Nice try, kid. Go back to sleep. We'll be there soon."

"Let me out," he demanded, his voice a hoarse shout.

"Kid, are you looking to get tazed again? Relax."

He fumbled for his phone in the pocket of his jeans, smiling when he realized his kidnappers had missed it. He freed it with effort, managing to unlock it with his thumbprint. He pressed the top number, still his emergency contact, and hoped he'd believe him.

The phone rang…and rang…and rang. Robby's heart sank. He was going to die in this smelly vinyl box surrounded by screaming. But then, "'lo?"

"Eli?"

The sound of rustling made Robby pull his phone away, and then a sleepy-sounding Elijah said, "Robby? What's wrong? It's, like"—a yawn broke his speech—"four in the morning?"

Robby's brain fought to put words together, wanting

to get the important stuff out first. "Kidnapped. I don't know where I am. I can't see anything. Can't move. So much screaming. I need you to save Casanova."

"Your dog? Robby? Have you been drinking? Where are you? You don't sound good. Is that a police siren? Tell me where you are, and I'll find somebody to come get you."

He didn't want somebody. He wanted a friend. "You, come get me. Please. You owe me."

Elijah's tone held just enough pity to twist the knife in Robby's heart. "Babe, I live hours away now, remember? Tell me where you are, and I'll get you some help? Do you need a lawyer? An ambulance?"

His heart sank. Elijah was married now. Married to that ginger psycho. They lived in the mountains far away. "Save my dog. Just do that. I don't care what happens to me. I probably deserve it."

He dropped his phone without hanging up and rolled over, burying his face in the crack of the smelly seat. He just wanted to sleep. He'd deal with his kidnappers later. Or maybe not at all. He didn't much care either way. He didn't care about anything really, just Casanova. The thought of his ugly dog made him think of the man he'd named him after. A long-haired, tattooed stranger who'd studied him during the worst day of his life, giving him 'fuck me' eyes in a room full

exasperating

of men in suits. He drifted with a smile on his face. If he was going to die, at least he had that memory.

Robby woke again to a sound like somebody ringing a bell before a boxing match. He scraped bleary eyes open to find a police officer staring at him from behind a set of iron bars. "Up and at 'em, pussycat. You made bail."

Robby groaned as he sat up, the world tilting on its axis until he thought he would vomit. He gripped his head and whimpered. What the hell had happened last night? He tried to recall even a single thing, but it was a giant black hole in his memory. "Bail?"

The officer scoffed. "Yeah, the money you pay to be released from jail after you've made an ass out of yourself."

"I didn't call anybody," Robby said, not entirely sure how true that statement was.

The cop chuckled. "Kid, you called everybody. By the time we'd gotten you to the station, you were ten seconds away from asking the tabloids to bail you out. Don't you have a manager? A lawyer? You're famous. Don't leagues of suits follow you around so you don't do something stupid…like this?"

Something withered inside Robby. He had all of those things. It was about all he had really. Suddenly, a memory flashed through his head. Elijah. He'd called

Elijah. Had Elijah come to bail him out? His heart soared at the thought, crashing and burning at a different question. Had he brought Shepherd? "Who…"

"I did, Obidiah."

That voice… It couldn't be. He never would have called *him*. "I didn't call you."

"Of course, you didn't. The police did. I'm still your father."

Robby drew his knees up to his chest and circled his arms around them. The man—Jebidiah—examined him as if he could see inside, see Robby's intentions. It was strange seeing him again after three years, but he looked much the same. He still wore those same black trousers, the same white collared shirt buttoned all the way to the top. His brown beard was more salt than pepper, and his hair was thinning at the top. The only difference Robby could see was how the lines around his eyes and forehead had deepened to grooves from hard labor under the sun.

"You're not my father. You said so yourself." He looked to the officer. "Give him back his money. I'll just stay here if it's all the same to you."

"Kid, we can't keep this jail cell closed just for you all day. Just 'cause he posted your bail doesn't mean you're required to go with him. But I highly recommend you not stay here. You spent the night

exasperating

calling a lot of people in your drunken stupor. I can only imagine the amount of press outside. I suggest you overlook this little family squabble and maybe take the back exit."

Robby's blood curdled at the idea of accepting anything from that man, but if he could get to his wallet, he would pay him back and then he could walk away. For good. He sighed, forcing himself to his feet, only then becoming aware of the coolness around his midsection. He stumbled to the sink in the corner, splashing water in his face before looking at himself in the shiny metal surface that acted as a mirror. He frowned at his reflection.

His caramel-colored hair stood up in all directions. The skin around his hazel eyes appeared puffy and swollen, his eyes themselves bloodshot. He had a split lip and blood on his earlobe. He wore tight black jeans with rips down the front, leaving his skin peeking through, and white high-top Versace sneakers, but it was his top that left him racking his addled brain. He wore a black crop top hoodie that said 'meow' in large white letters. The sleeves were long, revealing little pink and white paw prints where they hooked over his thumbs. Had he been wearing this when he left the house last night? There was no way.

He stared at his exposed midriff and the two black

stars now tattooed on his hip bones. Those had definitely not been there yesterday. Fuck. He dug his palms into his eye sockets, desperate to remember anything. Anything at all. But there was nothing. He sighed, turning away from the mirror, cringing as the officer gave him a once over and a smirk. He walked past his father without a word, refusing to acknowledge his presence just as he'd done to Robby three years ago.

They stopped at the desk where a pretty uniformed woman with deep umber skin and wild black curls handed him a large clear plastic bag with his belongings, a slightly star-struck look on her face. He smiled at her, and she smiled back reflexively. "Thank you," he managed.

Once in the lobby, he freed his phone from the bag to call Jasmine, his publicist. She was the closest thing he had to a friend.

"Obi, at least let me drop you at your apartment."

He didn't want that man knowing where he lived. He opened his wallet and found his debit card, walking to the ATM in the corner of the precinct. "How much do I owe you?"

"It's not about the money. Come back to the compound with us. We can talk. All of us. Your brothers and sisters miss you."

exasperating

"You haven't worried about me for years. Nothing's changed, Father."

He saw his father step closer from the corner of his eye, his voice dropping to a harsh whisper. "But it has. Your mother saw you…with that girl. She seemed a bit loose of morals, but we are willing to take her into the fold. We're just so happy—"

Robby's lip curled as he cut his father off, raising his voice high enough to draw the attention of the few stragglers milling around. "Happy about what? Happy that I'm heterosexual? Well, plot twist. I'm not. I was just…experimenting. I'm still super gay, Father. Lots of gay sex. All the time. Can't get enough dick."

His father's face flushed an unhealthy red. He snatched Robby's arm, shaking him hard, saliva flying from his mouth as he spit his words at him. "That's enough. I will not stand here and listen to such…filth."

Robby shook his father off his arm. "Go home. There's nothing for you here." He withdrew the maximum the ATM allowed and stuffed it into his father's hand. "We're done now. Leave me alone."

"Wait—" his father started.

A shrill female voice cut him off as she hurried down the hallway from parts unknown. "Robby? Oh, thank God. We thought for sure somebody would have made you their bitch by now."

Robby blinked at the dark-haired girl running toward him with purpose, taking in her black leather romper, red suede thigh-high boots, and obviously fake red fur coat. She looked vaguely familiar. Her companion more so. "Wyatt?" he asked.

Wyatt gave a half-wave, his smile almost shy. "Hey. Elijah asked us to come rescue you from prison."

Robby's heart skipped a bit. "He did?"

It wasn't Wyatt that answered, but the girl. Wyatt's best friend…Magellen? Charlemagne. Charlie. Her name was Charlie. He narrowed his eyes as she spoke as if that might help him focus on her words. "Yeah, he said you'd been kidnapped."

"Kidnapped?"

"Yeah, said you asked him to rescue Casanova and that you'd been kidnapped. It took hours for us to track you down. All we knew was that you were probably being arrested."

Casanova. "What time is it?" He scrambled for his phone. "Oh, God. It's four o'clock in the afternoon. Casanova needs his meds. He needs to eat. He's… delicate. Oh, God. He's been alone for hours."

Robby could feel the tears coming, and the last thing he wanted was to fall apart in front of his father and two virtual strangers.

Wyatt put an arm around him, squeezing him in a

exasperating

side hug. "Hey, relax. Linc sent somebody to rescue Casanova after Elijah's phone call. Don't let anybody in here see you fall apart. It will be all over the news."

Charlie crowded his other side, effectively blocking him from the onlookers. "Are you ready to leave? We have a car waiting out back. We'll take you to Linc's office so you can get your dog, okay?"

He gave a nod, sagging against Wyatt. To his credit, the older boy didn't let go, just steered him towards the hallway, which turned out to be the station's back entrance.

"Obidiah, we aren't finished with this conversation," his father shouted, following behind but not closely.

"Obidiah?" Charlie and Wyatt repeated at the same time.

"That's not my name. Not anymore. Not ever again," Robby snapped. "We are finished, Jebidiah. Go home."

Robby refused to look back. He let Wyatt and Charlie shuttle him into the back of a large SUV. She slammed the door, knocking on the glass that separated them and the driver. As soon as the car lurched into motion, Robby sagged back against the seat, feeling like somebody had exposed every nerve in his body, leaving him raw.

"That's some outfit you got there, kitty cat," Charlie

said before hissing and meowing.

"I don't think anybody dressed like a mobster's mistress gets to point fingers at my fashion choices," Robby managed, not even bothering to open his eyes.

Charlie snickered. "Oh, kitty's got claws. I like it. You're way more fun since Elijah broke your heart."

Robby tried to ignore the way said heart squeezed, a sudden knot forming in his throat. It wasn't Elijah, not really. It was all of it. His pounding head, his burning eyes, seeing his father standing there after all that time, his fear for his dog. The fact that the only people who had come to his rescue were two people he barely knew. He'd never felt so utterly alone…and so very tired.

"Charlie!" Wyatt snapped.

"What? Are we just supposed to pretend all of this is normal? We just rescued our friend's ex-boyfriend from prison where he's dressed like an underage male prostitute and talking to a dude who looked like he should be holding a sickle for a little kid named Malachi in some Nebraska cornfield. I have a lot of questions, so let's just confront the Elijah-shaped elephant in the car. Is this Miley level meltdown really because Elijah broke your heart?"

To Robby's horror, the sob he'd been holding back escaped. He pressed his fist to his lips but it was too

exasperating

late. Tears welled in his eyes, burning his already irritated skin.

Wyatt shot Charlie a scathing look. "See what you did?"

Charlie sucked in a breath. "Oh, no. I'm sorry. Come to mama. Let it all out." She patted her lap.

Robby eyed her warily, annoyed that he wanted to let this strange girl comfort him, but Wyatt gave him a gentle shove and a reassuring smile. "Go ahead. She won't stop nagging until you do. She's powered by gay tears."

Robby didn't have the emotional capacity to even try to fight her. He just let himself slump over until Charlie cradled his head in her lap. "That's it. Go ahead and cry it out."

He did. Not gross body wracking sobs, but tears streamed down his face as he lay there feeling sorry for himself. Charlie's scary claw-like nails felt nice as they combed through his hair and she crooned nonsense at him like a baby. At some point, he dozed off, but not before an awful thought struck him: What if this was all there was for him?

two

CALDER

CALDER SETON HAD BEEN GIVEN MANY STRANGE TASKS since he'd started working with Elite Protection Services, but babysitting the world's ugliest dog definitely topped the list. Lincoln had called him before the sun came up with a strange request. Go to the address given and retrieve the hideous beast, gather his supplies, and take said beast back to his apartment until further notice.

It had taken forty minutes to coax the dog out of hiding and longer still to gather up the list of supplies. He wasn't sure whose apartment he had skulked around in but they clearly loved this dog. He'd taken

exasperating

the containers full of fancy dog food from the fridge and the sparkly red bowls from the floor before spending far too much time searching for the box Linc said would be in a cabinet somewhere in the owner's tidy bedroom. He'd finally found the black and white polka dot box with 'Casanova' emblazoned across it in red glitter letters under the bathroom sink. Inside was an assortment of medications and tubes full of creams for what Calder imagined were the dog's many ailments.

Calder had spent the next ten or so hours in his apartment having a staring contest with the creature, now convinced it was more muppet than canine. It clearly had an unfair advantage as Calder was almost positive the dog's eyes were looking in different directions, which made him feel unsafe somehow. It was tiny, like the kind of dog one of his socialite clients carried in their overpriced handbags. But no self-respecting socialite would be caught dead with this dog.

The thing was pale and hairless except for the strange tufts of black fluff growing sparsely at its ankles and the tip of its tail. The small amount of hair on its head formed a mohawk, but Calder thought it looked deliberate, like a defense mechanism to warn people away, as if that would ever be a problem.

Its teeth were too big, giving it an overbite, and his tongue lolled out of his mouth at all times.

Despite its demonic appearance, the dog made no noise. It never growled or barked. Even when he'd entered the overpriced apartment, it was painfully silent. It took him forever to find it, lurking like some mutant sewer rat just behind the toilet. He couldn't even begin to imagine why his boss would have need for such a creature, but it wasn't his place to ask questions. He was just glad his babysitting duties had finally come to an end.

As he passed the conference room, he saw the boss's husband, Wyatt, sitting on the conference room table with his friend, Charlie, who dressed like she'd just left the night shift off Hollywood and Vine. They faced away from him, talking to somebody who sat in a chair in front of them, but he couldn't see who it was. He could only make out ripped jeans and pristine white sneakers. He shrugged off his curiosity, eager to unburden himself of the gremlin trembling in his arms.

He didn't knock on Linc's door before entering as it already sat slightly ajar. His boss sat behind the huge mahogany desk in jeans and a black EPS polo shirt that hugged huge biceps, signing papers while his assistant, Emma, sat in the chair opposite him. Emma leaned forward, pointing at things on the page. "And

exasperating

sign there, too. And then that's it. I'll get these over to Jack, and then I'm going to dinner if that's okay with you?"

Linc grunted in the affirmative, glancing up when Calder entered, one brow hooking upward at his new canine companion.

"You wanna tell me why I just had to spend hours guarding the world's ugliest dog?" Calder drawled, holding up said dog.

Linc ignored his question. "Emma, can you take the animal to the kids? Then you can have the rest of the evening off. It's already pretty late in the day."

Emma nodded, scooping the dog out of Calder's arms and taking the bag full of supplies off his shoulder, glowering at him all the while.

Calder grinned at her retreating back, amused by her mysterious hostility. "What'd I do to her?"

Linc gestured for Calder to sit. "She's the one who took the call from Kirsch yesterday."

Calder fought the urge to roll his eyes. It *was* a trap. Linc had only asked for his help to lure him into the office for yet another talking to. Were bait dogs a thing? He really wasn't cut out for the politics of corporate work. There were just so many rules.

He sprawled in the chair opposite Linc, sweeping his long dark hair off his shoulders and securing it with an elastic band. "What about Kirsch?" he asked, hopeful he read the situation wrong.

Linc scoffed. "What do you think? He's furious. He's demanding his money back."

Outside, the sun pierced the veil of clouds, sending a beam of light through the window, pinning him in place and forcing him to squint. "He's overreacting, man. You know how these rich folks are," Calder hedged, refusing to admit to any wrongdoing until he knew what Linc knew.

Charged silence filled the room as Linc fixed him with a dead stare. "You fucked his wife…and his son."

Yep. There it was. What could he say? "Not at the same time?"

Calder wondered which one of them blabbed. Probably the housekeeper. At least Linc didn't know about her. He hoped.

Linc flopped back in his chair, exasperation leaching into his tone. "Your job is to keep his family alive, not stick your dick in them."

Calder snorted, another grin spreading over his face. "Did they die?" he drawled, letting the Texan seep into his voice. "No. In fact, it might be the first time they ever truly lived. My dick changes lives, man."

"Stop sticking your magical dick in my clients," Linc boomed. Calder winced, glancing towards the

exasperating

windowed wall where the rest of the office all stood frozen, staring at the two of them with interest. Wyatt and Charlie both faced him now, laughing, but Calder's eyes locked on the boy sitting between them. Robby Shaw. The jilted cupcake of Oscar-winning actor, Elijah Dunne. The boy didn't laugh like the others. If anything, he looked shocked. Almost as shocked as Calder felt seeing the boy again after all that time. Something about the way that kid looked at him still went straight to his dick. Now was definitely not the time to get a boner.

He forced himself to look away, turning back to his furious friend. "Linc, I'm not trying to be an asshole, but I feel the need to point out that both you and Shepherd married the only clients you were ever charged with watching. Hell, at this point Jackson might as well call this place Elite Protection and Matchmaking Services. I submit that I'm being unfairly targeted and punished not because I fuck our clients but because I just refuse to marry all of them afterward, and honestly, it's starting to feel a bit like discrimination."

The vein on Linc's forehead started to throb. Calder may have felt sorry for the man if he didn't know Linc lived for this shit. He loved running a command, even if his team consisted of misfits and headcases. Calder had a foot firmly in each camp. "Come on, man. I promise I'll try to stop being so goddamn irresistible." Linc shook his head. Calder assumed that meant the verbal spanking was over. "So, tell the truth, did you have me kidnap that...mutant as some kind of punishment?"

Linc nodded toward the conference room. Robby snuggled the hideous dog against his chest, feeding him something from a dropper. Once more, the boy's gaze met Calder's, like he sensed him watching. It sent a jolt of adrenaline through him. Calder felt like he was held captive by the boy's stare, freed only once he dropped his gaze back to his canine companion. "What's he doing here?" Calder managed.

"Not sure. Shep said Elijah got a call at four in the morning their time with the boy out of it, claiming he'd been kidnapped. Shep heard a police siren and figured the kid was drunk or high in the back of a police car, which proved to be correct. He just kept going on and on about his dog. Shep called me, asked me to ping the kid's cell phone, Wyatt stuck his nose where it didn't belong as usual, and he and Charlie went to spring the kid from county lockup where he'd been picked up for a drunk and disorderly and assaulting a police officer."

Calder snorted. "Assaulting a police officer? Angel face in there? The kid is the personification of a basket of kittens. What did he assault him with? Kindness?"

Linc's lips twitched as he tried to keep a straight face. "A twelve-inch black dildo known as the 'hole wrecker.'"

Calder turned back to look at the boy who was adamantly not looking in their direction any longer. When he turned back around, he and Linc both started to laugh. "Well, that would definitely piss off a patrolman."

"Oh, he was pissed alright. He pepper sprayed and tased your adorable basket of kittens in there."

That wiped the smirk off Calder's face, a tightness forming in his chest. "That's fucking excessive. What does he weigh? A buck fifty, maybe? We should be suing for excessive force."

"We?" Linc inquired.

Calder snorted. "You know what I mean. He's friends with Elijah. He's friends with Wyatt and Charlie. He's in the fold. He's one of us." Linc examined Calder without speaking until he said, "Don't look at me like that. He's not a client."

There was a knock on the door, and then Wyatt entered without waiting for an invitation. He sauntered past Calder and walked to Linc, helping himself to the man's lap. Linc automatically curled an arm around him. "Robby wants to go home and shower. You think he should see a doctor first? That taser burn looks pretty bad and his eyes are swollen."

"I'll take him home," Calder heard himself volunteer.

Wyatt locked eyes with Calder, both brows raising before a smirk crossed his lips. "Yeah, okay. You should take him home and maybe stay with him for a little bit. He's kind of shaken up."

"Wyatt…" There was no mistaking the warning in Linc's voice.

Wyatt turned those guileless green eyes on his husband, batting his lashes. "Well, I guess I could go spend the night with Robby. I mean, you and I had plans, but if you're that worried about Calder potentially having his way with a fully grown adult not paying Elite for services…I'm willing to put off our plans. But tonight was the night we were going to…" He leaned down and whispered something in the boss's ear. Linc's hand squeezed Wyatt's thigh reflexively as the boy talked.

His eyes flicked to Calder. "Fine, go. Just don't… You know what? It's not my business."

Linc bent to kiss Wyatt's neck. The boy winked at Calder and gestured for him to get lost. Calder shook his head but left before he was as traumatized as everybody else on the other side of Linc's glass walls would likely be in five minutes.

exasperating

Calder stopped at the conference room door where Robby sat snuggling his demonic looking dog. "Come on, angel face. I'm gonna give you a ride."

Charlie choked on a laugh. "Well, damn, Calder. Right here in the conference room. I thought only Linc was allowed to do that."

"Get thee behind me, hooker Barbie. I have no time for your forked tongue today. I've been asked to take the boy home and make sure he gets to his apartment okay."

"Asked by who? 'Cause there is no way Linc dangled this sweet little morsel in front of you and asked you to take him home…to his apartment…where he lives all alone."

"Don't listen to her, angel face. I'll be a perfect gentleman…if that's what you want."

Charlie rolled her eyes. "Robby, I'll take you—"

"No, it's fine. He can take me, er, us. He can take us," Robby stammered, dropping the dog's things back into the bag and pulling it onto his shoulder. "I just really need to get home and take a shower."

"I can help with that." Calder grinned. When the boy's eyes went wide, Calder said, "Getting you home, that is."

"Gross," Charlie muttered before sliding off the conference room table. "Don't fall for his stupid lines,

Robby, or the only shower you'll need is one of those Silkwood decontamination showers. That dude's dick has given more rides than Uber."

Calder clicked his tongue. "Oh, don't be like that. I heard you *love* Uber."

Charlie flicked him off. "I will not be shamed. That dude was hot and definitely not a virgin, unlike this pristine, untouched boy."

The boy in question made a face at both of them. "Uh, this is getting weird. Can he just take me home now?"

Calder put an arm around Robby's shoulder, guiding him from the conference room. "Of course, I can."

When he looked behind him, Charlie wasn't looking at them but at Wyatt who was no longer making out with his husband but watching them with a look that Calder could only describe as conniving. What the hell were those two up, too? It was probably better not to know.

three

ROBBY

ROBBY TRIED TO CALM HIS NERVES THE ENTIRE RIDE home, but it was impossible with the man who starred in all of his most recent jerk-off fantasies sitting not two feet away from him in the front seat of his fancy pickup truck. He felt like he should say something, but he just couldn't seem to find his tongue. By agreeing to allow Calder to take him home, to escort him up to his apartment, it was like he had agreed to something more, and now Robby's heart was a snare drum, pounding an offbeat rhythm in his ears.

For all of Charlie's talk, she was right about Robby. He was a virgin. In every sense of the word. Other than three fake kisses he'd shared on camera and the chaste pecks he'd exchanged with Elijah for show, the only real kisses he'd ever had were with a girl he was too drunk to even remember. He was starting to think there was something really wrong with him. He was twenty-one years old and people treated him like he had an invisible forcefield nobody wanted to penetrate, and Robby really wanted somebody to penetrate him. He glanced over at the man behind the wheel singing softly and tapping out a rhythm on the steering wheel, completely unaware of Robby's panic. He didn't want just somebody. He wanted Calder.

Calder was perfect. He was a self-proclaimed manwhore, so maybe Robby shouldn't be surprised the man made no effort to hide that he was willing and able to tend to Robby's immediate needs. Maybe Calder just never said no to anybody. Maybe he was literally working through a list of everybody in LA and this was just his day to scratch Robby off his to-do list. The thought made his chest feel tight, so he pushed it away. Robby had wanted Calder since the day he'd spotted him in that conference room, watching Robby like he was the only person there. It had made him feel vulnerable, like somebody had ripped off his invisibility cloak and left him standing naked in a room full of strangers. But it had also warmed his insides. Somebody had finally noticed him.

Robby sneaked another glance at the man beside him. Calder was beautiful in a roughneck kind of way, like the boys Robby would see in town growing up back home in Kentucky. His chestnut hair was looped onto his head in a messy top knot that should have looked ridiculous but on him just managed to highlight how little he gave a shit about rules. He wore a sleeveless Metallica shirt covered in holes and paint splotches, and his well-muscled arms were covered in gorgeous swirls of colorful ink, all tribal in nature. His beard managed to accent his perfect jawline instead of hiding it, and he had chocolate brown eyes that looked almost black in the shadows of the truck cab.

"You seem to be thinking some awfully deep thoughts over there. You alright?"

No. That drawl of Calder's did things to Robby. That slow, easy way he talked, like he liked to taste the words before he released them into the universe. Robby wanted to know what those words sounded like whispered in his ear or growled against his skin. He shivered, shifting uncomfortably, his cock semi-hard at the thought.

"You cold, angel face?"

"Why do you call me that?" Robby blurted.

Calder chuckled. "You're joking."

Robby shook his head, swallowing hard. "Why would I joke about that?"

"I call you angel face because you have the sweetest face I've ever seen."

"Like a baby?" Robby muttered, his heart sinking.

Calder risked a glance at him. "Don't pout, sweetness. I've spent more than one night thinking about dirtying up that angelic face."

Once more, a nervous thrill shot through him. He wasn't entirely sure what that meant but it sounded promising. "You're coming upstairs with me, right?" Robby asked as they crept to a halt at the valet.

This time, Calder looked him in the eye, his gaze weighted with promise. "Is that what you want?"

Robby nodded, trying to find his voice. "Yeah," he finally managed. "That's what I want."

Calder grinned. "Well, alright."

Calder hopped from the truck, tossing the valet his keys before coming around and opening Robby's door, taking the bag, and leaving Robby to carry Cas. The ride up to the tenth floor seemed to take forever, especially with six other people on the elevator, giving Robby's ridiculous outfit a curious stare, and Calder standing close enough for his thumb to trace over the back of Robby's hand, making his stomach do cartwheels.

exasperating

By the time the doors opened, Robby was rock hard and Calder had barely touched him. He was pathetic. His hand shook as he fumbled with his keys until Calder took them from him and opened the door. Robby immediately put the dog down and turned, running straight into a wall of muscle.

Calder gripped Robby's hips, steadying him, his thumbs tracing over the new ink on his hip bones. "I really like this top you're wearing, but I bet you'd look even better without those jeans on."

Robby was almost positive his heart stopped. Calder was close enough for Robby to feel the heat of his body, to smell peppermint and something slightly chemical. Robby gripped Calder's shirt in his fists, feeling the need to hold onto something. He needed to speak but fear had robbed him of his voice.

Calder leaned in close enough for his beard to scratch against Robby's cheek. "You scared of me, angel face?" he asked, tone teasing but not mean.

"I'm scared of everything," Robby heard himself whisper.

"I won't hurt you," Calder promised, all traces of teasing gone. "I can go anytime you want."

Frustration leached into Robby's voice. "I don't want you to go… I just don't know what to do," he admitted, wanting to crawl into a hole. There was nothing sexy about this conversation. Robby refused to look at him. He couldn't. "Never mind. Let's just forget…whatever this was."

He turned to head to the bedroom but found himself turned right back around, Calder's finger under his chin, forcing his gaze upward. "Is that what you really want?"

A million thoughts assaulted Robby at once. *No. Not at all. Stay with me. Fuck me. Spend the night. Spend the rest of your life. Or mine.* All Robby could do was shake his head.

Calder's lips grazed Robby's forehead. "You want to take a shower with me?"

"Yes, please," Robby whispered, breathless.

Calder cupped his face, gazing at him with a look Robby just couldn't place.

"Jesus, you're sweet," Calder finally said. "Lead the way."

Robby did as Calder asked, feeling like he had stopped breathing an hour ago. He had no idea what he was doing or how this had happened, but it seemed inevitable, like this was the final domino to fall in a line they'd pushed over months ago.

Calder took the lead, which Robby appreciated. His hands were shaking too hard to be of use anyway. He watched as Calder turned on the tap to the fancy rain shower, testing the water. Once he seemed to decide it was the right temperature, he released his hair from its elastic, letting it waterfall down his broad shoulders, before peeling his shirt over his head and dropping it to the floor. Robby itched to touch the springy hair on Calder's chest and taut ridges of his abdomen but couldn't seem to move. He swallowed hard as Calder moved into his space. He picked Robby up, depositing him on the lip of the sink, spreading his legs and stepping between them.

"Your turn," he murmured, large hands caressing over Robby's skin as his hoodie went over his head to join Calder's shirt on the floor. He traced the words scrawled in ink over Robby's heart, causing goosebumps to erupt along his skin. He blushed. He hated that tattoo. *Daddy issues*. "Mm, is that so?" Calder asked before his fingers found the bars that pierced the stiff peaks of Robby's nipples.

He sucked in a shaky breath but sat frozen.

"You are just full of surprises, angel," Calder whispered before his lips found Robby's.

Calder kissed like he talked, slow like he was in no rush, brushing his lips over Robby's again and again, each time lingering a bit longer until Robby opened up for him, wanting more. When Calder's tongue slipped inside, Robby whimpered, overwhelmed. Was this what kissing always felt like? If kissing Calder felt like this, what would actual sex feel like?

"Fuck, so sweet," Calder drawled against his lips once more before pulling back and unbuttoning his jeans. "Water's gonna get cold."

Robby couldn't look away. He licked his lower lip as Calder removed his jeans and underwear, leaving him naked and hard in Robby's bathroom. Everything about Calder was beautiful, even his erection, flushed red and twitching under Robby's scrutiny. "Now you, angel face. What else are you hiding underneath that choirboy exterior?"

Once more, his inner voice flooded his brain with answers. *Fear. Anxiety. Loneliness. An unhealthy obsession with gangsta rap and mochi.* Robby let Calder pull him to his feet, trying not to orgasm on the spot as Calder dropped to his knees to remove Robby's sneakers and socks before undressing him. Calder was close enough to feel his breath on Robby's thigh. He bit down on his lip as Calder examined his hard and leaking cock. "Uncut," Calder whispered. "Christ, you're perfect."

Robby didn't think it was possible to blush harder but he did. He let Calder lead him into the shower, sighing as the hot water pelted his aching body. He leaned his forehead against the cool tiles, wondering if he still

exasperating

looked like somebody had thrown battery acid in his eyes. That couldn't be sexy. Could Calder see the burn on his hip where the taser prongs had pressed against his skin? Before Robby could spiral further down the rabbit hole of crippling insecurity, Calder pulled him from the wall and began shampooing his hair.

Robby had never had anybody wash his hair before outside of a salon. Calder massaged his scalp, the blunt scrape of his nails dragging a moan from Robby. Was this what real relationships were like? He sagged against Calder, just letting the man take care of him. Soapy hands began to move along Robby's chest and belly, scrubbing each part of him. When Calder went to his knees behind him once again, Robby held his breath, but Calder simply washed his feet, dropping kisses to the dimples on his back and the painful burn on his hip before standing again. It was maddening. Why wasn't he doing more?

Robby made a noise of frustration.

Calder chuckled. "What's wrong, angel face? You want something?"

He nodded, before whispering, "Yes."

Calder's lips found the spot just behind Robby's ear, and his fingers tugged at Robby's nipples hard enough to make his whole body feel like one live wire. "This what you want? You want me to play with you?"

"I… Yes… I don't know. I just want more. I need you to touch me."

Calder bit down on his earlobe, one hand sliding low on his belly. "I am touching you. Can't you feel me?"

Robby could feel him, could feel Calder's erection pressed against his lower back, could feel his arms around him. It was perfect, but it just wasn't enough… not nearly enough. "Don't tease me."

Calder turned him around, capturing his lips once more. "I haven't even started teasing you, sweetness. But I'll give you what you need."

Robby almost cried when Calder wrapped his slick fist around Robby's cock, his eyes sliding closed and his hands gripping Calder's biceps. "Oh, God."

"Open your eyes, angel. Look at me." Robby forced himself to comply. "Fuck, you're so fucking beautiful. I wanna watch you come."

That was all it took. Robby cried out in surprise as waves of pleasure rolled along his body, his knees all but giving out on him. Calder's arm kept him upright, his hand pumping Robby's spent cock until there was nothing left. He clung to Calder long after his hand disappeared, feeling embarrassed by this sudden need to hold onto something.

To his credit, Calder didn't seem in a hurry to release him. They just stood there, testing the limits of Robby's hot water tank, his forehead resting on Calder's shoulder and his arms around him. The older man was probably regretting ever offering to give Robby a ride home. He glanced down, looking at Calder's still hard cock. Robby's hand was moving before he could talk himself out of it, wrapping around Calder, marveling at the velvet feel of his skin.

Calder moaned, and Robby's heart did somersaults. He did that. He did it again, experimenting. He had no other frame of reference, so he did what he liked, twisting as he stroked, letting his thumb tease over the head before sliding back down. Calder leaned his shoulders back against the shower wall. "Fuck, that's it, angel. Keep going."

Robby did. He jerked Calder, studying his face, watching how every stroke, every squeeze affected him until he was only doing the things that pulled low moans and deep groans from him. This was the real drug, this heady power of making somebody fall apart. He understood why Calder had wanted to watch Robby's face, had needed to see the fruits of his labor. Robby wanted to make Calder orgasm almost more than he'd wanted to come himself. By the time Calder was panting, fists clenched, eyes closed, Robby was half hard again just from watching.

"Oh, fuck. I'm gonna come." He was thrusting

himself up into Robby's fist now, doing most of the work himself. Then he was giving a rough shout, his body going rigid.

Robby didn't know where to look. He was addicted to the shocky look of ecstasy on Calder's face, but he also liked watching Calder's cock erupt, his seed coating Robby's fingers before washing away under the water. Calder took the choice away from him, pushing his hand away and spinning him until he was the one pressed against the wall, Calder's mouth on his, tongue sliding over Robby's. He could only hang on as Calder pressed words against his lips. "Fuck, you did so well. God, you're fucking perfect. So fucking perfect."

four

CALDER

CALDER WAS IN OVER HIS HEAD. AFTER THEIR SHOWER, he'd dried the boy off and put him to bed. Now, he lay beside him, watching him sleep. Robby was a walking contradiction. He was a famous Hollywood actor. Maybe not household name famous but certainly recognizable on the street, yet it was clear the moment Calder kissed him that Charlie had vastly underestimated exactly how virginal Robby was. He kissed with abandon, touched Calder like he was a work of art, and came apart in the sweetest way imaginable. It stirred something in Calder, something deep inside that he'd worked hard to wall off years ago.

Fuck. Linc was right. Calder was a fucking liability. He'd been so determined to have Robby, to test this strange pull he'd felt toward the boy, that he'd completely ignored every red flag. He could have ended it with a kiss when he realized how little experience Robby had. He could have walked away. He should have just walked away. Virgins came with feelings and responsibilities. All the things Calder avoided like the plague. But Robby had just stared up at him with those innocent eyes, frustration leaching into his voice as he'd tried to ask for what he'd wanted. Calder wasn't strong enough to resist a temptation like that. He didn't understand how any man could.

It was hard to imagine how somebody like this boy had gone unnoticed, but he'd clearly been neglected. Daddy issues. That's what the boy's tattoo said. He believed it. Robby had been running amuck since Elijah had 'cheated' on him with Shepherd. It was clear their fake relationship had been plenty real to Robby, no matter how mismatched the two had been. Now, he took his pain out on himself, drinking, partying, turning his body into a roadmap of piercings and poorly thought out tattoos.

Calder liked the boy's piercings, liked the way he gasped when he played with his nipples, and liked the odd little piercing that sat just inside the boy's upper lip, resting against his two front teeth. He wanted to play with him, was hard as steel imagining coaxing the boy's body to let him inside. He couldn't remember the last time anybody had captured his attention the way Robby did. Calder was content just to watch the boy sleep, liked knowing he was safe at home and not out being abused or accosted by police officers or worse…strippers.

Except, this wasn't Calder's home and Robby wasn't his to watch. He was just some kid he'd crossed paths with whose big hazel eyes and infectious smile had gotten under Calder's skin. Maybe it was that Robby never smiled anymore. Before Elijah, there wasn't a single photo of Robby where he wasn't flashing his gorgeous smile and perfect teeth. Now, Robby always looked guarded or angry or too drunk to stand.

Calder rolled off the bed and dressed, taking Casanova's food from the fridge and placing it on the floor in his bowl, so the dog would let the boy sleep for a little while at least. He had to get out of there. Every minute he stayed, he just wanted to stay longer. That wasn't going to work. Still, he felt like a dick just sneaking out, so he snagged a paper towel and a sharpie.

Had to go. Didn't want to wake you.
Call if you ever need me.

XO Calder

He scrawled his number along the bottom, then stared at the XO. Why had he done that? This kid was a Jedi, playing mind games with Calder. He slipped back into the boy's darkened bedroom and set the note on the side table, hesitating before he dropped a kiss on the boy's slightly gaping mouth.

Calder replayed their shower on repeat the entire ride home. It shouldn't have affected him like it had. It was just one fumbling handjob. He'd been with countless men and women who knew tricks that would make porn stars jealous. Hell, he'd even been with an actual porn star once or twice. But the way Robby had gazed up at him, bottom lip trapped between his teeth as he'd worked Calder's cock, laser focused on what Calder liked and what made him moan… It was like the kid was trying for an A plus. He'd earned it. Calder's orgasm had ripped through his body like lightning, leaving him drained and shaken.

Part of him knew it wasn't the technique but the boy, but that part of him needed to shut the fuck up. There was no room in his life for somebody like Robby. That boy was so desperate for love that it practically oozed from his pores. He needed somebody who could give him constant praise, constant attention, could wrap him up and be the safety net he clearly needed. That wasn't Calder. It couldn't be. Calder couldn't be that person for him, for anybody. He'd proven that a long time ago.

Once inside his small apartment, he tried to shake off the nagging feeling tugging at his insides. He went to the fridge and cracked a beer before heading into what would be the dining room for most people. He flipped on the lights and set a new canvas on the easel before pulling his hair back up and off his face. He slipped his phone from his pocket to turn on his music but paused when he saw he had a new voicemail. He keyed up his messages and sat on top of the old butcher block table that subbed as his desk.

"Mr. Seton, this is Ginger at Vista Palms Funeral Home. We've been trying to reach you for several weeks regarding the remains of—"

Calder hit the button to delete the message and picked up his beer, draining half in one swallow before he pulled up his classic rock playlist and cranked it up as loud as he could. Mrs. Leighton across the hall was deaf as a post and the apartment below him had sat empty for months. His music wouldn't bother anybody, but maybe it would drive the memories from his head.

He skipped his paints, instead grabbing a charcoal pencil, roughly sketching an outline of a boy with a sharp jawline, wide almond-shaped hazel eyes, and swoopy caramel-colored hair. Maybe he could draw the boy out of his system, pour his need onto the canvas, and then burn it. Even the thought of burning the boy's face sent a pang through him. This kid was so deep under his skin and they'd only ever interacted twice. It didn't make any sense. Calder didn't form attachments. Not to anybody. Not anymore.

After he'd constructed a rough sketch, he switched to his paints, losing himself in the broad strokes and the minute details, anything to keep from thinking about the real boy whose likeness he created or the task he'd been putting off for weeks. He found himself mixing brown and green and gold to try to create Robby's eyes, layering each one onto the canvas until the boy on the canvas stared back at Calder with the same wide-eyed expression he'd worn just before they'd showered together. That look was like a punch to the gut, and Calder immediately wanted to cover it up.

It was early morning before Calder considered the painting done. If he'd hoped to excise Robby from his brain, the project was an epic failure. He cleaned up the space and washed his hands in the sink before throwing a microwave burrito in to cook. Linc needed to find a job for him soon or he was going to go crazy. He couldn't stay cooped up in this apartment, but he had no interest in going out since Carley had called with the news.

He ate his burrito in front of the television, staring at the blackened screen as if it might contain the answers he sought. He needed to do it. He needed to go pick up her ashes and do…something…with them. He didn't know what. He'd hardly known her, not really. He hadn't known her as a person. Would she want her ashes scattered along the ocean waves? Would she want to be sprinkled in a forest somewhere? Hell, maybe she wanted to be a tree? He didn't know and the not knowing was what left him paralyzed, unable to pick up the phone, refusing to return their calls. If he just ignored them, maybe they'd go away. What did it matter in the long run? In the end, she was just a pile of dust in a cardboard box.

He finished off his burrito and his third beer and got ready for bed, hoping that the food and alcohol would be just enough to make him sleep. It wasn't. He lay there, staring at the ceiling, wondering if Robby had woken up hours ago and found Calder had crept out like a jerk or if he was still sleeping soundly after his rough night and mutual orgasms.

Calder slid his hand into his black cotton pants, his fist gripping his cock as he thought about Robby and their brief time together. The whimper he'd made when Calder kissed him. How he'd gripped Calder's shirt when he slid his thumbs over his hips. He was so fucking gorgeous. Everything about him was bright and vibrant. He just radiated this energy, even after everything he'd been through, and Calder wanted to bathe in it, wanted to see Robby discovering what he liked and what he didn't, wanted to feel him coming apart beneath him, wanted to be the one who worked him open and showed his body how to yield to Calder's invasion. He'd never been anybody's first anything, but the idea of being Robby's first had him coming hard, a hoarse shout penetrating the silence of his room.

He lay there, panting, cum cooling on his skin and his pants sticking to him uncomfortably, wondering what the fuck was wrong with him. It was clearly just the stress of the phone call. His past coming back to bite him in the ass. He'd been better off when all he'd had to do was send a check every month. He hadn't signed on for funerals or burials. That was for the old Calder, the responsible Calder. The ranger Calder.

That Calder was dead.

This Calder lived free of commitments and responsibilities, fucked like a rock star, and screwed up as much as possible. He liked being this Calder. He needed to be this Calder. It was the only way for him to stay sane.

five

ROBBY

"SO, YOU JERKED EACH OTHER OFF, AND THEN HE SNUCK out in the middle of the night. Hate to say I told you so…" Charlie said, scratching her nails along Robby's scalp before she took another sip of her wine.

Robby's head swam from too much merlot. He didn't know what was more disturbing, how comfortable he was around Charlie and Wyatt or the fact that Charlie wasn't talking to Robby when she said 'I told you so.' That comment she aimed at Wyatt who sat opposite her at the other end of Robby's sofa.

Wyatt scoffed. "What do you mean? It totally worked."

"How?" Charlie all but shrieked. "All our sweet baby gay got was a handjob and heartache."

"I wouldn't say I'm heartbroken—" Robby started only to be cut off once again by Wyatt.

"Exhibit A," Wyatt crowed, waving the paper towel Calder had left behind. "He put his personal phone number, not his work phone."

Charlie waved her wine glass precariously over Robby's head, her words slurring. "Okay, that's flimsy at best."

"I'm not done. We also have this." Wyatt stabbed at the paper where Calder had scrawled XO.

Robby's heart tripped in his chest. He'd folded and refolded the paper towel enough for it to look battered even though it was only three days old. It was the XO that had thrown Robby, too. What did it mean? Did it mean anything? It was hard to know.

Charlie blew out a breath through her nose. "Okay, that is…odd. I'll give you that. But still, something spooked him." She turned an accusatory gaze towards Robby. "Did you do something clingy? Did you cry or say 'I love you'?"

Robby swung himself into a sitting position, the world tilting on its axis. "What? No. I didn't do anything… I mean, I don't think I did. We did…what we did, and then he just dried us off and tucked me

exasperating

in and told me to get some sleep. Then he crawled in beside me. I fell asleep. When I woke up, he was gone and this"—he plucked the note from Wyatt's fingers, refolding it carefully—"was on the bedside table." He sighed. "He even fed Cas before he left."

Wyatt and Charlie exchanged glances.

"Will you two stop doing that?" Robby snapped. "It's creepy. What is going on?"

Charlie refilled Robby's wine glass and handed it to him. "Drink," she commanded.

He did as he was told, annoyed with himself for giving in to her so easily. When he'd drained half his glass, she seemed satisfied. "Okay, so we just think that Calder needs to settle down. His horndog ways are fucking with Linc's business, which puts Linc in a bad mood, which fucks with Wyatt's getting laid on the regular."

Robby blinked at Charlie. "What?"

She rolled her eyes as if Robby was dense. "Calder needs to settle down with someone, and the only person who can tame a manwhore is a virgin, and of-age virgins are like unicorns."

"The virgin being you," Wyatt supplied.

Robby felt himself sulking. "What makes you two think I'm a virgin?"

Charlie gave him a pitying gaze. "Oh, sweetie. If we

were villagers, you'd be the first one we'd chuck into a volcano to appease the gods."

"Wow. Am I that obvious?"

"Well, yes. But that's a good thing. You're a unicorn. Now you get to offer up your virginity to Calder in exchange for living happily ever after together. That's a good thing. I mean, a guy who's fucked as many people as he has must be aces in bed. Why bother with some sad little dweeb who wouldn't know your ass from your elbow?"

Robby's face was in flames, but he didn't know if it was the alcohol or humiliation. He tried to focus, but his head was full of bees. "So, you guys dangled me in front of him like a piece of meat 'cause you thought… what? He was going to fall in love with me? You bet on the wrong version…er, virgin. I'm invisible to guys. They just look right through me."

Robby bit down on his lip to keep from confessing any more of his secret insecurities.

Wyatt scoffed. "Calm down, Mr. Cellophane."

Charlie shook her head, her wine sloshing dangerously close to the top of her goblet. "Nope. No way. Calder was all over you. He zeroed in on you so fast it was like he could smell your virginity."

"Gross," Robby muttered, still not really buying that somehow he was the one Calder wanted. If that was true, why hadn't he called? "It doesn't matter anyway. It didn't work. I'm still a vers-vers-I'm still volcano bait. He prob-a-ly just felt sorry for me. My tongue's not working," he confessed. "I'm sleepy."

Charlie ignored him. "We just need to keep putting you in his path. Like, he can't resist those big doe eyes and your gorgeous face forever. Not to mention your ass."

"Shh," Robby said, pushing his finger against her lips. "Don't mention it."

Wyatt snickered. "I think you got him wasted. We should go."

Was he wasted? Probably. His head buzzed and his tongue felt like a spongy sour grape and his limbs were heavy in a not unpleasant way. He'd hoped Charlie and Wyatt would take his mind off of Calder, but instead his whole night was just one big Calder-fest. Calder. Calder. Calder. Robby couldn't even get a total manwhore to fuck him. He was pathetic.

"No," Charlie cried. "We need to plot a plan or plan a plot. What am I saying?"

"Beats me, Dr. Seuss," Wyatt muttered.

"We need to plan a plot to get Robby inside Calder's world, so he can get inside Robby's ass," she said before erupting into a fit of giggles.

Wyatt stood. "Okay, that's enough for tonight. I'm

getting really tired of being the sober friend."

Charlie sputtered, spraying Robby with saliva. "That's not my fault. Lincoln log said you lost your drinking priv-privadges when you were doing stupid stuff, like cutting yourself. I don't have any rules, and I like it that way. But this isn't 'bout us. This is 'bout Robby. Oh, and Calder. We need to get them together. Ooh. Ooh. Project. Let's make up a stalker. Robby can hire Calder, and then he'll fall in love with him. We can teach Robby how to seduce him. Yeah. Let's do that!"

Robby stared at Charlie in horror. "No. No way."

"It's perfect," she cried. "You can be all like, 'Oh, Calder. I'm so scared. Come sleep in my bed and keep me company.'"

Wyatt got to his feet. "Yeah, okay. That's enough out of you. I called us an Uber. They'll be downstairs in five. Let's go."

Robby watched them leave before lying back down on the couch. He attempted to put his wine glass back on the table but missed. The glass didn't break but it spilled. He rolled onto his stomach to watch the wine spread across the hardwood floors. He should probably clean it up, but he was just too tired.

exasperating

IT WAS A STRANGE SOUND THAT WOKE HIM, LIKE somebody popping the seal on a vacuum. He forced his eyes open, even though his lids felt weighted. He frowned into the darkness. It wasn't dark when he'd fallen asleep. He heaved himself upright, stomach sloshing and head pounding. He needed water. Water and a thousand aspirin. He had to stop drinking. It never ended well for him. He only prayed he didn't wake up with another tattoo. Drunk him loved tattoos…and honesty. Never a good combination.

A high-pitched whimper came from far away, sending a shock of adrenaline through him, his heart racing as he fought to place the sound. "Cas?" he whispered, not sure why he was afraid to call out in his own home. The sound came again along with scratching on glass.

Robby sucked in a breath as he realized the sounds were coming from outside the sliding glass door. The one that went to the balcony. A balcony with only thin bars protecting Casanova from plummeting to the ground below. He lurched to his feet before stopping short. How would Cas get out onto the balcony? There was no way. He'd been sleeping in his bed the whole time Wyatt and Charlie had visited and had curled up at Robby's feet on the sofa as soon as they'd left. Not even drunk him would have put Cas out on the balcony. Would he?

Robby snatched the only thing in his immediate vicinity, the short, sharp, triangular cheese knife from the remnants of the charcuterie board. He held it before him as he crept towards the balcony. Had that been the sound he'd heard? Was there somebody lurking in the shadows, waiting for him to rescue Cas? He considered calling the police but couldn't risk Cas wiggling between the bars and falling.

Was he just being paranoid? Had somebody broken in? It seemed hard to believe. This was a secure building. Well, more secure than most. But it wasn't a new building and he hadn't locked the door when Wyatt and Charlie left.

He forced himself to creep through the darkness, feeling like he had found himself in a Scooby-Doo episode. He breathed a sigh when he reached the door without incident and Cas bolted back inside, giving him a look of betrayal with his one good eye.

He bent down to try to pick him up, but the dog cowered away, pulling his lip back in an uncharacteristic snarl.

"What's wrong with you, baby? How'd you get out there?"

He sensed another presence behind him a split-second before something solid swung into his periphery, missing his skull by a millimeter and crashing to the floor. It was a heavy stone sculpture shaped like a goddess. His heartbeat pounded in his ears as his brain tried to make sense of what was happening. He staggered forward, still hunched over, rearing up as he turned to face his attacker. The man grunted, lunging at Robby once more. He swung wide with his knife just as the man grabbed him. There was a slick sucking sound, and then something warm and sticky poured over Robby's hand.

The man stumbled back, his hands holding the side of his neck. Robby followed without thought, unsure what had happened. He flung the cheese knife away from him, watching as the man fell to the floor, a puddle forming beneath him, looking like black ink in the shadows of the room. Why was there so much blood? It was such a small knife. He stood for far too long just staring as the stain crept towards him. When it almost touched his sock, he finally jerked into motion. He flipped on the light and ran to the man. He was large, like a wrestler or a linebacker, but it was the slit in the side of his throat that had Robby's eyes going wide as a fountain of thick red blood poured from the wound. He put his hands over it, but the man's skin looked wrong, waxy and gray in the soft lights.

"Oh, fuck. Oh, fuck. Oh, God. Please don't die in my

apartment. Fuck. Fuck. Fuck."

After a few seconds, the blood stopped pumping, instead oozing out slowly. The man gazed upward, his mouth slack as a strange rattle escaped from the back of his throat. Robby scooted away, snatching Casanova and his phone, before retreating to the only spot he could find in his small apartment not stained crimson. A sob caught in his throat as his fingers slipped each time he tried to unlock his phone with his blood-slicked hands. "Fuck. Come on," he whimpered.

Finally, his phone relented, and he stabbed at the contacts, calling the only name that came to mind. The name he'd focused on for the last three nights.

six

CALDER

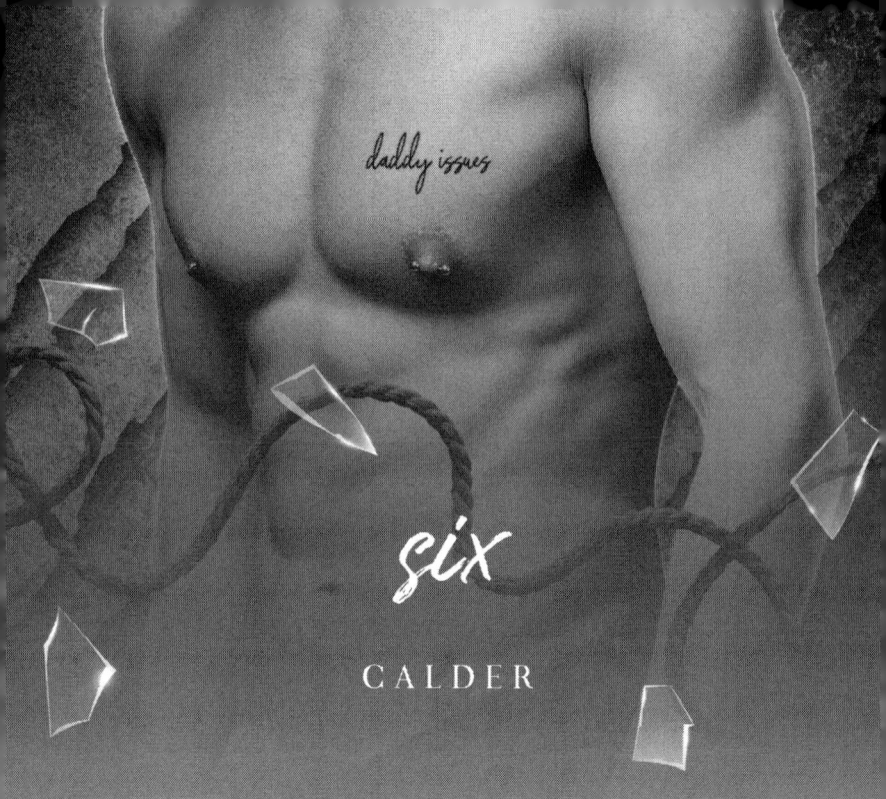

"'ELLO," CALDER MUMBLED, HIS EYES STILL CLOSED.

"Calder... It's me, Robby." Calder's eyes flew open at the tear-soaked voice on the other end of the phone. "I-Oh, God. I think I killed someone."

Calder jerked to his feet. "Where are you?"

"My apartment. He's-I think he's really dead." The last words were a frantic whisper.

"Are you safe? Is there somebody else in the apartment? Why are you whispering?"

"I don't know. I've never killed somebody before," Robby shot back. "I'm scared."

Calder put his phone on speaker, shoving his legs

into the jeans he found on the floor. "Listen, angel face, I'm on my way. If you're sure you're safe, you need to hang up and call 911. Do you understand?"

There was a shuddery sob. "He looks really bad. I don't think he's breathing."

The kid was clearly going into shock. "Hey, I know you're scared. I'm on my way. But you *have* to call the police. Do you hear me? It's already going to look suspicious that you called me and not them. Hang up and don't say a word about what happened until I get there."

"You're coming?" Robby asked, sounding uncertain.

"I'll be there before you know it."

"Hurry," Robby begged before disconnecting the call.

Calder shoved a white t-shirt over his head, stuffed his wallet in his back pocket, and pulled the pistol from its hiding place in his top drawer. Once he had his keys in hand, he called up Linc.

"It's three in the morning. Somebody better be dead," Linc growled into the phone.

Calder gave a humorless laugh. "Funny you should say that. I need a criminal defense attorney."

"Christ, Calder. Tell me you didn't kill some hookup's spouse. Or worse. A client."

"Not me. Robby Shaw just called me in a panic

saying he killed somebody in his apartment."

"What? What happened?" Linc asked, sounding much more alert than just a moment ago.

"No idea. But the kid sounded real shook up."

There was silence on the other end of the phone for so long Calder checked to make sure the call hadn't disconnected. "Wyatt just left his house a few hours ago," Linc finally managed. "Why the hell did he call you? You messing around with this kid?"

"Hey, he's not a client," Calder said by way of an answer. "Are you going to help me out with an attorney, or do I need to Google while I'm driving?"

Linc grunted. "I'm on it. I know a guy. I'll have him call you."

When Calder pulled into the lot of Robby's building, the place already crawled with patrol cars. He walked towards the building's entrance with purpose, flashing his credentials at the officers and closing them too quickly for them to get a good look. He ducked beneath the crime scene tape, making his way past a group of shell-shocked building staff toward the elevators in the middle of the hall.

A pale, sweaty, plain-clothed detective with a receding hairline and a paunch over his waistband held out a hand to stop him once he reached Robby's floor. "I'm sorry, but you can't be up here."

Calder didn't even hesitate. "That's my boyfriend's apartment." He pointed to the open doorway.

The man's brows shot up. "Is that kid even legal?"

"Can I see him or not?" Calder drawled, refusing to take the bait.

"Don't touch anything," the man snapped, stepping aside.

Calder tipped his head. "Much obliged."

The detective rolled his eyes, following Calder into the apartment. He stopped short just inside the doorway. It looked like a massacre had taken place. On the floor was a large middle-aged man with a neat inch-long gash in the side of his neck. He had a pasty gray pallor to his skin, and his jaw hung in a grotesque caricature of a scream. Robby sat on the sofa, his once white long-sleeved henley now mostly rust-colored. He cradled Casanova on his lap, the dog's body covered in bloody handprints.

When Robby noticed Calder, his face collapsed and he started to cry. Calder's heart seized at the boy's tears. He couldn't think of anything else to do but wrap his arms around him.

"I didn't mean to do it," he said, his words muffled against Calder's chest.

"Shh, I know. It's going to be alright. We'll get it sorted out. I called an attorney."

exasperating

"What's the kid need an attorney for?"

Calder turned to look at the detective, not relinquishing his hold on Robby or the dog squirming between them.

"Because he's a celebrity and there's a dead body in his apartment. I just want to make sure he isn't about to be railroaded for what was clearly a home invasion."

The detective scoffed. "You've seen one too many movies, buddy."

Calder scoffed. "I was a Texas Ranger for over a decade. I know exactly how these things go. He'll be happy to answer any questions down at the station with his attorney present. Take it or leave it."

The detective turned around, muttering under his breath as he walked away. Calder turned his attention back to Robby. "They are probably going to photograph you, and they'll likely collect your clothes as evidence. I'm going to grab something for you to wear home. Don't move, and don't talk to anybody."

Robby just nodded, his red eyes glassy.

Once an officer had escorted Calder to collect Robby's necessities, he carefully took the dog and placed him in his crate, which still sat where Calder had left it three days ago. Three fucking days. Why couldn't this have happened the night Calder was there? *You snuck out on him. Left him with a note. He still would have been alone when he was attacked.*

Robby almost had another meltdown when the detective told him they'd have to escort him to the precinct to preserve any evidence on both him and the dog. Calder assured him he'd meet him there with the boy's attorney, a man named Stanton Fields. Calder had never heard of him, but his name sounded lawyerly, so he'd just have to trust that Linc knew what he was talking about.

Hours passed as Calder sat outside in the waiting room of the precinct with the now processed Casanova. Robby wasn't alone in the interrogation room. His attorney had arrived about an hour after Calder, but the detectives were leaving Robby to wait, likely hoping to rattle the kid. They clearly didn't understand who they were dealing with. Robby couldn't hurt a fly. Except, he had. He'd killed a man and, just four days ago, had assaulted an officer. Shit.

Calder was playing a game on his phone when the plain-clothed detective from the apartment stomped his way into the lobby and stared Calder down with daggers in his eyes. "Come with me."

Calder frowned but complied, gently slinging Casanova's crate over his shoulder. "What's wrong?"

"The kid's refusing to speak without you."

exasperating

"Me?"

"Yeah, you," the man grumbled.

Odd, but okay.

Outside the door, the detective shoved a fat finger into his chest. "One word out of you and you're back on the bench. Got it?"

Calder merely nodded. Once he entered the room, Robby's shoulders sagged, his relief evident. He took the bag from Calder and pulled the ugly mutt free from his canvas prison, snuggling him close.

Calder took a seat beside him, his stomach churning as he looked around. All of these rooms looked the same, smelled the same. They all had the same eggshell-colored walls and uncomfortable plastic and metal chairs. They all smelled faintly of stale sweat and bad decisions.

The detective sat opposite Calder, Robby, and his attorney, flipping a switch on the table that turned a green light on. "This is Detective Michael Grady interviewing Obidiah Shaw. Also present in the room is his attorney." He looked at the older man with his salt and pepper hair and thousand dollar Brooks Brothers suit. "State your name and title for the record, please."

"Stanton Fields, litigator."

The detective rolled his eyes. "And also in the room is…"

He flicked his gaze to Calder. "Calder Seton, private investigator and personal protection agent."

Calder's response had Grady sneering as if Calder had said he was a professional kitten mangler. He was used to it. It didn't help that Calder had lied to the man upon their first meeting. Robby had likely explained that Calder was not, in fact, his boyfriend, but then again, maybe not. Was that why Robby had asked for him, had called him and nobody else?

Beneath the table, Robby's leg jiggled fast enough for him to power all the electricity in Los Angeles. The boy looked two seconds away from having a stroke.

"Obidiah—" Grady started only to be cut off immediately.

"Robby. My name is Robby. I had it legally changed."

"Robby," the detective said through gritted teeth. "Now, would you please explain what happened in your apartment?"

"I don't know what happened," Robby said, his voice thick. "My friends, Wyatt and Charlie, came over last night and we were drinking wine. A lot of it. When they left, I fell asleep on the couch. I didn't even walk them out, I just passed out on the sofa." Robby swallowed hard, his hand stroking Casanova's fur almost compulsively.

Calder slid his hand beneath the table and pressed

exasperating

down on the boy's jittering leg. He released a shuddering breath.

"So, you were asleep on the couch and then what happened?" Grady pressed.

"A noise woke me. At the time, I couldn't place it, but now, I think maybe it was the sliding glass door closing. It makes a weird sound. I was dizzy, and I heard Cas whimpering and scratching, but it was far away. That's when I realized he was outside on the balcony." He clutched the dog tighter, kissing his head. "I got scared. I thought somebody must be in the house."

The detective leaned forward. "Why didn't you call the police?"

Robby's hand fluttered into the air as he shook his head. "I don't know. All I could think was that I had to get Cas off the balcony before he fell. I was drunk."

"When did you grab the cheese knife?"

A cheese knife? Seriously?

Calder massaged the boy's knee, hoping it helped somewhat.

"I grabbed it from the coffee table as I walked toward the back door. I couldn't see anything. Somebody had turned all the lights off. I thought someone was lurking in the shadows."

When Robby didn't continue, the detective

prompted, "And they were?"

"Well, yeah, but not in front of me. Behind me. I was bending down to pick up Cas. He tried to hit me with this giant ugly stone sculpture my designer picked up in Peru, but he missed. It startled me, and I turned and swung my hand and"—he shuddered—"then I felt it."

"It?" the detective asked.

"The knife blade sinking into his skin." The boy paled. "It made this wet sound and—" Robby jerked from the table, shoving Casanova at the lawyer before he lurched to hover over a small rubber trash can, losing the contents of his stomach. Calder went to crouch beside him, rubbing his back as the kid heaved over and over again. Oof. He was not lying about the red wine.

"Can he get some water or a soda or something?" the attorney asked.

The detective left and came back with a ginger ale and a paper cup. Once Robby was no longer green, they continued the interview. "Mr. Shaw, do you know the man who broke into your apartment?"

Robby shook his head. "No."

Grady leaned back in his chair, rubbing the back of his neck. "Anybody you know might want to hurt you?"

Robby started to shake his head but then froze,

staring at the wall long enough for Calder to exchange a confused glance with Fields.

"No," Robby finally said, but it lacked any strength.

"If you know something, you need to tell them, angel face," Calder urged.

"I don't know that he'd hurt me exactly, but he'd definitely make somebody come get me and try to bring me back."

"Who?" Calder asked, earning a glare from Grady.

"My dad."

Grady stared down Robby. "Now, why would your father have somebody break into your home to 'come get you'?"

"Because he thinks he can get me back into the fold now that he saw me kiss a girl," Robby said as if that made a lick of sense to anybody in the room.

"I'm going to need you to speak plainly," Grady snapped.

Calder agreed but he didn't appreciate the man's tone. He turned furious eyes on Grady, but Fields spoke first. "My client has been through a very rough night. Somebody broke into his home, and he defended himself. We're under no obligation to answer your questions unless you plan on arresting my client. Give him a minute."

Calder relaxed but placed a hand on the back of

Robby's neck, massaging gently.

"My father is Jeb Shaw." At everybody's puzzled looks, he said, "The leader of the Church of Magnus Dei."

"That's not a church. It's a cult," Grady spit.

"Yes," Robby confirmed.

The detective frowned down at his file. "Your IMDB profile said your father was a preacher and your mother was a school teacher."

Calder shook his head. Even the cops in LA were Hollywood. Hopefully Grady had done more than a quick Google search before he'd questioned Robby.

"Son of a notorious cult leader doesn't sell well when you're trying to make a name for yourself in Hollywood. It was my father's idea," Robby finally said.

"Why would your father want you to lie about who you are?" Grady asked.

Calder was curious, too.

"He thought if my siblings and I became famous, we could recruit other celebrities into the fold. Celebrities bring money and legitimacy. My brothers and sisters couldn't book any jobs. I was picked up by an agency almost immediately. Then I got the television gig. Once I knew I had the ability to pay my own way, I came out to my family as gay. My father declared me dead in the eyes of Magnus Dei, which was fine by me. But he said I couldn't see my brothers or sisters anymore or my mom. Not that my mom wanted to see me after she knew. My publicist thought it best to just stick with the original story."

"But now he thinks you've gone straight and he wants you back on track?" Calder muttered.

Robby shrugged. "Maybe. He bailed me out of jail the other day. Tried to make me go with him. I don't think anybody else cares enough to try to kidnap me. I'm not the kind of celebrity who has stalkers."

Calder felt like somebody had mule kicked him at the boy's words. Nobody else cared enough to kidnap him. Jesus.

Robby looked visibly upset, like the morning had finally caught up with him. "Look, I answered all your questions. Can I please go home now?"

Grady shifted in his seat. "Your apartment is still an official crime scene."

"Are you going to arrest my client?" Fields pressed.

"That's up to the prosecutors, not me. He's free to go, for now. But he needs to make himself available if we have questions in the future."

Stanton Fields was already on his feet. "You know how to get in touch."

The three of them were almost to the door when Robby stopped. "If he was one of my father's followers, there will be a burn on his heel in the shape of a cross. If that helps."

Branded. Like Jennifer. Like all of Elizer's girls. What was it with men like Elizer and Robby's father that made them want to mark their flock like cattle? Did Robby have a scar on his foot? Calder couldn't remember. He felt like an even bigger asshole than before. He never should have messed with Robby. The kid needed help, not sex. Shit. Shit. Shit.

Outside the station, the attorney handed Robby a business card and then headed for the parking lot, leaving them alone. "Is somebody coming to pick you up?" Calder asked.

Robby scoffed. "Like who?"

Once more, Calder's stomach churned. "Come on. We're going to stop at the office, and then you're coming home with me."

"I am?"

Calder was sure he would live to regret this. "Yes, you are."

seven

ROBBY

IT WAS A TESTAMENT TO ROBBY'S EXHAUSTION LEVEL that he managed to doze off with Calder beside him in the truck, but he must have because Calder gently shook him awake.

"Come on, angel face. I need to talk to Linc for a few minutes, and I don't want you alone out here."

Nausea and fatigue warred within Robby, but he didn't fight when Calder took Cas from him and helped him from the truck. On the ride up the elevator, he leaned against the mirrored walls with his eyes closed. Ten steps into the office, two pairs of arms enveloped him. Charlie and Wyatt. He wanted to cry for the hundredth time in the last twenty-four hours.

"Why are you guys here?" he asked, flushing at how rude it sounded.

"Are you kidding? It's all over the news. When Linc said you were on your way to the office, we hurried over to check on you. I can't believe this happened. We never should have left you alone last night," Charlie cried, her coconut shampoo overwhelming his senses as she clung to him.

"I don't think that would have helped," Robby managed.

"You stay here with them while I talk to Linc. Why don't you guys go hang out in the kitchen or the conference room? Somewhere quiet," Calder suggested, his large hand practically burning a hole into Robby's shoulder.

Robby let his two new friends drag him into the conference room and slam the door. Wyatt pushed a button, frosting over the glass for added privacy. Robby sat in the same chair he'd sat in just days before, and Charlie and Wyatt sat on the table. It was like deja vu, only with more blood and an unhealthy amount of guilt.

"Did you really kill somebody?" Charlie asked.

"Yep," he said, too exhausted to embellish and grateful that his body seemed to have run out of tears.

Charlie puffed up her cheeks and then let out a big sigh. "Like, way to commit to a plan."

Robby blinked at her. "What?"

"Getting Calder to guard your body," Charlie said as if reminding him they were part of some conspiracy. "I just thought you should make up a stalker, but you literally killed a dude. That's some Shepherd levels of commitment. I'm impressed."

"Charlie," Wyatt warned before looking at Robby. "What happened?"

Robby woodenly told the story for the second time that day. Or maybe it was the third. He honestly couldn't remember. Everything was running together except for the feel of the knife penetrating that guy's skin and the wet sound it made and the feel of hot blood running over his hands and the stink of a million copper pennies still stuck in his nostrils, making him shudder.

"Holy shit," was Wyatt's only reply.

Charlie shrugged, tossing her chestnut hair over her shoulder. "I mean, it's extreme, but it worked."

"He didn't kill a home invader to get laid," Wyatt exclaimed before asking, "Did you?"

Robby sighed. "Seriously?"

Wyatt held up both hands. "I was just asking. But why call Calder and not the police?"

Robby's cheeks flushed. "I did call the police."

"After Calder told you to. What made you call him first?"

Robby swallowed the lump in his throat. What was he supposed to say? Because he literally had nobody else? Because he was scared and somehow knew if he called, Calder would answer. That Calder wouldn't leave him alone to face any of this. That, more than anything, Robby was sick of being alone?

That was just way too pathetic.

Instead, he just shrugged. "I was drunk. I wasn't thinking clearly. There was a guy bleeding out on my living room floor. I have no idea why I called him." But he was glad he had. He liked having Calder by his side. He felt safe. Something he rarely felt when he was alone.

"What do they know about the guy who broke in?" Wyatt asked.

"Nothing much, yet. I think my dad sent him after me."

Charlie leaned forward until Robby was sure she was going to fall from the table. "Like a hit?"

He shook his head. "No. At least, I don't think so. I think he was trying to take me back to the compound."

"Your dad wanted to kidnap you and take you to a compound. Is that code for like a conversion therapy program or something?" Wyatt asked.

"My dad doesn't believe in conversion therapy so much as there's no behavior that can't be beaten out of a person. He saw me kissing that girl in the paper, so it's possible he thinks he can somehow persuade me I'm straight or at least that I'm straight enough to marry some girl and tithe all my money to his creepy cult."

Charlie rested her elbows on her knees and her chin on her fists, her eyes wide. "Cult? I thought your dad was a preacher? Not that I don't think most religions are just cults anyway."

Robby could lie but why bother? If it was all over the news, the world was bound to find out the truth soon enough anyway. "My dad is the head of Magnus Dei."

"Holy shit," Wyatt whispered. "They make Jonestown look like Disneyland. No offense."

"None taken," Robby muttered.

He was so tired. He wanted a shower and food and to sleep for at least a year. He'd settle for showering. He felt dirty in a way he'd never be able to explain, like killing somebody had left a permanent stain on his skin. One he'd never be able to wash away.

"Do you think your father will try to snatch you again?" Charlie asked.

"I don't know. I hope not."

Wyatt shook his head. "We can do better than hope. You need to hire Elite to protect you. That way Calder is duty-bound to guard your hot little body all day and all night. He could barely keep his hands off you after one car ride alone together. Twenty-four hours a day? He'll be in love with you in no time at all. It's perfect."

Robby's heart twisted. "Or he'll want nothing to do with me because I'm a client."

Wyatt scoffed. "Calder has fucked so many of Linc's clients, they think it's part of their service contract. Trust us, he will never be able to resist you."

"I don't know. If the last twenty-one years of my life have taught me anything, it's that I'm really, really resistible."

"Okay, that's just not true. You are only resistible because of this energy you put off. You have a giant 'keep away' sign around your neck."

Robby rubbed his eyes. "That's not true. I was with Elijah for months, and he never even noticed me."

Wyatt sighed. "Okay, real talk. Do you really believe you and Elijah were a good fit?"

No. "Yeah. Why not? Because he was too good-looking? Too famous for me?"

"No, you idiot, because he was a total bottom and so are you. Like, you need somebody to take care of you,

exasperating

and let's be real, that was never going to be Elijah. You need a Daddy, not a boy," Wyatt explained.

"Don't listen to him. He thinks everybody just wants to be spanked and have their hair pulled," Charlie said.

Robby wasn't sure if he'd like that or not, but he was willing to try. He wanted to try a lot of things. Would Calder teach him?

"Hello?" Charlie sang, snapping her fingers in front of his face, ripping him from his thoughts. "I think you were with Elijah because that meant you didn't have to try. Your fake relationship with him was much easier than a real relationship with somebody who could care about you like you cared about them. You definitely have baggage, probably stemming from your abusive childhood and the fact that you were raised in a cult. Which is a way better bio for IMDB, just FYI. That Jasmine chick isn't doing you any favors as your publicist. My publicist, Mario, would have killed for a client with a backstory like that."

Robby really didn't know how to address any of that, so he focused on what he did know. "You guys are putting a lot of faith in me somehow getting Calder to fall in love with me. You, yourself, said he doesn't do commitments. He fucks anything that moves. Even if he sleeps with me, I doubt he'll fall for me. That's not how the real world works."

Charlie rolled her eyes. "Who lives in the real world? We live in Lalaland. You are a twenty-one-year-old virgin who was raised in a cult. I'm in the movies. Wyatt makes money on YouTube. Your ex-boyfriend left you for a dude who's probably a serial killer. The real world doesn't apply to people like us. In LA, we make the rules, and I'm telling you, Calder is the guy for you. We just have to make him understand that."

Robby wanted to believe Charlie's pep talk. He wanted to think that they lived in a world where somebody like Calder, the guy who refused to settle down, would look at Robby and see somebody worthy of happily ever after, but no matter which way he turned the thought, it just didn't fit. But it didn't change how unsafe he felt. Maybe it was a fluke, just some random break-in, but Robby wouldn't be able to sleep at night until he knew the truth.

"Fine. I'll hire Elite, but that's all I'm agreeing to. I'm not going to waste my time trying to seduce Calder. I just need his help, that's all."

Wyatt and Charlie looked at each other before Charlie smiled and patted him on the cheek. "Whatever you say, angel face."

"Don't call me that." Only Calder could call him that. Even if it did things to his insides every time he did.

exasperating

Charlie smirked. "Whatever you say, buttercup. Let's go tell Linc the big news."

Was he really doing this? Agreeing to having Calder in his life, day and night? This would be torture. Why was he like this?

Why did Robby keep putting himself in situations where he never got what he wanted? Where he was forced to pine for a guy who didn't even know he was alive. What if this was just another Elijah situation, only worse, because Robby already knew what it was like to kiss Calder, to feel his hands on his body? It would hurt so much more to be so close and yet so far from getting what he wanted, and he couldn't have what he wanted.

But he'd do it anyway because the tiniest part of him kept hoping there was a chance. A chance that maybe, just this once, he could.

eight

CALDER

"A CHEESE KNIFE?" LINC ASKED, INCREDULOUS. CALDER could only nod. "First, he beats a cop with a sex toy, and now, he's murdered a man with a cheese knife. This boy is either a secret assassin or a walking disaster."

Calder was leaning towards the latter. "Yeah, so you can see why he needs constant supervision until he's safe."

Linc hooked a brow upwards, leaning forward. "Supervision you want to provide." It wasn't a question.

Calder shrugged. "I'm sure you can spare me."

exasperating

Linc frowned. "You want to do this free of charge? Why? It's not like the boy can't afford to hire us."

Calder squirmed beneath Linc's weighted stare. "The kid doesn't have anybody else."

"But he has you?" Linc asked.

Yes. "It's not like that, man."

"You're not fucking this kid, are you?"

"No." *Not yet.* He shook the thought away. "It's not about that."

"It's clearly a little about that," Linc chided. "There's something about this kid that's got you by the short ones, which I have to admit, I find…amusing."

"Happy to help," Calder muttered.

Linc scrubbed his hands over his face. "Look, what you do in your off time is none of my business, but on the clock, no more fucking the clients. This is your last warning. I don't want to have to fire you."

Hence the reason Calder wanted to keep Robby off the payroll. He couldn't trust himself to keep his hands off, but he also knew he wouldn't trust anybody else to keep him safe.

"Oh, and if you do plan on doing this boy in your off time, don't bring the drama into my office. We're getting a reputation here."

Before Calder could respond, the door burst open and Charlie and Wyatt spilled inside, Robby in tow.

"Robby wants to hire Elite to guard him until we figure out what's going on, and he wants Calder as his security detail."

Calder's head swiveled to Linc. A wide grin spread across the man's face. "Is that so?"

"Yeah," Robby confirmed, his voice squeaking a bit at the end.

Calder sat upright. "Wait. That's not—"

"Excellent," Linc said, cutting Calder off. "We'll get the paperwork drawn up so we can start right away. You don't have a problem with that. Do you, Seton?"

Calder could feel a headache start to form behind his eyes, but the dejected look on Robby's face had him saying, "No, not at all."

Calder wanted to kick himself. He should have never tipped his hand. He'd been pushing Linc's buttons for way too long. He had to know that Linc would take the opportunity to teach him a lesson if one presented itself. Fuck.

Thirty minutes and one signed contract later, it was done. Robby was officially a client and Calder was officially neutered. The kid looked exhausted, his hair matted to his head and his skin pale. Most clients preferred to stay in their homes, but Robby's apartment was still a crime scene, so that meant coming up with another plan.

exasperating

"You could take him to the safehouse off of Cresthill," Linc offered.

Calder shook his head. "If it's alright with…my client," Calder forced himself to say, "I'd rather take him to my place." Four sets of eyes bored a hole into him. "What? My place is more secure than any of our safehouses."

"It's fine," Robby said, directing his answer to Linc. "I just really need to get somewhere I can shower, and Cas needs to eat and take his medicine."

"Okay. The client comes first," Linc said, glaring at Wyatt and Charlie when they giggled like small children.

Calder couldn't help but feel like the two had lured him into a trap, but it was too late now. He pressed his hand to the small of Robby's back, leading him towards the office door.

"Don't forget our talk, Calder. Last warning," Linc reminded one final time.

"Yeah, yeah. I hear you." No fucking the clients. No matter how sweet and soft and delectable they were, and Robby was the sweetest of them all.

The boy slept before Calder even made it out of the parking lot. He didn't blame the kid. He'd had one hell of a week and the truck was a safe space. But Calder found it hard to keep his eyes on the road, hard to tear himself away from the boy's softened features and the way his lips parted in sleep. Robby tugged at some long dormant part of Calder's soul, a part he'd thought he'd excised long ago. It didn't make sense, but he just wanted to protect this boy's soft heart but also couldn't stop thinking about all the ways he wanted to violate his perfect body.

The boy sucked in a startled breath as soon as Calder shut down the truck's engine. His neighbor, Mrs. Leighton, stood at the security gate, her groceries at her pink-bunny slippered feet as she attempted to swipe her key fob to allow her access into the building. Calder reached around the old woman who jumped, then laughed, when she realized it was him. When the door buzzed, he swept her bags up with one hand while guiding Robby with the other. The boy's skin was pleasantly warm.

Mrs. Leighton beamed at him before following them up the stairs at a snail's pace. Calder didn't understand why the older woman never took the elevator, but he lacked the nerve to ask. She probably wouldn't hear him anyway. Calder punched in the access code to his door lock and slid the keycard in before scanning his thumb print on the pad. Robby frowned at the elaborate security system, probably wondering why Calder felt the need for such measures, but he

exasperating

remained silent.

Once the door opened, he gently pushed Robby inside. "Give me a minute to help her and I'll be right in. Make yourself at home."

Robby didn't speak, just nodded.

Calder helped Mrs. Leighton put her groceries away and feed Mr. Pickles, her—in Calder's opinion—entirely too fat, orange and black cat.

"It's nice," Mrs. Leighton said, seemingly out of the blue.

"What's that?" Calder asked, stooping to scratch the cat under his chin.

"Seeing you finally bringing somebody home."

Calder stood. "It's not like that. He's a…friend."

She turned away from him with a noncommittal, "Hm."

Don't 'hm' me, old lady. He gave her a wave as he made his escape from her apartment.

He found Robby in the dining room, staring slack jawed at Calder's paintings. He was relieved that he'd stuffed Robby's portrait to the back of a stack of finished canvases leaning against the wall. He seemed hesitant to touch any of the paintings, which suited Calder just fine. He didn't invite people into his apartment. He kept his art to himself. He couldn't remember the last person he'd allowed to breach the walls of his sanctum.

Robby seemed transfixed by a particular canvas. A painting of a red-haired woman sitting on the side of a bathtub, her robe down to her waist, exposing her naked back as she gazed out the window. It was her elegant neck that had snagged Calder's attention. She'd worn her hair in a bun at the diner where she'd worked, and Calder had just had to paint her. He stepped behind Robby, close enough to smell that the boy still desperately needed a shower. He smelled like blood and sweat, which should have turned Calder off but didn't.

"Who is she?" Robby asked.

There was the slightest tinge of something in his voice. Jealousy, maybe?

"Just a girl who let me paint her. I don't even remember her name." It was the truth. Calder had slept with her, too, but he didn't think that information would help his case. Not that he was trying to make a case.

Then why did it matter so much?

"She's...elegant."

Calder didn't acknowledge the boy's words. She had looked elegant, but she was just another face in the crowd to Calder. More art than human. A temporary muse who was happy to leave the next

exasperating

morning. "Come on. I'll show you where the shower is, and I'll throw together something for us to eat. I'm sure you're starving."

Robby nodded, his top teeth sinking into his lower lip like he was nervous about something. Calder wanted to tug that lip free and kiss it, kiss him until he didn't look timid or anxious around him. He wanted Robby to trust him, needed him to even, but Calder wasn't sure he deserved the boy's trust.

He led Robby to the bathroom and showed him where everything was and then went to the kitchen and tried to pull enough food together to create a meal. He'd left a steak marinating in the refrigerator, but it wasn't big enough for two. He found white rice, corn, frozen peppers, and avocado and decided he could turn that into a southwest stir-fry type meal. It would be quick, and then he could get the boy to bed. *To sleep,* Calder corrected. Alone. He'd take the couch.

Robby appeared just as Calder finished putting the food into two bowls, one plastic, one glass, neither remotely similar looking. He almost dropped the pan on his foot when he saw Robby standing there, wet and naked, a small towel slung low on his narrow hips. His hair stuck up in all directions like a baby bird, his eyes glassy and red. "I don't have anything to wear," he managed, his voice just slightly past a whisper.

Good, a voice whispered in Calder's brain. The idea of keeping Robby naked and slippery had Calder's cock hardening behind his zipper. He'd pulled clothing for the kid the night before, but he'd worn them at the station. Fuck, this was going to be impossible. "I'm sure we can find you something," Calder said, voice cracking slightly. He cleared his throat. "I have some sweatpants that will fit."

Robby followed Calder back to his room, and he kicked himself for not thinking to clean up the mess strewn everywhere. He opened his bottom drawer and pulled a pair of black sweatpants and a paint splattered t-shirt free. "They might be a bit big, but they should do the job."

Robby nodded, dropping the towel right there and stepping into Calder's pants. He jerked his head away, staring at the wall.

"It's not like you haven't seen me naked before," Robby reminded him.

That was the problem. Calder had seen the boy naked. He'd touched him. Caressed him. Kissed his perfect lips. Heard him gasp with pleasure and felt him cling to him after climax. Yeah, he'd done so much more than see Robby naked. Clothed, the boy was beautiful, but naked, he was perfection, and Calder wanted to pick him up and dump him on the bed and lick every drop of water from the boy's smooth skin.

"I'm aware, angel face. But we have to keep things professional now." Calder cleared his throat again. "Once you've eaten, you can sleep in here. I'll take the couch."

Robby nodded, pulling the shirt over his head, before following Calder back out to the kitchen. They ate in silence, Robby staring out the window but not really like he was seeing anything, just zoning out. Casanova had made himself at home on the back of Calder's sofa, his eyes somehow watching both sides of the room at the same time, his tongue lolling out of his mouth.

"I gotta ask. Where did you get that dog?"

The boy glanced over at Casanova and smiled the first genuine smile Calder had seen in a while. "The Glendale Humane Society."

"Did you lose a bet?"

Robby shook his head. "I helped raise money for them a couple of months ago, and we shot the commercial there with all the puppies and cute kittens, but they had Cas hidden in the back. They said nobody wanted him, that he'd lived in that cage for over a year. He's old, and he's got a lot of problems. He has no teeth and he has bad skin and, sometimes, he faints when he gets scared."

Calder tilted his head. "Seems like a lot of responsibility at your age."

Robby shrugged. "I know what it's like to be invisible, for nobody to want you. I couldn't stomach the thought of him living the rest of his life feeling unloved."

Calder's chest ached at the rawness of the boy's words. The kid was just twenty-one years old and it was like he'd already decided he'd spend his life alone. How could somebody work in front of a camera and still feel so invisible? It seemed impossible, but Calder knew, deep down, Robby wasn't fishing for compliments or even just feeling sorry for himself. He believed he was unworthy. It was crazy. Robby deserved everything he desired. He deserved to have somebody who would love him through his insecurities. Somebody who would let Robby adopt a thousand special needs dogs if that was what he wanted. Calder was certain that man existed out there somewhere, but fuck if he didn't wish it was him.

nine

ROBBY

ROBBY LAY IN CALDER'S BED, IN CALDER'S CLOTHES, his face buried in pillows that smelled just like Calder, like oil paint and peppermint. It was torture. He'd taken the couch—had insisted on it. But Robby hadn't wanted him out there. He wanted to sleep wrapped in Calder's arms. He'd thought of nothing else for days. Instead, it was only Cas snuggled against him, his tiny body curled up on the pillow beside Robby's head. Did Calder sleep on this side of the bed?

Robby flopped onto his back, earning a grumble from his dog. He was pathetic. It was no wonder Charlie and Wyatt wanted to chuck him into a volcano.

At this point, he was starting to think his virginity was bulletproof. Even the manwhore didn't want to fuck him. Maybe he hadn't made it obvious enough? Was standing naked in front of him not obvious? Last time, Robby hadn't had to do anything. Calder just took control. Why couldn't he just do that now? Had one handjob been all Calder had needed to realize Robby was too inexperienced to satisfy him?

The thought settled in Robby's belly like spoiled milk. He needed to take his mind off the gorgeous man in the other room, but each time he tried to shift his thoughts to something else, it was the open mouth of his attacker and the hot sticky blood on his skin, which led to thoughts of jail and sharing a toilet with other people...in front of other people. No. Just no. How had his life spun so far out of control in such a short time?

Robby couldn't just lay there, crawling out of his skin. He was on his feet and moving before he could change his mind. Maybe he could find a way to be brave enough to just kiss Calder, to remind him that he liked to break the rules. Robby wanted to be worth breaking the rules for, just once.

Calder wasn't sleeping. He was sitting on the sofa in red boxer briefs, eating dry cereal straight from the box and watching an old movie on tv. He glanced up and smiled when Robby entered the room, seeming genuinely happy to see him. It warmed his insides.

"I thought I put you to bed already, angel face?"

Robby shivered at Calder's low drawl. He wanted to wrap that voice around him like a blanket.

"I can't sleep," he said, flopping down beside Calder without waiting for an invitation, acutely aware of their sides touching.

He was warm, and Robby fought the urge to lean in. Calder glanced over at him and grinned, tipping the box of cereal in his direction.

Robby's heart fluttered at Calder's perfect teeth, but he shook his head, declining the cereal. There was no way he could eat with his stomach in knots. "What are you watching?"

Calder cocked a brow at him. "*Rear Window*."

Robby shrugged. "I've never seen it."

Calder shook his head. "Shoot. An actor who's never seen *Rear Window*? They should revoke your SAG card," he teased.

Robby glanced at the screen where a man with two broken legs sat at his window in a wheelchair, gazing into the courtyard below.

He'd come out here to try to seduce Calder, but he could already feel himself losing his nerve. "Can I stay out here with you for a while?"

Calder's expression softened. "You don't have to ask."

Robby chastised himself for the flush of heat that ran over him. It wasn't a marriage proposal. Calder just said he could hang out on his sofa. Robby needed to calm down. He yanked the soft black blanket off the back of the couch and laid down, using Calder's thigh for a pillow, praying he didn't reject the overt demand for affection he was asking for from a virtual stranger. The muscle beneath his head tensed briefly before Calder's large hand settled on his head. Robby shivered when fingers began to comb through his hair. It was nothing, hardly a seduction technique, but Robby's cock hardened just the same. He was grateful for the blanket covering his lower half.

"Get some sleep. You've had a long night," Calder said, his finger tracing the shell of Robby's ear before returning to his hair.

"I don't know if I can sleep. My brain won't shut off," Robby mumbled.

Calder turned the lamp off, plunging the room into shadow except for the large tv screen with its soft technicolor images and hushed tones. Within seconds, Robby's thoughts grew hazy and his lids grew heavy. Calder's touch was addicting, pulling Robby under the blanket of sleep in minutes.

exasperating

He woke to find himself in Calder's bed, his morning hard-on tenting his borrowed sweatpants. Had Calder carried him in there? Robby flushed at the idea of being bridal carried through the apartment by the large Texan. It was alarming how much he wanted it to be true.

He could hear Calder moving around out in the other room but was in no hurry to have another awkward encounter. He picked up his phone only to find messages from Wyatt and Charlie.

Wyatt: Well?

Charlie: Did you bone?

Robby sighed before tapping out his reply. **Wow, so romantic.**

Three dots danced before Charlie's response appeared. **Romance, schmomance. First, you get in his pants, then you get in his heart. That's how this works.**

Wyatt: Charlie! Focus. Did you see the news, Robby?

His stomach plummeted into his feet. **No. Why?**

Charlie: The media. They know.

The spoiled milk feeling was back. **Know what?**

Wyatt: That you killed a guy and your dad is a cult leader.

Charlie: I definitely wouldn't go back to your

apartment.

Robby: My apartment is a crime scene.

Wyatt: All the more reason for you to stay at Calder's.

Four devil faces followed.

Robby: Whatever you're planning won't work. He's not interested.

Wyatt: False. He's interested, but my idiot husband is cock-blocking you.

Robby: What? Why?

Wyatt: Revenge? Amusement? General fuckery? He told Calder if he fucks you, he's fired.

Robby thought about the words. If he fucks him… For as much as Robby wanted to lose his virginity, he had never contemplated what that entailed. A picture of Calder on top of him, inside him, took root at Wyatt's message, sinking its hooks into him and refusing to let go. He wanted Calder inside him, wanted it more than he could ever admit to anybody, including himself, because the likelihood was slim to none. He didn't want to get Calder fired. He told them as much.

Wyatt: Linc isn't going to fire Calder for getting laid. He's just giving him a little payback.

Robby: Does Linc know you're telling me all this?

Wyatt: Oh, God. No. I wouldn't be able to sit

down for a week.

Robby: Oh. So, why are you telling me this?

Charlie: Because he's hoping Linc punishes him hard enough that he won't be able to sit down for a week.

Robby sometimes felt like these two were speaking an entirely different language.

Robby: So Calder won't sleep with me because Linc said he'll get fired? But only if he fucks me... right? So it all depends on his definition of sex?

Charlie: Oh, I'm picking up what you're putting down. You wanna pull a Clinton. That's perfect. Get him to do everything but the sexing, and eventually, he will throw it all away for that sweet ass of yours.

Robby: Why are you like this?

Charlie: Hard to say, really.

Wyatt: Ignore her. You've got this. Be brave. Be bold. Be flexible.

Charlie: Yeah. Go out there and suck a dick for the greater good.

Robby didn't bother to answer, just tossed his phone aside and went to use the bathroom off of Calder's bedroom. There were paint brushes in the sink and paint splotches on the shower wall. Robby smiled. He never would have pegged Calder as an artist, much less an amazing one. Though as messy as he was and as wild as he seemed, maybe it made perfect sense. He was definitely a free spirit.

Once Robby had answered nature's call and splashed some water on his face, he brushed his teeth with the toothbrush Calder had found for him under the sink. Robby didn't want to think too hard about why Calder kept new toothbrushes at the ready. He supposed he should just be grateful it was there.

His hair stood on end, and nothing he did would get it to lay down, so he left it as it was. He held the shirt he wore—Calder's shirt—to his nose, inhaling deeply. It smelled like him. Robby shook his head, dropping it back into place, before venturing out of the bedroom.

Calder stood at the kitchen counter in the same red boxer briefs he'd slept in. How could anybody look that good just standing there? His ass was perfect. His everything was perfect. Calder glanced over at him and grinned. "Good, you're up. I made breakfast."

Calder held out his offering.

"A burrito?" Robby questioned, then flushed bright red. Obviously, it was a burrito.

"A breakfast burrito," Calder clarified.

Robby sniffed at it, and his stomach growled loudly. "Thank you."

They ate leaning against the counter. Robby made it

halfway through his breakfast before he said, "Wyatt and Charlie said the papers know about my dad…and the other thing," he hedged.

Calder paused, the burrito halfway to his lips. "The other thing?"

"Yeah, the…dead guy in my apartment."

"I'm surprised Jasmine didn't call." Calder's eyes went wide as soon as he realized what he'd said.

Robby's gaze flicked upward. "Jasmine? How do you know my publicist's name?"

Calder's gaze turned back to his burrito before he stuffed the whole thing in his mouth, mumbling something Robby couldn't make out.

His heart sank. "Please, don't tell me you fucked my publicist, too."

Calder swallowed audibly. "Fucked…no."

Robby's stomach dropped. "Seriously? Is there anybody I know who you haven't slept with? Other than me?"

Calder flashed him a grin. "I don't know who you know, so it's hard to say."

Robby huffed a breath out through his nose and set his burrito down, walking into Calder's space. "I know Linc told you not to fuck me."

Calder seemed to choke on the air. "What?"

"Wyatt said that Linc told you that you aren't

allowed to fuck me. Is that true?" Calder blinked down at Robby who plopped his hands on his hips. "I can practically hear you thinking. Did he say that or not?" Calder nodded, looking at Robby with just enough surprise to embolden him. "Is that why you said we had to keep things professional?"

"Yes," Calder confirmed, his voice low.

"Is that the only reason you want to keep things professional?" Once more, Calder seemed to short circuit. "Don't think, just answer."

"No."

That one hurt. It was like he'd been kicked in the stomach. "Are you just not interested in me now that we've fooled around?"

"No, angel face. That's not it at all," Calder drawled.

Robby folded his arms across his chest as if that could protect him from the answer to his next question. "Then what is it?"

Calder's lips twitched in an aborted smile. "You're being awfully aggressive."

"Because I'm tired of turning this over and over in my head. You don't understand what it's like up here. I can't stop thinking about it, about you. You couldn't keep your hands off me four days ago, but now, it's like I have the plague. Is it because I didn't do something right? Because you realized I'm a virgin?

I'm a really quick study, you know."

Calder made a noise that sounded like something between a grunt and a growl and pinned Robby against the counter, invading his space in a way that stole his breath. "You are killing me here, kid. I'm trying to be the bigger person. You deserve better than me."

Robby sucked in a shaky breath, dropping his hands to his sides. "But I just want you."

Calder leaned in until his lips almost touched Robby's cheek. "You have no idea what you're saying. This is a very bad idea. I'm not a good guy."

"Then prove it," Robby murmured. "Be the bad guy. Use me up. Teach me."

"But Linc—"

"Linc said you can't fuck me," Robby reminded him. "There are a lot of other things we can do between nothing and everything…isn't there?"

Calder's lips dragged along Robby's cheek. "What'd you have in mind, angel face?"

Robby froze. What did he have in mind? He hadn't gotten that far.

Suddenly, Charlie's words reverberated through his head. *Suck a dick for the greater good*. Robby gently shoved Calder back just enough to drop to his knees, his hands reaching for the band on Calder's underwear. Could he feel Robby's hands shaking?

ten

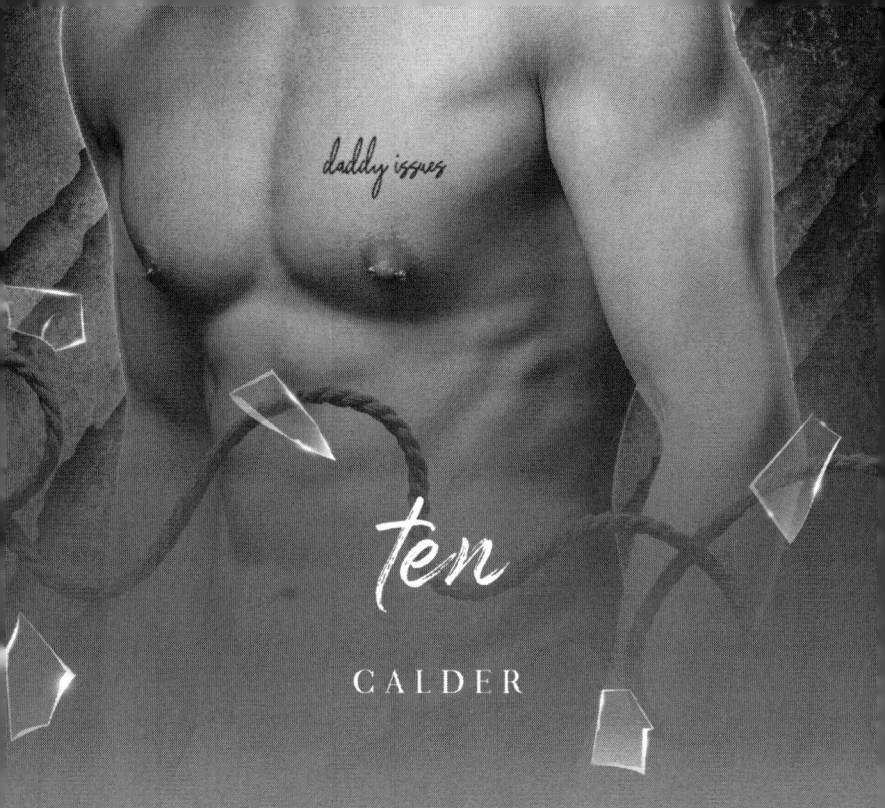

CALDER

CALDER CAME TO HIS SENSES THE MOMENT ROBBY WENT to his knees before him. It wasn't that he didn't love the sight. His rock hard cock was two seconds away from peaking above the band of his underwear with no help from Robby's hands or his lips, but Calder would have to be blind to miss the terror in the boy's body language. He wasn't ready for this. He deserved better than this.

"Wait. Stop," Calder said, cursing himself. He tugged Robby to his feet. His already flushed face grew splotchy as he blinked back unshed tears. Shit. Why was Calder always making him cry? "No. Don't do that. Fuck.

exasperating

You're breaking my heart here, angel. I'm not saying no to…something…but not kitchen blowjobs. Not yet. You gotta crawl before you can run, right?"

Robby blinked rapidly, his arms once more crossing his chest. Calder hated that he was always upsetting him. He was so…tenderhearted. Calder didn't want Robby to lose that. He definitely didn't want to be the reason he did. But he also wasn't strong enough to say no. If Robby wanted Calder to teach him, then he would but on Calder's terms.

Calder took Robby's hand and led him back into the bedroom. "Get on the bed," he said, all traces of humor gone.

Robby all but fell backwards onto the mattress, scooting himself upwards until his head was on the pillows. Calder spread the boy's legs, settling himself between them and bracketing his forearms on either side of his head.

"Is this crawling?" Robby whispered.

Calder brushed his lips over Robby's. "This is kissing. Just kissing. With no expectation of anything more. So relax."

Robby gave a hesitant nod before lifting his head to capture Calder's mouth in a kiss that sent their teeth clacking together. Robby flushed, flopping back down. "I'm a disaster. I suck at this."

Calder smiled at the disgruntled look on the boy's face, which only deepened his pout.

"How about you just let me lead and stop thinking so hard?"

Robby slapped his hands over his face. "You have no idea what you're asking of me. I don't drive because I spend my life in fear of having to parallel park."

Calder barked out a surprised laugh, causing Robby to peek out at him from behind his fingers. "Then let me drive, okay? No thinking necessary."

Robby dropped his hands, his expression dubious, like he wasn't quite sure he could take Calder at his word. He understood what it was like not to trust somebody. He even understood what it was like to be afraid. "Or we could stop right here?"

Robby closed his eyes. "What if you're disappointed? What if I do something wrong?"

"Not even possible. Sex is like pizza. Even when it's bad, it's good. Besides, it's just kissing. We've already done this already, remember? I do."

Robby opened one eye as if once more gauging whether Calder told the truth, and again, he was struck by how truly adorable the boy was. If he'd ever needed more of a reason to get up and run, that was it, that was the moment. Something about this kid tugged at something inside Calder, and it scared the shit out of him.

"Do you want to stop?" Calder asked.

Robby shook his head, cheeks pinking.

Calder moved slowly, feathering kisses over the boy's cheeks, his chin, his nose, before tracing the seam of his lips with his tongue. He didn't remember the last time he'd kissed somebody without intent, without it being a means to an end. He stroked his thumb along Robby's jaw, coaxing the boy's mouth open beneath his.

Time slipped away. Kissing Robby was easily Calder's new favorite thing. He collected every whimper, every sigh, every moan. Each kiss lasted longer, grew needier and more frantic. They were both hard, but Calder was content to ignore that, focusing instead on exploring new territory—Robby's throat, his jawline, the shell of his ear, cataloguing every single response, every noise, the way Robby's blunt nails scraped over Calder's skin whenever he bit at the boy's lower lip or growled against his skin.

Calder was congratulating himself on his incredible restraint when Robby decided to let his mouth do a bit of exploring of its own, his tongue darting out to taste the dip in Calder's throat. He ground his hips down without thought.

Robby whined at the friction of their cocks slotting

together with only the thin layers of fabric between them and wrapped his legs around Calder's hips to rut against him. "Fuck, that feels so good," Robby said, his voice wondrous, sounding almost drunk on Calder's kisses.

"Yeah? You like that, angel?" he asked.

Robby didn't answer, just nodded, burying his face against Calder's throat like he was embarrassed to be enjoying himself. Maybe Calder was selfish but he wanted to hear it. "Tell me," he whispered against his ear.

"Yes. Please, don't stop," Robby begged.

Fuck. So much for taking it slow. He tried to appease his guilt by reminding himself that Robby had begged for it, had asked Calder to be the bad guy, to use him up. How could he say no? He shoved their clothes out of the way, gripping the boy's hips, helping him find a steady rhythm, losing himself in a dirty pantomime of the sex they could be having if not for Linc's edict. But this was good, this was amazing. The feel of the boy's cock, slick with precum, rubbing against Calder's was perfect.

Robby was right. He was a very quick study, and Calder knew he wouldn't stop, couldn't even, especially if the boy kept whimpering, "Please, please," against Calder's skin desperately, like he

exasperating

might change his mind.

Not a chance. They weren't kissing anymore, just gripping each other tight, rubbing off on each other like teens, and Calder couldn't remember the last time he felt so present, so in the moment. His only intent was to give Robby what he needed, knowing the boy wanted just him.

Robby came first, nails digging into Calder's back, gasping his name in his ear almost like his pleasure surprised him. That shocky, startled breath was Calder's undoing, just like last time. Calder lifted himself off enough to see the evidence of Robby's orgasm, thrusting against him until he came hard, his own cum mixing with the boy's. He ran his fingers through it before slipping two fingers between Robby's lips. The boy sucked them clean, teeth scraping across Calder's skin. He kissed him deep, tasting them on Robby's tongue before dropping his head to Robby's shoulder. "Fuck."

They both laid there, panting and sticky, clothes askew. Robby clung to him just like he had that day in the shower, like he was afraid Calder would run. It caused a strange ache in Calder's chest, one he couldn't let himself get used to. Robby could count on Calder to keep him alive and could count on him for some no strings hookups, but he couldn't count on Calder in any personal way. He couldn't let himself care for Calder, and he definitely couldn't allow himself to fall for Robby. Love made Calder stupid, it got people hurt, and he couldn't live with himself if he was the reason anything happened to Robby.

He pressed a kiss to Robby's forehead and then rolled off and into a sitting position, reaching for the wet wipes in the top drawer and quickly cleaning up and righting his underwear before handing two to Robby. This was the part where he usually made up an excuse about work or just left to head back to his post. But he couldn't do that. Not this time. So, he grabbed his phone to keep from having to think too much about the hazel eyes burning a hole into his back and the boy who was thinking loudly enough for Calder to almost feel ashamed of himself. Almost.

There was a text from Linc: **The shit's hit the media. It might be best to keep the kid away from the internet today. The tabloids are going crazy.**

Calder clicked on Google and searched Robby's name. Linc wasn't kidding. The headlines were not only outlandish and incorrect but insulting.

Home Invasion Nightmare:
Ex-lover of actor Elijah Dunne Accused of Murder

exasperating

They couldn't even mention Robby by name while falsely accusing him of murder? Not that the ones who did mention his name were much better.

**Robby Shaw's Downward Spiral
Ends with One Dead**

**Kid's Channel Star Rocked by Scandal:
Angelic Robby Shaw Son of Devilish Cult Leader**

The boy had been in the tabloids for weeks now, but Calder wasn't sure if a breakup meltdown ranked anywhere near having killed a person who may or may not have been sent by your father to harm you. But the boy was stronger than Linc gave him credit for. He asked for what he wanted even when terrified. He braved a potential killer with only a cheese knife to save his dog and had come out of it without a scratch. Still, Calder would feel better if the boy wasn't winging it in the event his father tried again. Maybe he needed to show Robby how to defend himself?

The mattress shifted behind Calder and then Robby was peering over his shoulder. Calder quickly set his phone face down on the side table, gripping Robby's forearms and tipping his head up to kiss his lips. He narrowed his gaze. "Wow. Must be pretty bad if you're trying to distract me with kisses when you were contemplating jumping out your own window to get away from me sixty seconds ago."

Calder's brows went up. "You literally say whatever pops into your head, yet you claim everything scares you?"

Robby shrugged, expression glum. "When everything scares you, what have you got to lose? You miss a hundred percent of the shots you don't take, right?" he mumbled.

"Life lessons from the world's grumpiest motivational speaker," Calder drawled with a smile.

"Mockery from a guy who thinks his dick is literally magic," Robby said, a hint of laughter in his voice.

Calder launched himself backward, trapping Robby beneath him. "Do me a favor, angel. Stay off the internet today, okay?"

Calder's head rose and fell as Robby took a deep breath. "That bad, huh? What are the tabloids saying today? Am I the AntiChrist? Am I secretly indoctrinating actors into Magnus Dei? Oh, God. Did they say I was getting fat?"

Calder shook his head. "Stay off the internet. I mean it."

"Fine. Can I at least call Wyatt and Charlie and ask them to bring me some clothes? Yours all smell like paint thinner."

Calder flipped over in one graceful move, pinning Robby beneath him. "Wow, you sound mighty ungrateful. I gave you the very shirt off my back—"

"You pulled it from your bottom drawer," Robby corrected with a giggle.

"—off my back," Calder continued as if he hadn't heard the boy. "And this is the thanks I get."

He skimmed his hands up under the shirt the boy still wore, tugging it up and off, earning an involuntary bark of laughter as his fingers snaked along his sides. Robby cut his laugh off abruptly, biting down on his lip as if he'd accidentally revealed some deep dark secret. "Are you…are you ticklish, angel face?"

"What? No."

Calder sat up, straddling Robby's hips. "No?"

Robby's gaze landed somewhere over Calder's left shoulder. "Nope. Not at all. Are you?"

Very. "Now, now. Focus. This ain't about me. This is about you, and I think you're a dirty, rotten liar."

Robby's mouth fell open, looking truly insulted. "Rude."

Calder's fingers skimmed along the stars at Robby's hip bones. Once more, the boy's teeth sank into his lower lip. He was so easy to read. So open. So afraid but always so willing. Even now. Calder teased over

Robby's sides, heart skipping as the boy giggled. "What was that?" Calder asked, tickling the boy until he was squirming and breathless with laughter, hands wrapped around Calder's wrists in a half-hearted attempt to displace them.

Calder found himself on top of Robby again, their mouths almost touching, his hands no longer at the boy's sides but tugging at the bars through each nipple. Robby moaned against Calder's lips. He supposed if they had to spend the day hiding from the press and ignoring the internet, there were worse ways to spend it than figuring out what Robby liked and what he didn't. He definitely liked having his nipples played with. His hands were restlessly flexing against Calder's back, his breath panting against Calder's mouth. He liked where this was going. At the rate Robby was learning, maybe kitchen blowjobs were on the menu at some point in the near future.

Calder's head jerked up as rap music began to blare from the side table of his bed. "I think your phone's having a seizure."

Robby didn't try to wiggle free of Calder, just bent impossibly far behind him to reach his phone. He was bendy. Calder filed that away for later.

"It's my ringtone."

"Why is it so angry?" Calder asked.

exasperating

"Don't disrespect Tupac," Robby mumbled before frowning. "It's the lawyer."

Calder grimaced. "Well, don't leave him hanging. Answer it."

All the joy seemed to leave Robby, like somebody had dropped heavy curtains across a sunny window. Calder dropped a kiss to Robby's lips without thought before adding, "It's gonna be okay, angel face."

Robby nodded, but it was clear he didn't believe it. "Hello?"

eleven

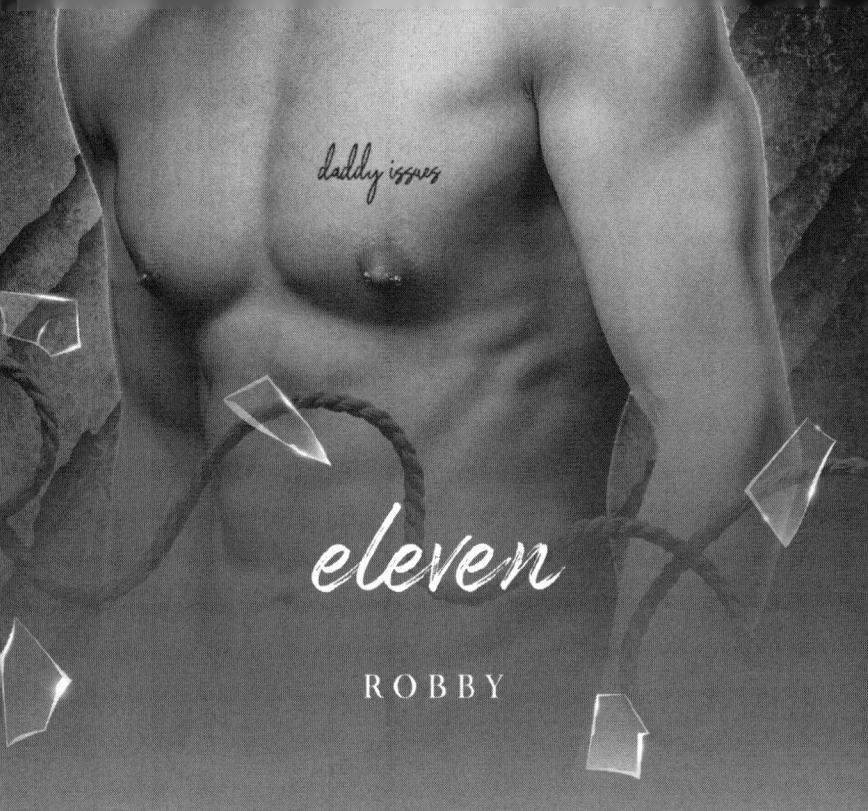

ROBBY

"ROBBY? STANTON FIELDS."

"Hello, Mr. Fields," Robby managed, feeling like his heart had physically lodged itself in his windpipe. He didn't bother to sit up, just let his head hang over the side, certain that Calder wouldn't let him fall.

"You're not staying at a hotel, are you?"

Robby frowned at the strange question. "What? No. Why?"

"The press is all over this. They know you're not at your apartment. I wanted to warn you if you had decided to stay at a hotel. You shouldn't go out right now, and you definitely shouldn't be going out alone.

exasperating

It could be dangerous."

"I hired a security detail. I'm staying…at a friend's. I wasn't planning on going anywhere."

That was true, at least. The last thing Robby wanted was to have to muscle past paparazzi screaming at him, trying to get a reaction from him since the only reaction they were likely to get was him bursting into tears, and he was already an embarrassment.

"Good. Good. This investigation will blow over sooner rather than later, but we have to let the detectives do their job and explore all avenues. In the meantime, I suggest getting with your publicist and hiring a PR team."

"A PR team? Why?"

"Because your father has one and he's already out there in front of the cameras claiming that he's the victim of a smear campaign and threatening to sue you for defamation of character."

Robby felt like he'd fallen down a rabbit hole. "Defamation of character?" His father had no character. Besides, how could he be defaming his father? Nobody had even known who his father was… except, now, somehow they did. "How did the press even get a hold of this?"

His attorney scoffed. "The LAPD leaks like a sieve. I'm sure somebody tipped them off before we'd even made it out of the building. It'll get kicked up to HSS now, and then this is about to get real Hollywood. I hope you're ready for it."

Ready for it? For what? To be the star of a crime drama that possibly ended up with him doing time in a real life jail cell? Was anybody ready for that? "HSS?"

"Homicide Special Services. They handle all the cases with high-profile suspects."

Was he high-profile? Was *he* a suspect? Robby's stomach sloshed. What was happening? How was this happening to him? He had the worst luck in the world. Only he could be the victim of a break-in and still somehow be the one under suspicion. "Am I going to jail, Mr. Fields?"

The attorney snorted. "I'm not going to let that happen. Like I said, this investigation should close rather quickly, but the press is gonna make a meal out of it regardless. Just do what I say and you're going to be fine. But you should seriously get with your publicist and hire a team quickly. You need to get out in front of this. The world thinks your father is a quack, but you've done some pretty damning things in the court of public opinion lately. You might need to start triaging your image."

Triaging his image? "Yes, sir."

exasperating

"You'll hear from me shortly."

There was no goodbye, just silence as the man ended the call. Robby dropped his phone to the mattress, feeling dizzy and sick. Calder gently tugged him into a sitting position. "What was all that about?"

Robby sighed. "My father is threatening to sue me for defamation, and the media is trying to hunt me down. I need to call Jasmine. Mr. Fields thinks I need a PR team now."

"What do you think?" Calder asked.

"I think it doesn't matter what I think. I need to know what Jasmine wants. I have to do what I'm told, at least until the end of the year."

Calder tipped his head like a curious puppy. "What happens at the end of the year?"

"My contract with the show is up and so is the contract with my publicist. Then I can…reevaluate."

"Reevaluate?"

"Yeah. I became an actor because it was a way out from underneath my father's thumb. I don't know if I want to do it anymore. I don't know if somebody like me is cut out for Hollywood."

To Calder's credit, he didn't tell Robby he was crazy or try to tell him he was squandering an opportunity most people would kill for. Robby lectured himself about those same things enough for ten people. He lived in a constant spiral of shame and guilt.

"What would you do if you weren't an actor?"

Robby shifted, uncomfortable with the level of attention Calder now lavished on him. Nobody had ever asked him what he wanted. It was a strange feeling. Not only that Calder asked but that he examined Robby like he actually cared about the answer. "I don't know. I just always wanted to work with animals."

"Like a lion tamer or like a vet?" Calder asked, giving Robby a half-smile that probably melted the panties off women everywhere.

Robby's cheeks flushed. "I don't think I'm smart enough to be a vet or brave enough to be a lion tamer. I would just like to take care of the animals nobody else wants."

A strange expression crossed Calder's face. "I think you would be perfect for that."

Robby wasn't sure if Calder was making fun of him or not, but it didn't really matter. Despite Wyatt and Charlie's scheming, whatever this was with Calder was temporary. They'd fooled around twice, and both times, Calder had looked like he was fighting the urge to run away. Robby tried not to let that hurt, but it twisted his insides anyway.

"Do you show your art anywhere?" Robby asked,

hoping to deflect the attention away from himself.

Calder's head turned towards the dining room. "My paintings? Nah. I just do that for me."

"But you're really talented. Don't you want to share that talent with the world?" Robby asked.

"You're a really talented actor. Do you really want to stop acting and deprive the world of your talent?"

Robby scoffed. "Thanks, but I'm a mediocre actor on a good day. Most people over the age of ten only know me because I'm Elijah Dunne's ex-boyfriend."

"Well, I'm a mediocre painter, but I like that you think I'm not."

Robby smiled. "I should probably call Jasmine now." His gaze flicked upward. "Should I tell her you said hi?" he asked, voice deadpan.

Calder snickered. "Uh, that won't be necessary."

Robby batted his lashes. "Are you sure? I don't want to keep you from anything."

Calder caught Robby's mouth in a dirty kiss that left him semi-hard. "I'm positive, angel. I've got my hands full at the moment, unless you've tired of me already?"

Robby's heart cartwheeled behind his ribcage, but he shrugged, turning his attention to his phone screen. "I suppose not yet."

"Oh, well that's good. I have some calls to return of

my own. So, I'll leave you to your planning."

Once Calder had left the room, Robby called Jasmine who answered on the first ring. "Where have you been?"

"In hiding. In case you haven't noticed, I've been accused of murder and my father is all over the news."

"I've noticed. Why do you think I've been freaking out? Are you okay? Where are you staying?"

"I hired a security company. I'm staying with the guard who's looking out for me. Calder Seton."

Robby took some pleasure in the long silence on the other side of the line and the way Jasmine cleared her throat uncomfortably. "Oh, good. Uh, good plan. I think we need to get out in front of this. The tabloids are all over it and CNN has been running stories about Magnus Dei all day."

"My attorney says we need to hire a PR team."

"Okay. That makes sense. I'll call Marin Bridger. Her team handles murderers all the time…not that you're a murderer," she finished lamely.

He was, though. Technically. He'd stabbed somebody in the neck. Didn't that make him a murderer by definition? How did things get so out of control? "It's fine. Don't tell anybody where I'm staying."

"I'll be in touch shortly."

For the second time that day, somebody hung up

exasperating

on him. He shook his head. He was the one facing jail time. Why did people keep acting like he was the one who was inconveniencing them? He grimaced as he thought about the people he might actually be inconveniencing. Charlie. Wyatt. Calder.

He quickly texted Wyatt and asked if there was any way he could bring him some clothes. He let him know he was essentially on lock-down until further notice. Wyatt shot back a thumbs up.

With that handled, Robby tossed his phone and went in search of Calder. He found him in the kitchen, facing the open window to the parking lot below. He had his phone in his hand and a woman's voice came through the speaker. "—several attempts to reach you regarding retrieval of your loved one's ashes. Please call us back at your earliest—" The voice disappeared as Calder hit a button on his phone.

Loved one? Ashes? That didn't sound like a pet. Had Calder lost somebody recently? If he had, he clearly wasn't interested in sharing that information with Robby. He backed up a few steps and made a production of clearing his throat so Calder wouldn't feel like Robby had snuck up on him.

"That was fast," Calder said, turning around to look at him, that slick half-smirk on his face. The one Robby hadn't seen since their shower that first day. Robby called it Calder's 'casanova look.'

"Shit, Casanova," Robby cried, earning a confused look from Calder. "I didn't give him his meds or his breakfast."

He noticed then that his beloved dog was curled up sleeping on the back of Calder's couch. There was no way Cas would have let him forget to feed him. Robby turned to narrow his eyes at Calder. "Why's he so quiet? Did you drug him?"

Calder shook his head. "Yes, I did. I fed him, too. Before you even got your butt out of bed this morning."

"Oh. How did you…"

"There are pet-sitting instructions in that box of his. I took care of him while you were in the clink, remember?"

Robby flushed. "Thank you."

Calder backed Robby up against the wall. "Well, I figured if I let that gremlin die, you wouldn't let me see you naked anymore."

"You're right," Robby murmured, initiating a kiss. "What should we do until Wyatt and Charlie get here with my clothes?"

Calder wrapped his arms around him and kissed him thoroughly. "I'm going to teach you something useful."

Robby liked the sound of that. His hands slid down

to Calder's ass, pulling him closer. "Oh, yeah? Like what?"

Calder grinned. "Self-defense."

Robby could feel his face contorting into a sour look against his will. "What?"

"Self-defense. I'm worried you won't know how to protect yourself when this is all over. I can be your Mr. Miyagi."

Robby blinked at him. "My who?"

Calder gaped at him. "Mr. Miyagi? Daniel-san. The Karate Kid? Christ, angel. We've got to get you up to speed on your classic films. This is downright embarrassing."

"I was raised in a cult. I didn't see a computer until I was fifteen. Movie nights weren't really a thing until my dad took over and decided we needed to modernize," Robby reminded him.

Calder shrugged in a 'fair enough' gesture. "Good point. Luckily for you, angel face, I happen to be gifted in many things. We will watch all the movies, I'll teach you all the ways to protect this hot body of yours, and I'll teach you all the fun things to do with said body… Well, not all, but almost all."

Who was this man? How did he let everything just roll off of him like life was just one big joke while Robby felt like every decision was life or death?

Maybe Calder could show him how to not take things so seriously? "Calder Seton, life coach. How very LA of you," Robby mused.

Calder grinned, wiggling his brows. "I prefer your sexual sensei."

Robby rolled his eyes. "Of course, you do."

"Come on. Let me teach you how to protect yourself."

Robby's heart sank. That was the thing, though. Calder couldn't teach him the one thing he truly needed to know. Robby didn't care about protecting his body. That was what he had Calder for. What he needed was to protect his heart, and he was pretty sure it was far too late for that. "Okay, fine. You win."

twelve

CALDER

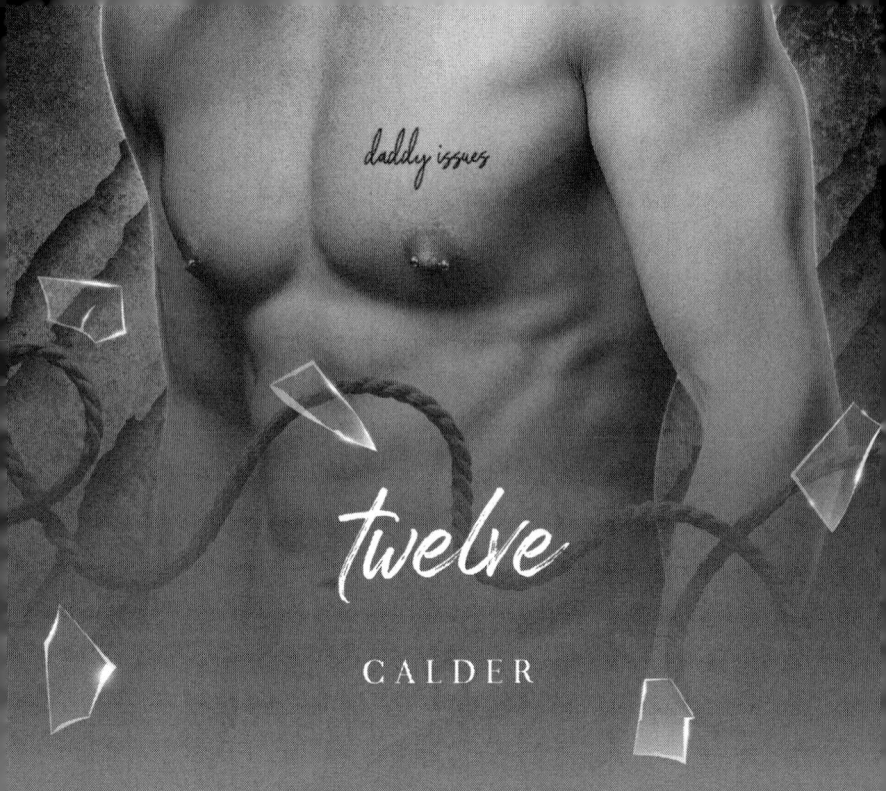

"GOTTA HIT HARDER THAN THAT, ANGEL FACE."

Robby blew air out through his nose, his jaw clenched tighter than his fists, which he dropped to his sides as he glared at Calder with a hostility he hadn't thought the boy possessed. Sweat glistened off his chest and forehead, Calder's borrowed joggers hanging low on his hips. "I'm hitting as hard as I can."

Calder let his eyes roam Robby's well muscled body. "I find that hard to believe, beautiful. You don't get a body like yours without working out hard."

Robby flushed and glanced down at himself as if he'd never seen his body before. "I got this body because a guy named Sven yelled at me every morning for a year and forced me to lift weights and eat things that taste like cardboard. If I wasn't an actor, I'd probably be a big pile of mush because working out sucks and food tastes good."

Calder barked out a laugh. "Well, for now, you *are* an actor and you can hit way harder than you are, so come on, let's do this." Calder slapped the pads covering his hands together. "Pick up your fists. Protect your face with your left and jab with your right."

Robby did as Calder instructed. Despite his lack of enthusiasm, his irritation seemed to grow with each swing until he was snarling whenever he jabbed or crossed, hitting harder, making Calder's palms sting. Every time Robby dropped the arm guarding his face, Calder thumped a pad against the boy's cheek hard enough to remind him to pick up his hands.

As time passed, the boy's fatigue grew evident. His swings became more wild, less accurate. When he missed Calder's pads entirely and socked him in the jaw, Calder dropped them to the floor and caught his fist with his hand, spinning the boy around and pinning his arm behind his back, careful not to hurt him. "And here I thought you didn't have a mean bone in your body. That hurt, angel face."

Robby panted hard as he craned his head back to

look up at Calder, blinking sweat out of his moss green eyes as he fluttered long lashes at him. "It was an accident," he said, voice filled with mock innocence.

"I think you're lying to me," Calder purred against his ear.

Robby shrugged, his expression flirty. "Prove it."

Fuck. Calder knew he needed to keep the boy focused, but it was awfully hard when everything about him screamed for Calder to pin him to the wall and fuck him. He let himself trace the shell of the boy's ear with his tongue. He tasted like salt and clean sweat. "If I didn't know better, I'd say you were trying to distract me so you could get out of practice."

Robby turned his head and let his lips graze Calder's jaw, ducking out of his grip just as Calder tried to capture his mouth, dancing away with fancy footwork like he was suddenly Mohammed Ali. "Then I guess it's a good thing we don't know each other," he quipped, grabbing his water bottle off the table and taking a big swig.

Calder raised a brow. "Careful, angel. Nobody likes a tease."

Robby locked eyes with him as he drained the bottle, water escaping the sides of his plush mouth to fall on his chest and slide down the ridges of his abdomen. "You're the one who decided this would be a better use of our time, not me."

Calder gave him a half smile. He wasn't wrong, but it was a job and he had to at least try to earn his paycheck. "We have plenty of time for whatever dirty thoughts are swirling around in that pretty head of yours later . This is important."

Robby stomped his foot and whined in what Calder could only describe as a hissy fit. He bit down on his lower lip to keep from laughing as the boy said, "Is it? Why? I hired you to protect me. I don't want to hit anybody, and I don't want anybody hitting me. I don't like being hit in the face. I don't like being hit at all. The whole point of hiring you was so that you will keep people from hitting me."

The boy was a ball of emotions, the living embodiment of chaotic energy. Loud one minute, quiet the next. Timid one minute, bold the next. Scared all the time but had no filter at all when it came to his thoughts. Calder couldn't figure out how the world seemed to just pass Robby over. It was like Calder had some supernatural gift to see something the rest of the world couldn't. Robby was a ghost that seemed to appear only to him. It seemed a shame to squander such a generous gift, but now wasn't the time.

"Okay, how about this? I'll teach you some basic self-defense moves and then we'll call it a day. I'm going to come at you from behind, and I want you to just do your best to try to get away. Okay?"

Robby eyed him warily but eventually nodded before turning away.

Calder allowed himself a moment to appreciate the swell of the boy's ass and the perfect dimples that sat just above it on the boy's lower back. Calder wanted to lick his way along Robby's spine, wanted to dip his tongue in those dimples. Wanted to spread Robby open and taste the very core of him. He shook the thought away, noting the boy's tension. "Relax, angel. You're not supposed to see this coming. You need to be able to respond instinctively."

Robby shot him another sour look over his shoulder. "We've been at this for two hours. I'm tired. I'm obviously not a fighter. Why is that a bad thing?"

"Ordinarily, it's not," Calder drawled. "But somebody broke into your house with nefarious intentions, and even if you can't—or won't—throw a punch, you still need to be able to defend yourself if somebody comes after you again. If you hate fighting that much, I won't make you, but you have to know some self-defense strategies. At least give me that."

Robby rolled his eyes. "If they come at me from the front, hand to nose, knee to groin. If they come at me from the back, elbow to the ribs, heel to instep. I've seen *Miss Congeniality*, too, you know. I've got it."

Calder sighed. "Please take this serious, angel. I don't want you getting hurt."

"Then you should stay close and do your job," Robby snarked.

Calder shook his head at the sass. "I have every intention of staying close, very close, but I need to know, for my own peace of mind, that you can take care of yourself."

"I mean, I've only been attacked twice and both times I walked away," Robby pointed out, his tone almost smug.

Calder grinned. "Well, you won't always have a cheese knife or a sex toy to defend yourself with."

Robby's cheeks went pink, and he whipped his head back around so Calder could no longer see his face. He was so easily embarrassed. Calder had never thought he'd find this shy, bashful shit attractive but everything Robby did turned him on. He just always found himself wanting to touch him, inhale his scent, taste his skin. Calder drifted closer, all thoughts of safety gone by the wayside. He slid his hands around Robby's waist, pulling him back against him.

"Is this your attack?" Robby whispered, breathless.

Calder's hands slid up, playing with the bars through Robby's nipples. "Depends. Is it working?"

exasperating

Robby moaned, his back arching to rub his ass against Calder's already hard cock, straining against the zipper of his jeans. "I don't feel much like defending myself."

"No?" Calder murmured.

"Uh-uh."

"What do you want?"

"Kiss?" Robby asked, his chest rising and falling rapidly beneath Calder's splayed hands, like he anticipated Calder's refusal.

As if Calder would say no to that. He turned him around and tilted his chin up. Robby lifted up on his toes to lick over Calder's open lips once then twice before closing the distance between their mouths. He wrapped his arms around Robby, hands sliding over the slick muscles of the boy's back. But he didn't stop there, he slid his hands into the boy's pants, gripping his ass and lifting him up. Robby didn't hesitate, his legs wrapping around Calder's waist, his arms encircling Calder's neck.

He briefly thought of dropping the boy onto the sofa but decided the living room wall worked just fine. Robby must have thought so, too, because he moaned into Calder's mouth, biting at his lips the way Calder had done to him earlier. There was nothing gentle or slow this time. Their kisses were all teeth and tongue and then Calder was fucking his hips up against Robby without any thought to technique or Robby's lack of experience. This was just about getting off.

Calder shifted Robby's weight, bracing him against the wall so he could shove their clothes out of the way and grip both their cocks in his hand. Robby's pupils were blown wide and he swallowed hard as he watched Calder jerk them off, tiny half-bitten cries falling from his mouth before he clamped his teeth down hard on his bottom lip and let his head fall back against the wall.

Calder worked them both hard and fast, helped along by sweat and precum. Robby's heels spurred him on, digging into his thighs as he drove himself into Calder's fist with abandon. "I'm gonna come. I'm gonna come," he chanted, almost like he didn't know he spoke, then Calder's fist was slick with Robby's release. He continued to jerk them both, using Robby's cum as lube. Robby brought his forehead to Calder's whispering, "I love that I can make you come. I want to feel it. Please."

It was the please that did it, rocketing Calder over the edge, pleasure licking along his spine as he came hard between them. "Christ, kid. The mouth on you. Who would have thought it?"

This time, it was Calder who didn't let go, clinging to

exasperating

him as he waited for his heart rate to return to normal. Robby took advantage of their close proximity, reaching between them and gathering their cum on his fingers and holding it up for Calder in silent askance. Calder took the boy's fingers between his lips, sucking his fingers just as Robby had his that morning. The boy's eyes grew wide, like part of him had expected Calder to refuse.

He should have refused. He shouldn't have let Robby lick his fingers clean that morning. He should have warned him about safe sex and condoms, that was the responsible thing to do. But Calder knew he was clean. He used condoms. He was tested frequently, used PrEP. He was careful and Robby was a virgin, completely untouched in almost every sense of the word. The one type of lover Calder had avoided like the plague. Yet, now his worst nightmare had somehow become his hottest fantasy. Calder wanted to pretend it made no sense. That it was the novelty of the boy, but some annoying voice in the back of his head kept calling him a liar and Calder had yet to figure out a way to shut it up.

Robby jumped as a loud buzz echoed through the space. Calder sighed, setting the boy on his feet and righting his jeans. "I'm pretty sure that's gonna be Wyatt and Charlie. You should probably go clean up real quick if you don't want to answer a million questions."

Robby gave a hesitant nod before fixing his joggers and walking towards the bathroom, head down like Calder had done something wrong. Had he? Probably. It was just who he was as a person. It was better if Robby got used to disappointment now. When it came to Calder fucking up, that train was never late.

Calder let Wyatt and Charlie in while Robby cleaned up and then excused himself to the bedroom to let them talk in private. He needed to start doing his job. Robby had hired him to keep him safe and Calder intended to do just that, but guarding Robby's body wasn't Calder's only skill. He was a private investigator. He didn't need to sit back and wait for the officers to do their job. Somebody had tried to harm Robby, and it was imperative that Calder determined whether this was just an accident of circumstance—wrong place, wrong time—or whether Robby actually had a target on his back.

He pulled up a number on his phone and hit call.

A smooth, unbothered voice answered. "Tex-ass. What's up, brother?"

Calder rolled his eyes at Webster's nickname. "Sup, poindexter. Think you could step away from your mirror for five minutes? I need a favor."

exasperating

Webster was Elite's resident computer expert, though he looked more like an underwear model who was trying to make himself look like a computer nerd. Nobody would really know he was actually a fairly lethal fighter, too.

"What's the matter? Give your laptop herpes again looking at porn?" the man quipped. There was a sound like movement, and then Webster was mumbling something Calder couldn't make out to whoever he was with. Suddenly, he was back. "What do you need?"

"An ME report."

There was a long-suffering sigh. "Can't you just request the findings like a normal person? Hacking municipalities is boring. It takes literally no skill on my part. It's insulting, really."

Calder snickered and shook his head. "How quick can you get it to me?"

"Twenty minutes if it's in their system. Anything in particular you're looking for?"

Calder knew what he was looking for but he didn't want to get so focused he missed something. "Yeah, but just get me everything that's back."

"Yeah, man. You got it."

Webster disconnected the call without another word, and Calder opened his laptop, positioning himself in the chair in his bedroom that allowed him to keep Robby in his line of sight while he started digging into Magnus Dei. Twenty minutes into his search, he stumbled upon a group on reddit started by former members. The horror stories turned Calder's stomach and left him looking at Robby in an entirely new light.

What the fuck had this kid been through? How had he remained so positive and sweet after a monster like Jeff Deaton, aka Brother Samuel, had entered their lives, and later, the evil machinations of his own father? Would Calder end up being another monster who hurt Robby? Deep down, he already knew the answer, and it made him hate himself even more.

thirteen

ROBBY

ROBBY WAS BOTH RELIEVED AND DISAPPOINTED to take off Calder's clothes and replace them with Wyatt's. The white joggers and black Chanel hoodie fit perfectly and were far more luxurious than anything Robby currently had in his closet. But they didn't smell like Calder and Robby found he really liked smelling like the older man, even if he smelled like oil paints all the time. His visit with his friends hadn't lasted long because Wyatt had therapy and Charlie had an audition, but it was still nice that they seemed like they weren't bailing on him despite how high maintenance his friendship probably seemed to them now.

Robby put the duffle bag full of borrowed clothes on the floor of Calder's bedroom and wandered around the house aimlessly before settling on the sofa and flipping on Calder's huge television and surfing through the channels, unable to focus on anything for more than a few minutes. His head swam with thoughts of dead bodies and paparazzi swarming around his old place just waiting to grill him and ask him invasive questions he had no way to answer.

Calder emerged from his bedroom and sprawled on the opposite end of the sofa, kicking his legs up and tangling them with Robby's without acknowledging him in any other way. Calder didn't glance up, intently focused on whatever was on the screen of the laptop balanced on his flat belly. Robby hesitated before sliding lower on the sofa, resting his head on the arm and slotting his legs on either side of Calder's. The older man's foot began to idly rub against Robby's inner thigh, not in any overtly flirty way but in a familiar way, a boyfriend way, like he just needed to touch him. It warmed Robby's insides.

Robby was cycling through the channels when a picture of his attacker came into view in the upper righthand corner over the shoulder of a woman in a red blazer with a head full of blonde hair and a serious

exasperating

expression. He froze, turning up the sound until her measured voice filled the room.

"A home invasion turned deadly just forty-eight hours ago when the occupant of the residence, Kid's Channel star Robby Shaw, allegedly killed an assailant who forced his way into his home. While there has been no confirmation, sources say the weapon was believed to be a cheese knife and that this man could have been sent by none other than Shaw's own father, the notorious leader of the Magnus Dei church, Jeb Shaw. Detectives could neither confirm nor deny these allegations but say if anybody can help identify this man they should contact LA county's homicide division and that, for now, the investigation remains open."

"Thanks, Sharon," the other anchor said as the picture disappeared and another appeared behind the man's head. "In related news, Magnus Dei leader, Jeb Shaw, has himself released a statement regarding the incident. Here's what he had to say."

Robby's stomach sloshed as his father came into view wearing a suit that probably cost more than a Kia. "Folks, it's a sad day when a man has to defend himself against slanderous allegations from his own blood, but I'm afraid that's where we're at. I've never been anything but supportive of my son's career and even brought him out to Los Angeles myself so he could fulfill his dream of being an actor. To hear now that he believes I'm somehow capable of sending a man to assault him is not only insulting but outrageous. I can't help but feel this is some kind of retaliation against me for not condoning his deviant lifestyle of sodomy, drugs, and alcohol. Had I known I was sending my boy out to Sodom and Gomorrah, I would have simply kept him close. I can only hope my son turns away from the devil and this wicked lifestyle and comes back to Jesus's light. I don't wish to get attorneys involved but if he keeps bringing these lies against me and the church I've built up from nothing, I'll have no choice. Please, Obidiah, call me. Your mother and I are here for you. Your brothers and sisters are here for you. It's not too late."

The video faded away, and the news anchor cleared his throat. "Well, there you have it. We'll continue to cover the story as it unfolds."

Robby blinked back tears, his face on fire, humiliation consuming him. Calder was no longer looking at his screen but at Robby. He thought about bolting. He couldn't stand the thought of crying in front of Calder again. He'd cried more in the last week than he'd cried in his entire life, and Calder had been there every single time. Robby couldn't even imagine what he thought of him. When his phone rang in his pocket, he

exasperating

jumped, heart sinking, as he saw his attorney calling once again.

"Hello?" he managed.

"Robby, sorry to call twice in one day, but the detectives want us back for more questions tomorrow morning. Meet me out front at nine-thirty so we can walk in together."

"Y-Yes, sir," Robby stuttered. "Did they say why they wanted to talk to me?"

"No but don't worry. Everything is going to be fine. You just listen to me and do as I say, and everything will be right as rain. See you tomorrow."

Robby set the phone on the table and attempted to flee to the bedroom, but Calder raised a leg, barring him from standing. "Hey. Where are you going? Are you okay? Who was that?"

"They want me back to answer more questions tomorrow morning," Robby said, hot tears spilling over his cheeks. He tried to wipe them away before Calder saw them, but it was no use.

"Okay. Don't panic."

Tears flowed freely now, and his nose started to run. "Easy for you to say. You aren't the one who's being accused of murder and threatened with a law suit."

He sniffled, looking at his hands, too embarrassed to look at Calder.

"Come here, angel. Please don't cry," Calder crooned in a voice so sympathetic it only made Robby feel worse.

Robby just shook his head. But then Calder's hand closed around Robby's wrist, tugging him across the couch and into his arms. Robby didn't quite make it all the way, his cheek resting against Calder's stomach. It didn't matter, though. Robby could barely talk as he wailed, "I swear I don't usually cry this much. It just seems like my life is falling apart."

"Shh, you have the right to be emotional, sweetness. This is a lot for anybody to take."

"You wouldn't cry at the thought of going to prison," Robby said between racking sobs. "I don't want to go to jail. I won't do well in prison. Look at me."

Calder's fingers combed through his hair, and his stomach jiggled with laughter. "I don't know about that, angel. I was a cop for over a decade. We definitely don't do well in prison. I might shed more than a few tears at the notion," he said. "But I promise you, I'll never let you see the inside of a jail cell, even if I have to smuggle you out of the country to some place without extradition. But I sincerely doubt it will come to that."

Robby knew Calder wasn't serious, but it made him feel better anyway. His panic slowed, even if his tears didn't. Robby wrapped his arms around Calder's waist, closing his eyes, letting the warmth of the older man's skin and even the sound of his stomach growling sooth him. He didn't open his eyes again until the sound of the Paramount music swelled into the room.

Robby took in the soft, slightly fuzzy movie on the screen. "What's this?"

Calder glanced down at him with a smile. "*Vertigo*. We're going to fix this insane lack of knowledge you have about classic films. Now, pay attention."

Robby wiggled a bit higher to snuggle under Calder's chin. His fingers stayed in Robby's hair, but his free arm came around Robby's back as he covered them both with the black blanket from the back of the sofa. If he could have burrowed under Calder's skin, he would have. Nobody had ever held him before. Not when he cried and not when he was happy. Positive touches had never been a part of his life and he craved it more than anything. His parents didn't believe in physical affection. If only they had carried the same convictions about punishments. Robby forced thoughts of his parents and lawsuits and police officers aside to focus on Calder and the movie he was so eager to show him. He deserved a few hours of peace.

ROBBY WONDERED IDLY IF THE POLICE PROVIDED barf bags. Being back in the interrogation room had his stomach sloshing. Why did everything smell like stale air and sweaty socks? Why was it so cold in there? Shouldn't the cold have killed the smell at least? His attorney, Mr. Fields, sat on his left just like last time. Calder sat to his right, his hand resting on Robby's knee under the table.

Mr. Fields had advised Robby not to answer any questions unless he said it was okay and not to volunteer any information. He'd also somehow managed to get them to allow Calder to sit in on the questioning provided he said nothing. Robby almost wished he'd brought Casanova. He always calmed Robby's frazzled nerves.

There were now two detectives in the room, a tall man with a bald head, flawless umber skin, a full beard, and eyes so brown they looked black. He dressed casually in blue jeans and a white t-shirt, his gun at his hip, and his badge on a lanyard around his neck. He'd identified himself as Detective Mayhew. The detective from the other day was there as well, still pale, pudgy, and sweaty, looking like he had worn the same rumbled shirt and dress pants since the last time they'd interviewed him.

Once everybody had introduced themselves, Mayhew flipped open a folder. "Mr. Shaw, can you please walk me through the events of the other night, just so I'm up to speed?" he asked, clicking his pen and pressing it to a paper within the folder like he was going to take notes.

"Again?" Robby asked before looking at Mr. Fields.

"My client has already been through this story twice. I think that's enough. I assume you brought us down here for more than just that?"

"Mr. Shaw. Tell us why you think your father sent somebody to kill you?"

The question hit Robby like a bucket of ice water, sending shockwaves over his body and causing goosebumps to erupt on his skin. His brows knitted together, his voice raising an octave. "What? I never said that."

Mayhew leaned back, lacing his fingers together on the table. "You said your father was the only person you could think of who would want to hurt you."

Robby was shaking his head. "But I didn't say that. You're twisting my words."

The look on Mayhew's face made Robby feel like his insides were shriveling up. It was the same type of look Brother Samuel would give them when they cried during punishment. This sort of sneering condescension. "Tell the truth. You suspected your father because you know the man you killed. Don't you?"

"What?" Robby said again, bewildered, looking to his attorney for some kind of help.

Mr. Fields just tilted his head. "You can answer."

Robby's hands flailed in a helpless gesture. "No. I have no idea who he is…was, and I never said my father wanted to kill me."

Mayhew didn't even acknowledge his answer. It was almost like he didn't even care what Robby said. "How can you be so sure that the man from your apartment was sent by your father?"

Robby bit the inside of his cheek to keep from crying, trying to focus on Calder's thumb stroking the inside of his knee. "I'm not sure of anything."

Mayhew made some kind of notation on his notepad, but Robby couldn't see what it said.

"Is it true that three days prior to killing the man in your apartment, you assaulted a police officer and were arrested?" the detective asked.

Robby's gaze flicked to his attorney. Finally, Mr. Fields spoke, his tone dripping with boredom. "Gentlemen, why are you asking questions you already know the answer to? This whole thing is ridiculous, really. It's not my client's job to figure out who broke into his apartment and why. It's yours. If you can't do that, perhaps you should find another profession."

Mayhew smiled this slick smile, like they had some kind of ace up their sleeve. "We have reason to believe that your client is lying to us about knowing the victim. We have recently uncovered some evidence that says the victim and your client were seen together prior to the night of the break-in."

Robby shook his head, his voice cracking. "No! No way. Not possible."

Mayhew once more ignored Robby's outburst. "Tell us about the night you assaulted Patrolman Penski. The night of the eleventh."

Robby licked his lower lip, his leg tapping double time beneath the table as he started to sweat. Fuck. Fuck. Fuck. "I-I can't."

Mayhew arched a brow at Robby, expression curious. "Why is that?"

"I-I blacked out. I don't remember anything about that night at all."

"Seems convenient that you can't remember assaulting a police officer with a sex toy," Mayhew spit, his expression bordering on disgusted.

Robby could feel himself getting emotional. "Does

it? Because it doesn't feel convenient. Some guy breaks into my apartment, tries to kill my dog and do god knows what to me, and I'm the one being interrogated. What the fuck is going on?"

"Relax, angel. They're just trying to get you riled up."

"Quiet," Detective Grady snapped. "Or I'll have you removed."

"You have me removed and this line of questioning ceases. Period. As for the assault charge, that officer assaulted *him*. He pepper sprayed him and tazed him with enough force to leave a wound that still hasn't healed," Calder growled. "That patrolman should be thanking his lucky stars we didn't file an excessive force complaint…yet."

Robby's heart felt light enough to float from his body. He couldn't remember a time when anybody had ever defended him like that. Ever. Including his own attorney who seemed to finally come to his senses. "Gentlemen, I think this has gone far enough. Are you planning on arresting my client?"

The detectives looked at each other before Detective Grady shook his head. "He's free to leave…for now."

"Excellent. Let's go."

Just like last time, Mr. Fields said his goodbyes on the steps of the police station. Robby managed to keep it together until he'd snapped his seatbelt into place in

exasperating

Calder's truck. Then he just burst into tears. "I don't know that man. I've never seen him before. What evidence could they possibly have that says I did?"

Calder gathered him into his arms awkwardly, pressing kisses against his temple and forehead. "I hate when you cry, angel. You're breaking my heart. I've got you. Okay? We're gonna get this figured out. You hired me to keep you safe, but I'm also a private investigator. Let's go home and do a little digging. I have a friend who can help us figure out what they know. But please, please don't cry."

Calder's words made Robby ache in a way he'd never be able to describe. It was like he was in a completely different kind of fake relationship, one where Calder would be every single thing Robby had always wanted but never dared hope for, but only for a limited time. It was perfect. Calder was perfect. But there was a clock ticking over their heads.

Robby had told himself that nothing could be worse than pretending to be Elijah Dunne's family-friendly boyfriend, but he was wrong. So wrong. Losing Calder was going to hurt like losing a limb, a phantom pain that would twitch and burn long after Calder moved on from Robby for good.

fourteen

CALDER

CALDER SAT IN THE LIVING ROOM READING THE ME report. Beside him, Robby napped under the fluffy black blanket they'd used yesterday, his head resting on Calder's thigh, Casanova snuffling like a winded gremlin in Calder's ear as he perched on the back of the sofa behind his head. The tv was on, playing a movie he'd turned on then quickly ignored, when Webster emailed the medical examiner's report.

Calder had pulled up the report on his tablet, unwilling to disturb the peacefully sleeping boy just to go get his laptop from the bedroom. As he read, he stroked Robby, his fingers playing with the boy's hair, mapping the shell of his ear, tracing his jawline. Calder didn't want to admit how much he enjoyed this…connection he had with Robby. It seemed foreign to feel so close to another person. He'd spent years perfecting the art of being physically close to somebody while avoiding intimacy like the plague. But it was impossible to keep Robby at arm's length. No matter how much Calder tried to think of him as temporary, it just felt like a lie.

When he cupped Robby's cheek, the boy nuzzled into Calder's palm and sighed, seeking his touch even in sleep. Calder never would have guessed that the one person to sneak past his defenses was this complete mess of a kid and his ugly as sin dog, but he couldn't worry about that now. He had a job to do. He'd figure out how to untangle himself later.

His phone buzzed and his stomach dropped as the name of the funeral home appeared on his screen. He ignored the call, but he couldn't ignore the guilt eating a hole through his belly. He couldn't avoid them forever. They insisted there was nobody else. He knew it was true. He'd looked far and wide, but if anybody had ever loved the girl, they were now long gone. He was all she'd had, and even in death, he was still letting her down.

Robby rolled over, rubbing his face against Calder's

leg, before sighing deep and sinking back into sleep. The boy was exhausted. He'd cried for an hour before sleep had finally come. Calder had tried to make him feel better, had wanted him to understand that Calder wouldn't let anything bad happen, even if it meant breaking the law. Hell, even if it meant breaking *every* law. The kid had been through enough in his life. There was no way Calder was letting them add a prison sentence to that hardship. Though he doubted it would come to that.

Calder took a sip of his coffee and turned his attention back to the report. It was depressingly unenlightening. The assailant who'd entered Robby's apartment had a heart two sizes too big. Literally. According to the pathologist, Dr. Gupta, if Robby hadn't killed him, his next cheeseburger probably would have. Three out of four of his major arteries were occluded by plaque. She'd also noted severe cirrhosis of the liver, diabetes, and a suspicious mass on the man's pancreas. What she hadn't noted was a burn mark in the shape of a cross on the man's foot.

Calder wasn't sure if that meant Robby's father hadn't sent the man or if Jeb Shaw was just smart enough to avoid detection by not sending someone bearing the mark of his cultish church. It also did nothing to help explain the detective claiming they

exasperating

had evidence that Robby had met the man before the night of the break-in. Were they bluffing? He doubted it. They wouldn't have tag-teamed Robby like that in interrogation if they truly believed Robby's story. Something had led them to believe Robby and this John Doe had met before. Calder needed to figure out what they knew and how they knew it.

As soon as they'd gotten into Calder's truck, he'd texted Webster and asked him to run a search on Robby's social media for the night of his arrest since it seemed to be the only day the boy couldn't account for. He said he'd compile a report and see if he could create some kind of cyber timeline to map Robby's whereabouts that night to try to determine where he could have run into a fifty-something-year-old stranger. Was it a random encounter? Crazed fan? Had he followed Robby home? How did he get past security at Robby's apartment complex? Had they had an altercation at the club? On the street? Had the man also taken a dildo to the face? Calder imagined if a cop was mad enough to taze and pepper spray Robby, John Doe might not have been above murder.

Before he could put too much thought into it, the buzzer to the callbox downstairs beeped out a weird rhythm and then began to screech like somebody was holding down the button. When it finally stopped,

Calder said, "What the fuck?"

"It's us, let us up."

Calder sighed at the familiar voice and shook his head. Was this what it would be like if he and Robby were together? Wyatt and Charlie bursting into his apartment uninvited at all hours of the day and night? He tried to muster up the irritation that thought would have caused just a week ago but found he couldn't. He shook the thought away, unsettled at how much the idea pleased him. It was a great fantasy, but it was just that, a fantasy. Calder didn't deserve a happily ever after. Maybe Robby was his penance. Seeing what he could have had if he'd done the right thing, if he hadn't been so selfish when it truly mattered.

He pressed the button to unlock the front entrance. He opened the door just as Wyatt and Charlie were walking up the last step into his hallway. "You guys know you don't live here, right?"

Charlie rolled her eyes and waved a hand. "We might have just solved your case for you so you should be a little nicer."

"What are you babbling about?" Calder asked, a throbbing starting in his left temple.

"I'm talking about you needing to pull a *Hangover* and piece together Robby's blackout. If anybody knows how to do that, it's Wyatt and me. We've lost

exasperating

entire weekends. Shit, one time in Ibiza, we lost a whole week."

"It's true," Wyatt said as if imparting some sage wisdom.

"How exactly do you even know about any of this?"

Charlie gave him a look like his question was absurd. "You called Webster, Webster called Linc, Linc was getting a blowjob so he put it on speaker, Wyatt finished up his…husbandly duties and then called me, and here we are."

She brandished her phone from her purse. "So, I used this app that basically allows you to compile every pic or video or tag you were mentioned in within a specific timeframe, and I'm almost positive I can tell you everywhere Robby was from about five thirty in the afternoon until his arrest. Believe me when I tell you, homeboy was busy."

"What's going on?" Robby asked, voice thick from sleep.

Charlie beamed at him, but the look carried a fair amount of pity. "Hey, boo. We were just telling your knight in dirty denim that we may have pieced together where you were and what you were doing the night you were arrested."

Robby's cheeks flushed. "Oh, yeah? Great," he said, sounding like it was not great.

Wyatt went and sat next to Robby on the couch, throwing an arm around his shoulders. "So, the good news is, there are tons of pics and videos of you that night. The bad news is, there are tons of pics and videos of you that night and I'm about eighty-five to ninety percent sure the tabloids will find them eventually."

Robby groaned, burying his head in his hands. "Is it that bad?"

Charlie gave a malicious cackle. "Bad? Oh, it's glorious. I just wish I had been there as your wingman, er, woman. Whatever, the truth is, you had an epic night and you should never let anybody shame you for it."

Robby peeked at Wyatt from between his fingers. "Forget it. I don't want to know. Just let them take me to jail. It would be far less humiliating than whatever it is you two are so happy about."

"Oh, buttercup. Your ass is far too pretty for prison. You'd be holding somebody's pocket before dinner."

Robby's face crumpled, and for a split second, Calder feared the boy might start crying again. "Jesus, Barbie, stop helping. Also, for the love of God, never volunteer for a suicide hotline."

Charlie scoffed. "Like I'd ever make that mistake again. Laugh at one clown…"

Calder stared at her for far too long, unable to tell if

exasperating

she was joking but fearing she wasn't. "Show me what you've got."

"Can I borrow your tv?" Charlie asked, already flipping it on and linking it to her phone without waiting for Calder's permission. "Wi-fi password?"

Calder handed it over, feeling at that point like resistance was futile. This was his life now. Overrun and bossed around by two twinks and a scary brunette with no filter. As soon as she connected, she plopped herself onto the floor, folding her jean-clad legs beneath her and staring at Calder expectantly. He went and sat back in his seat, his weight displacing Robby so he shifted towards him. Before he could scoot to give the boy his space, Cas crawled down from the top of the sofa to curl up in Calder's lap and go back to sleep. All three of them stared at him as if he'd performed some kind of magic trick.

"Are we gonna do this or what?"

Charlie nodded. A picture popped up on the screen. Robby stood with a group of dude-bros in polo shirts and backward ball caps, shots of tequila lined up before them. The hashtag said Boardwalk 11.

"Do you know these guys?" Wyatt asked, threading his fingers through Robby's and squeezing.

Robby nodded. "Yeah, the guy in the pink polo is Marco. He's my dogwalker."

"You went day-drinking with your dog walker? I'm so impressed," Charlie said. "I know you're sad but heartbroken Robby is definitely more fun than fake boyfriend Robby. I stand by this. So, we know at five thirty you were doing tequila shots with a bunch of frat boys because they all tagged you in several pics. You must have stayed there until at least eight o'clock."

"Because that's when open mic night starts…and that's when you started performing."

Charlie keyed up another video, and all the color drained from Robby's face. "Please, tell me you're joking."

"Oh, buttercup. I wish I could. Brace yourself."

fifteen

ROBBY

ROBBY STARED IN HORROR AT CALDER'S TELEVISION. It was like a car accident. He didn't want to look but he couldn't look away. Why did they have to have a video of this? Robby couldn't sing. He sounded like somebody was trying to strangle a duck. As soon as Charlie hit the play button and the music swelled, Robby's fear of carrying a tune faded and a new terror gripped him as the music to Eminem's *Rap God* swelled. "Oh, please. No," he whispered.

"Oh, yes," Charlie confirmed, gleeful.

For the next two minutes, Robby could only sit frozen, staring as he stalked across the stage, arms swinging as he attempted to spit the lyrics to one of the fastest songs in existence, spurred on by the crowd who screamed for him like he was actually Eminem and not a kid who ironed his jeans. Maybe they just hadn't expected a kid in khaki pants and a button down shirt to know anything about rap, or maybe they were as drunk as he clearly was and couldn't hear him butchering the song. Either way, it now existed on the internet forever.

"I think we get the point," Robby muttered.

"Shh, this is my favorite part," Charlie said, waving her hand at him.

Robby's face was on fire as he watched himself lift the mic in the air and drop it before stalking off the stage. The crowd went wild. "Please, tell me that was the most humiliating thing I did that night."

Wyatt shook his head. "Sorry, sweetie, but this doesn't even make the top five."

Robby could feel his organs shriveling within him. "Can you guys just watch the rest of this without me?"

Charlie chuckled. "What kind of fun would that be? Besides, for a kid raised in a cult, you kinda nailed it."

"It's true. You were amazing, really," Wyatt confirmed.

Calder said nothing, his expression uncharacteristically stony. Robby buried his face

exasperating

behind Calder's shoulder as Charlie pulled up the next video. He forced himself to lift his head and look at the screen when he felt Calder tense beneath him.

Wyatt snickered at the picture on the screen, but Robby's brows knitted together. A guy in a realistic Spiderman costume hung from a street sign. Robby had unrolled his mask so only his lower face was visible and it appeared they were seconds away from re-enacting the famous kiss from the movie.

Robby cut his eyes to Calder who sat with his jaw clenched tight. Was he…was he jealous? Embarrassed? Robby didn't remember anything, but he prayed he hadn't kissed another stranger. He didn't want to kiss anybody else, just Calder. Except, maybe now Calder didn't want to kiss him anymore. That thought cut like a knife through his rib cage.

"Am I at the Walk of Fame?" he asked, if only to distract himself from the idea that Calder was angry with him.

"Yup," Charlie confirmed.

"What the hell am I doing there?" he wondered out loud.

"Making friends," Wyatt said, pointing to the screen.

He was talking to two men who were holding hands. One was enormous, easily six-foot-six and probably three hundred pounds of muscle. The other was built in a similar way to Robby. Robby recognized the boy's top immediately. It was the crop-top cat hoodie he'd been arrested in. "Who are they?"

"According to their profiles, they're married gay porn stars. Their instagram is super cute," Charlie said without looking at Robby.

Robby thought he might throw up. He didn't begrudge people making a living, but he didn't think he wanted to know how he ended up wearing the shirt of a porn star. He didn't have to wait long for the answer. The next picture showed the boy, shirtless, holding four hundred dollars and Robby wearing the cat hoodie.

"You paid four hundred dollars for a cat hoodie, angel?" Calder asked, sounding amused but also a tad relieved. Had Calder feared he'd sold his virginity for a cat hoodie? Robby couldn't be mad at him since he'd also feared the same thing.

They flashed through more pics of Robby on the Walk of Fame, taking pictures and signing autographs in his cat hoodie. He appeared to be alone. When had he lost the frat boys? How had he ended up there at night? He closed his eyes and tried to remember something—*anything*—that might answer that question but it was just a void. A big, gaping black hole in his timeline.

exasperating

The next picture was of Robby in his cat hoodie sitting among a group of girls, his cheek smooshed up against a pretty girl with red hair and a tiara on her head and a sash across her white tank top that read BRIDE in big pink letters. The other girls' tank tops designated them as various members of the red-haired girl's wedding party, but he didn't recognize the location.

"Where the hell am I?" Robby asked.

Several pictures flashed across the screen. All of them contained half-naked men. "That would be *The Hollywood Men* strip show," Charlie said.

As humiliating as it was, he was relieved to see he stayed firmly planted in his seat, though he couldn't say the same for the ginger-haired girl who was on stage in several pictures, looking like she was having the time of her life. "That isn't so bad, I guess."

"Buckle up, buttercup, 'cause here's where the road gets bumpy."

Once more, Robby appeared at a table. This time, he was seated among a group of hairy, barrel-chested men in leather while an Amazonian drag queen dressed as Cher spoke to him from the stage. Charlie hit play on the YouTube video.

"I know you, doll. Aren't you that sweet-faced kid from that show? Are you even old enough to get in here? Do your parents know you're here? Or did you bring your daddies?"

The crowd laughed, but Robby just randomly shouted, "It's my birthday."

Robby's face burned as Wyatt, Charlie, and Calder all looked at him. "That was your birthday?"

He closed his eyes and shook his head. "My birthday is in September."

Wyatt and Charlie laughed again before everybody turned their attention back to the screen. Robby was now face down over Cher's lap while she spanked him with a paddle and the crowd counted the blows. When they hit twenty-one, Robby jumped back up to his feet and put his hands over his head, cheering for himself before promptly falling off the stage. Charlie audibly gasped.

Suddenly, Robby bounded back to his feet, thrusting his arms into the air. "It's my birthday!" he shouted again. The crowd cheered. The video ended. Thank God.

"I don't think I can handle anymore of this trip down memory lane."

"Oh, don't be sad, pumpkin. Drunk Robby is a blast. You've got a shit ton of likes. Tons of celebs would kill for these numbers. This is Hollywood. There's no such thing as bad publicity."

Robby's breath caught as Calder's thumb began to caress the inside of Robby's wrist. Neither Wyatt or Charlie could see what he was doing from this angle but Robby was almost positive they'd notice a boner if he popped one in the joggers he wore. How could such a little touch affect him so much? How did Calder do this to him? He really liked Wyatt and Charlie but he'd never wanted to kick two people out more than he did right then.

Another picture caught his eye. He was lying on a chair in a tattoo studio, his jeans pulled down low enough that pubic hair was visible. Robby silently prayed he'd worn underwear. The tattoo artist was predictably covered in ink, but it didn't hide his gorgeous face, his perfect teeth, or his sparkling blue eyes. He appeared to be laughing at whatever Robby said. The group next to Robby looked like they'd escaped a rodeo. Five men of various ages stood around their friend, all wearing checkered shirts, Levi's, huge belt buckles, and ten gallon hats. Was there a rodeo in Los Angeles? Tourists maybe?

"At least I know I got my tattoos from an actual artist and not some weirdo in a back alley," Robby managed.

The image on the screen changed again. "Okay, this is where things get…confusing. There are a ton of sightings of Robby at the club where he beat up that cop with a sex toy, but in most of the videos, it's too dark and smoky to see. Then I found this."

There was no way to hear the sound over the music blaring from everywhere, but Robby could see the police officer he'd assaulted poking his finger into the chest of a woman. Well, a drag queen. It was Cher from the club. They both seemed really angry. There were a lot of head wobbles and finger pointing from Cher and the officer had his hand hovering over his taser like he was afraid for his life.

Suddenly, Robby was there, pushing his way between Cher and the officer, poking the man in his chest. The police officer shoved him back hard enough to topple into Cher who—to her credit—simply righted Robby onto his feet and handed him something from her handbag. Robby flushed. It was the sex toy. If it was possible, he would have melted into a puddle of shame right there on the floor. He watched himself slap the officer with the dildo hard enough to send the man reeling backwards into the crowd, hitting the man with the camera and sending it flying to land lens down, the screen going dark.

"And there you have it. That's your lost night," Charlie said. "It definitely could have been worse. It's hard to look for sub-tweets, but I'll keep searching through those, too. Not that I doubt Webster's skills, but when it comes to social media, I just work faster."

Wyatt helped her to her feet. "What are you going to do with this information?"

"I think you should retrace Robby's night and see if any witnesses remember him," Charlie volunteered.

Calder sighed in exasperation. "Yes, Barbie, that's the plan. Robby and I will retrace his steps and see what we come up with."

"Excellent. Happy hunting." She grabbed Wyatt's hand but stopped short with her fingers on the doorknob. "Oh, and if you ever want to party like that again, I'm always your first phone call. Toodles."

Then they were gone, leaving Robby and Calder alone with only Cas between them.

Neither of them said anything for so long that Robby's nerves started to fray at the ends. "Are you mad at me?" he finally blurted.

Calder glanced over at him, startled. "What? No, angel. Why would I be mad?"

Robby shrugged. "Because I humiliated myself on a global scale?"

Calder frowned. "What, that?" he asked, waving vaguely towards the television. "When I was a Ranger, I lost entire weeks to drinking. For a while, it was my way of coping. I was never an alcoholic but I wasn't far off."

Robby looked up at Calder, his deep chocolate brown eyes looking more like whiskey in the light. "It's hard to picture you as a cop."

Calder's lips twitched. "Oh, yeah? Why's that?"

Robby shrugged. "I always picture cops as strait-laced rule followers. Boy scout types."

"Are you telling me I don't seem like a boy scout, angel?" Calder murmured in that low sexy purr that went straight to Robby's cock every time.

Robby shook his head, scooping Cas up and gently placing him on the sofa, before climbing into Calder's lap, calves resting along the outside of his thighs. "Uh-uh," he whispered, lips hovering just above Calder's.

"What's on your mind, sweetness?"

A million answers raced through his mind. *Kiss me, fuck me, love me, keep me.* Instead, he just shrugged.

"Did you need something?"

Robby shifted his hips closer so Calder could feel how hard he was already. Calder's hands slid up under Robby's shirt, just teasing along his skin, not really touching him anywhere that counted. Robby whined.

"If you want something, angel, you gotta say it. I want to hear you ask for it."

Robby dropped his head to the crook of Calder's

shoulder with a groan. "Haven't I been humiliated enough for one day?"

Calder pushed him back gently until he was looking at him. "Why would you be embarrassed telling me what you want?"

"Because what if I say it wrong? What if you think I'm weird or perverted or a total freak of nature?"

Calder gave Robby a grin that rocked him to his core. "Damn, angel. What exactly is it you're into? Spanking? Bondage? Daddy kink? Furries?"

"What are furries?" Robby asked.

"Never mind. The point is, I might not be into everything you're into, but I'm certainly not going to kink shame you and I'll try to give you whatever I can. But I can't until you tell me because I like to hear dirty things come out of this innocent little mouth of yours. It turns me on."

Robby caught his bottom lip between his teeth, examining Calder for any sign he was lying or somehow setting Robby up to laugh at him. Before he could say anything, Calder grunted, tugging Robby's lip free to nip at it, whispering in-between kisses, "That. That right there. When you look at me with those wide green eyes and that bashful fucking look, all I can think of is you saying 'yes' and 'please' whenever my hands are on you. It makes me want to drag you into the bedroom and fuck you into my mattress. Because it's hot. You're so hot and sweet and perfect."

Robby's heart was slamming against his chest hard enough for him to fear it might leap from his body and run away. Nobody had ever talked to him like that before. "I like when you talk like that," he managed, face on fire.

"Yeah. What else do you like?"

"I like your hands on me." He gripped Calder's wrists, leading his hands up under his shirt to hover close to his chest. "Here. I like when you touch me here."

Calder's hands continued sliding up. "Lift up your arms, angel."

He did as Calder asked, his shirt landing in a heap on the floor. Before he could say anything else, Calder leaned forward, catching one of the bars through Robby's nipples with his teeth and tugging. Robby cried out more from shock than pain, but it didn't matter, Calder was soothing over it with his tongue. Robby moaned, his cock hard and leaking in his pants. "Do that again," he begged.

"Yeah?" Calder asked before giving his other nipple the same treatment.

"That's so good," Robby whispered, sounding awed.

"Oh, angel. It gets so much better."

Robby wanted to try it. Try everything. With Calder. He only wanted it with Calder. Fuck Linc and his no sex rule. How would he even know? "Show me?"

Calder kissed him deeply, his hands sliding into Robby's pants to cup his ass and drag him closer. "Show you what, angel?"

"Everything," Robby said, tilting his head to let Calder's lips continue their exploration. "How do I know what I like if I haven't tried it? Maybe I am into spanking or bondage or whatever furries do."

"They dress up as animals and rub off on each other," Calder explained.

Robby frowned. "Okay, we can skip that one, but can't you just…teach me? I've never even watched porn."

Calder stopped short. "You're kidding?"

Robby shook his head. "It seemed weird to watch porn alone."

"'Cause you're alone is precisely why you watch porn, angel."

"See, I didn't even know that. You told me to ask for what I want. This is what I want. For you to teach me what I want."

Calder leaned back to study Robby's face, like he was trying to decide if he could do it or not. "Fine.

Okay. But not right now. We need to go talk to some of the people from those pictures and see if they can help us figure out if and when you may have met that guy."

Robby's face fell. "Now?"

"We have a lot of places to stop. You were really busy."

"But…"

Calder arched a brow, lips twitching in an aborted smile. "But…"

Robby took Calder's hand and dragged it to his erection. "This."

"You want me to take care of you, sweetness?"

Robby bit his lip and nodded.

Calder's expression could melt steel. "Then tell me. If you're feeling shy, just come on over here and whisper it in my ear."

Robby swallowed hard, but he did as Calder said, leaning close to press his lips to his ear. "Make me come, please."

"See. You did so good. Good boy." Robby sucked in a sharp breath, cock throbbing at Calder's casual praise. "You like that, angel? You like being my good boy?" Robby couldn't even answer, just nodded against his shoulder. "Say it."

"Yes. I like being your good boy," Robby whispered.

Robby's eyes rolled and he bit off a sound of surprise

exasperating

as Calder's hand slipped inside his underwear and gripped him tight.

"Fuck, you really like it," Calder said, swiping his thumb over the head of Robby's cock, using his precum to slick his fist.

Robby didn't answer, just gripped Calder's shoulders, head buried against his neck as Calder worked him hard and fast, the friction almost painful. He couldn't stop the sounds coming from his lips no matter how hard he tried. He was so close, had been so close before Calder ever touched him.

"I'm gonna come."

"Yeah? Come for me. Come on."

"Oh, fuck. Oh, fuck," Robby chanted without thought as his brain short circuited and waves of pleasure crashed over him.

He bit down on Calder's shoulder to keep from screaming as he jerked Robby through the aftershocks. "Good boy. Such a good boy."

Robby tried to get Calder off, but the older man shook his head. "You can take care of me later, angel face. I've got to start earning my paycheck, and you need to get cleaned up so we can go."

Robby's face flushed. He was such an idiot. He was facing murder charges, and there he was, worried about sex and keeping Calder from doing his job.

"Sorry."

"Hey, stop apologizing. I wanted this. I have every intention of picking up right where we started as soon as we get back here. But for now, I can wait. Let's get cleaned up and do what we have to do so we can get back here. Okay?"

Robby nodded, feeling the knot in his stomach loosen a bit. "Okay."

sixteen

CALDER

CALDER WASN'T SURE WHAT EXACTLY HE'D EXPECTED from retracing Robby's footsteps but it was more than the big pile of nothing they'd found in the last three hours. The only place they'd yet to try was the club, and Calder wasn't optimistic. They parked around the back of the building where the employees parked, and he pounded on the back door. A few minutes later, a guy in jeans and a black t-shirt with the club's logo on it pushed the door open but didn't allow them in, blocking the entrance with his body. He wasn't imposing, but Calder wasn't looking to make any headlines. The dude was fit, Calder supposed. Good-looking too with his wavy black hair and pale blue eyes. *Just Robby's type.* The thought rankled.

"Can I help you?" the pretty boy asked.

"We're looking for this guy. Is he working today?" Calder asked, showing a still from the footage Charlie found. It was blurry, but Calder hoped that somebody who knew the man would still be able to identify him.

"Caleb? He works the bar. He doesn't get in until late. He's ten to three," the guy said, his gaze stuttering to Robby then back again as if he suddenly realized who he was. "Hey, you're the guy. The actor who killed that creep from your dad's cult, right?"

Robby flushed. "Yeah."

The guy grinned, arching a brow. "I'm Brandon. Listen, if you guys want to come back tonight and talk to Caleb, I can get you in."

"Yeah, I'm not really supposed to be out in public right now," Robby said, looking at Calder.

Before Calder could speak, Brandon did. "I hear ya, beautiful. Listen, come back about eleven tonight and come to the back door. I'll let you in before I clock out. Maybe I could even buy you a drink? You are old enough to drink, aren't you?" he asked with a wink.

Calder rotated his jaw and prayed for calm. He had a job to do, and he couldn't do that if he was sitting in jail for assault. "We'll be back at eleven," Calder all but snarled before gripping Robby's hand and spinning him around. "Let's go."

"It's nineties night tonight. You know, if you want to dress up like your friend is," Brandon shouted at their retreating figures. "You really nailed the grunge look, man."

Robby giggled as Calder looked down at his faded jeans, paint-splattered Pink Floyd t-shirt, and his black shitkicker boots. Grunge? What was this little asshole trying to say? "See you tonight, Brad."

"It's Brandon," Robby corrected.

"Whatever," Calder muttered, opening Robby's door for him and helping him up into the cab of the truck before slamming it shut. Calder climbed in, shoving the key into the ignition. "Put your seatbelt on."

Robby didn't put his seatbelt on. He just stared at Calder, brows furrowed. "Are you okay?" he asked before worrying his bottom lip between his teeth. "Did I do something wrong?"

Calder's irritation melted away at the fear in Robby's tone. "What? No, angel. That guy just got on my nerves."

"'Cause he asked if I wanted a drink?" Robby asked, tone almost hopeful.

He should have said no, gave a gentle reminder to Robby that what was between them was just sex, just short term fun. But that felt like the bigger lie, and he couldn't bring himself to hurt Robby, not when the rest of the world seemed hellbent on doing it for him. "Yes, sweetness, because he asked you for a drink."

"Did you think I wanted to have a drink with that guy?" Robby asked, voice small, almost like he worried he was in trouble.

"Did you?" Calder asked gently. "It's okay if you did. I don't control what you do and who you do it with. He does sort of look like Elijah."

Robby shrugged. "Maybe, but I didn't pick Elijah. Jasmine and Mark work for the same agency. Elijah wasn't really my type."

Calder turned in his seat to look at Robby. "No? Then what is your type?"

Robby slid along the bench seat until he sat on his knees beside Calder. When the boy's lips brushed against Calder's ear in a timid imitation of what Calder had done to Robby just hours ago, Calder's dick immediately took notice. Why was everything Robby did sexy? This kid was going to give him blue balls before the end of the day.

"My type?" Robby asked, biting at Calder's earlobe. "Tall, older, sexy, southern drawl, tough, a butt that looks really good in Wranglers, and has a truck with a bench seat." As Robby listed off these attributes, he kissed along Calder's throat, hand skating over his inner thigh.

Calder groaned, tilting his head so Robby could trace his tongue along the corded tendon of his neck. "Careful, angel. Don't start something you can't finish."

Robby undid Calder's belt and jeans with impressive efficiency, his hand slipping into Calder's underwear to wrap around his cock. "But what if I want to finish it?"

Fuck. Calder would be an idiot to refuse such a bold advance. He shoved his jeans and underwear to his thighs and leaned back. "I just can't say no to you, angel."

Robby's hand disappeared and Calder could only stare as the boy ran his tongue along his palm before returning it back to Calder's cock, jerking him in a lazy motion that had him squirming. "You're such a little tease," he groaned.

"I'm not being a tease," Robby murmured. "I'm just making it last. I've wanted to do this for a long time."

Calder smiled, rocking himself into Robby's hand. "Do what, sweetness? 'Cause we've done this before."

"Not here. Not in your truck."

Calder looked at him. "You've fantasized about jerking a guy off in his truck? Do tell."

Robby kissed Calder, his tongue teasing his way

into his mouth before breaking the kiss. "Not a guy. You. I've wanted to do this ever since I saw you climb into your truck that day."

"What day?" Calder managed, his voice catching as Robby's hand twisted on the upstroke in a way that made Calder see stars.

"The first time I saw you. That day in the conference room. It was like you were the only one who even noticed I was there. As usual, it was always about Elijah. Just looking at you gave me so many dirty thoughts. I couldn't wait to get back upstairs to my hotel room."

"Fuck, angel. Are you telling me you jerked off thinking about us fooling around in my truck? How'd you even know I drove a truck?"

"I saw you when you got there. I saw you get out of this fancy truck, and I couldn't imagine who you were or why you were there. I thought you had to be a tourist."

"I like where this is going, dirty boy. Tell me what you thought about. Was it this?"

Robby shook his head, kissing Calder as he worked him faster. "No. I thought about you fucking me. I wondered if you'd be rough or gentle. If you'd just use me all up and I'd never see you again."

"Fuck, you are killing me, angel. What did you

exasperating

decide?" Calder panted, pushing himself up into Robby's hand.

"I decided it didn't matter. Rough or sweet. I just wanted you to want me. I wanted you inside me. I wanted to feel like somebody like you saw me and still wanted me."

Jesus. Calder was talking before he could think better of it. His lizard brain was more than happy to tell Robby every fucking thought that was rattling around in his thick fucking skull. "Fuck. I do want you. You know that, right? I can't get you out of my head. You live there now and that's a problem, but it's a problem for another day because I need you to get me off. Please, sweetness. Be good for me." Robby kissed him, whimpering into his mouth as he fisted Calder's cock with purpose. "Oh, fuck. Yeah. That's it. Oh, fuck. That's it, angel. I'm so fucking close. Don't stop."

Two minutes later, Calder was coming, his release spilling over Robby's fingers as he worked every drop from him. Calder's spent cock jerked as Robby lifted his fingers, looking him in the eye as he licked them clean. Calder dragged him in for another deep kiss.

"Did I do good?" Robby asked.

"So good. You were so good, angel. Let me take care of you."

Robby flushed from his neck to the tips of his ears,

looking down into his own lap at the wet spot on his pants. Well, technically, Wyatt's pants. God, the kid had come just from jerking Calder off. Shit. What had Calder gotten himself into, and why the fuck didn't his brain have the self-preservation to want to get out? Why wasn't every single alarm bell telling him to ask Linc to reassign Robby to another security detail?

"Let's go home, get cleaned up, and eat dinner. We should probably try to get some sleep if we have to be back here at eleven. I don't know how long this will take."

CALDER WAS BOTH RELIEVED AND IRRITATED TO SEE Brandon waiting for them, as promised, when they arrived at five past eleven. Robby made no effort to even acknowledge the other man, instead breezing past him as if he wasn't there, leaving Calder to give the guy a wave. Once they made it to the front, Robby stopped short, laser focused on something across the room. At first, Calder worried maybe Robby had spotted reporters, but when he followed the boy's eyeline, he realized it was far worse.

Charlie waved to Robby from a table in the roped off VIP section. She wasn't alone. Wyatt didn't surprise

exasperating

Calder, as it seemed the two were always joined at the hip, but Linc and Shepherd were a complete shock. Where was Elijah? There was no way Shepherd would agree to go to a club without his famous husband.

Charlie waved her hands over her head, as if they could miss her in the packed club. She wore a skin tight red mini-dress with a black and white flannel and a pair of combat boots. She'd pulled half her hair up and teased the shit out of the front of it. Oh, right. Nineties night.

Elijah returned to the table from somewhere and also waved at the two of them, giving Robby a remorseful look. Calder sighed, placing a hand on Robby's back and pushing him towards the group. As soon as they reached the table, Charlie snagged Robby and Elijah by the arms and nodded her head at Wyatt. When Wyatt stood, she started herding the boys towards the dance floor.

"I love this song," she screamed over the base beat.

Calder watched them go, worry gnawing at him. Robby's attorney wouldn't like this. Robby's publicist and PR people certainly wouldn't like Robby and his ex-boyfriend out on a dance floor together while the ex's new husband looked on.

Calder refused to acknowledge his own feelings of seeing Robby and Elijah on the dance floor together. It was nothing. Robby had told him just hours ago that Elijah had never been his plan. He wanted Calder. Robby had jerked him off in his car and had whispered in his ear how he'd fantasized about Calder from day one. Not Elijah. Him. It did little to quell the jealousy burning a hole through his gut. He didn't want anybody touching Robby. The boy was his. Just his.

Except, he wasn't. Fuck. How had he let shit get so twisted in his head? He had too many other things to deal with in his life. He wasn't good enough for Robby. He made shit decisions when feelings were involved. Just ask the girl whose ashes were sitting in a cardboard box at the funeral home.

"You're staring," Linc shouted. "At least sit down and glare at the kid so it's not so obvious."

Linc kicked Charlie's empty seat towards Calder, but he shook his head, leaning down enough for Linc to hear him. "I need to go talk to the bartender. Keep an eye on him for me?"

Linc gave a curt nod, and Calder walked towards the massive bar, currently manned by four bartenders. Two women and two men. One of the two men was bald with dark skin, which meant the slightly built blond one had to be Caleb. He flagged the man down and received a curt nod. He waited as the guy helped the four to five people waiting for their drinks in front

exasperating

of him.

"What'll it be?" he shouted.

Calder reached into his pocket and pulled out a hundred dollar bill. "This is yours if you just answer a few questions for me about him."

He pointed to Robby who was currently jumping up and down on the dance floor with the others as Chumbawumba blared overhead.

The bartender's entire demeanor changed. "Listen, I get that you have a job to do but give the guy a break. You people are like fucking vultures."

"You people?" Calder asked.

"You're a reporter, right? Tabloids?"

"What? No."

"Well, you're definitely not a cop," Caleb said, eyeing Calder's clothes.

Calder reached into his back pocket, showing the man his PI license. "I work private security for Robby. He's having a hard time piecing together what happened the night of the fourteenth. The night he was arrested."

The bartender eyed Calder warily, like he was sizing him up. "Okay, look. The kid was bombed out of his mind. I'd stopped serving him, but he was flying on whatever it was he'd had before he got here. He made a big splash when he got here 'cause he'd shown up with three drag queens, which tends to stand out in this place. Everything was fine until he got into a fight with some old guy."

"Old guy?"

"Yeah. Big, overweight, sweaty, and out of breath. He came in not long after the kid and his queens. I only remember him because he ordered ice water. Nobody comes to a place this loud to drink water alone."

So, the guy from the break-in had been there that night. Had been following Robby. "So, what started the fight?"

"I don't know, man. I only know that the guy was pulling on the kid, like he was trying to get him alone, and the kid threw a drink in his face. Then all hell broke loose. Next thing I know, your boy is slapping the shit out of a cop with a fucking dildo the size of my arm."

Calder slid the money across the bar to Caleb. He didn't ask any further questions. It wasn't worth it. He had what he needed. The dead man had clearly been following Robby, even if it was only from the street. Calder wasn't sure what scenario worried him more. That this was a random encounter that had turned violent or that this man had an agenda when he followed Robby into the club that night. That he'd possibly been following him for days without the

exasperating

boy's knowledge. Robby was always so certain the world didn't see him that it would never occur to him he was in danger, that somebody stalked him.

He returned to the table and flopped into his seat. Shep nodded at Calder, who did the same before they all returned their gaze to the dance floor. The music had morphed into a song with a slow, throbbing rhythm. Charlie was dirty dancing with a girl dressed like Gwen Stefani, but it was the boys who had Calder's undivided attention. Robby was somehow the meat in an Elijah and Wyatt sandwich.

It was all in good fun. They were laughing and constantly losing rhythm. Robby looked like he was having a blast. It was the first time in a long time that Robby's infectious smile seemed on full display. Elijah had made him smile like that. Knowing that knifed at something inside Calder.

"You okay, hoss?" Linc asked.

Calder glanced at his boss. "Yeah, why?"

"You look like you're two seconds away from flipping this table. You wouldn't be jealous by any chance, would you?"

Yes. "What? No. He's a client." Christ. Even he didn't buy that delivery.

"Precisely why I'm concerned," Linc reminded him. "Please, tell me you're not fucking this kid."

Calder looked Linc in the eye. "I'm not fucking this kid." *Yet.*

Linc studied him for a minute. "Good. That's good."

"Doesn't it bother either of you that your husbands are all over another man?"

Shep and Linc exchanged a glance. "No," they said in unison.

"Oh," was all Calder could manage.

It bothered Calder. Robby faced Wyatt, his arms around his neck. Wyatt's hands shared space on Robby's hips with Elijah's hands. He was crowded up on Robby, pelvis pressed to his ass. They moved in unison now, having found a rhythm. Calder would have found it hot if he wasn't picturing ripping the boys' arms off and beating them to death with them.

The muscle in Calder's jaw ticked as he watched them, the rational part of his brain at war with the part of him that screamed *mine.*

"I should probably get him out of here. Jasmine and his attorney didn't want him out in public. This is going to be all over the tabloids tomorrow, and his team's going to be pissed."

Linc and Shep both smirked at him but said nothing. Fuck them. It was easy to be smug when they knew that Wyatt and Elijah were going home with them tonight, would be lying in bed with them, would wake

exasperating

up with them. They had access to their boys any time they liked. That was what marriage was.

Images flooded Calder's brain. Waking up next to Robby every day. Drinking coffee together. Feeding the dogs. Getting kids off to school. Having sex in the shower. Calder felt like he'd been mule kicked. Fuck. What was happening to him?

On the dance floor, Wyatt broke away from the trio to dance with Charlie, leaving Robby and Elijah to dance together. Robby leaned back, winding his arms around Elijah's neck, still facing away from him. Elijah's hands squeezed Robby's hips before sliding up under his shirt.

Nope. That was it. Calder couldn't sit there and watch this one more second. He stood, his chair rocketing back violently enough for Linc to have to snatch it before it hit the ground. He could feel the weight of Linc and Shep's judgment, as well as their amusement, but he just didn't give a shit. This stopped. Now.

seventeen

ROBBY

ROBBY SWAYED AGAINST ELIJAH, EYES CLOSED, enjoying the music and the easy weightless feeling inside him. This was the first time he felt on even footing. The first time he was part of the group. He had friends. He had Calder. He wasn't the fifth wheel for once. It made him giddy. The music was too loud to think about all the shitty things happening in his life. He could just feel. Could feel the heat of Elijah's body, could feel the weight of Calder's stare as he watched. It was perfect.

It was nice to see Elijah and not feel that seething jealousy, to know that just once, Elijah actually acknowledged he was there and feel as though he belonged there. Wyatt and Charlie were his friends, too. Calder was there, protecting him, just as Linc and Shepherd had for them. It might have sounded stupid if he'd said it out loud, but he allowed himself to just appreciate the feeling of not being alone.

Robby's eyes popped open as a hand closed around his upper arm and the warmth of Elijah's body disappeared.

Calder stood there in the center of the dance floor. He leaned in close enough for Robby to hear. "We need to get going, angel. There are cameras everywhere."

Robby's heart sank. "I don't want to go yet. I'm having fun. Dance with me."

Calder gave Robby a half smile. "I don't think that's a good idea. Linc's watching."

"I don't care. It's just dancing. Please? One dance and I'll go without a fight. Pretty please?" Robby begged, blinking up at Calder with as much innocence as he could muster.

"Fuck, kid. You are killing me."

Glory Box started playing, and Robby clutched at Calder's shirt. "Please. I love this song. Please, Calder? Dance with me?" He could see him wavering. He bit down on his lower lip.

Calder barked out a laugh. "Oh, you little fucking

tease. Fine. One dance. You're so going to get me fired."

Robby cheered a bit in his head as Calder pulled him to a shadowy corner of the dance floor, away from prying eyes. Nobody had ever responded to Robby like Calder. When he spun Robby away, his heart sank, but then Calder's chest was against Robby's back, his hips pressed to Robby's ass, just the way he'd danced with Elijah. Had that made Calder jealous? Robby's heart tripped at the thought. He pressed his ass back against Calder, looping his arms around his neck just as he'd done to Elijah, only this time the dance felt so much more…personal.

Robby closed his eyes, swaying his hips in time to the music. Calder gripped his hips, pulling him in close. Robby sucked in a breath at the feel of Calder's semi-hard-on pressing against him. With his hands looped around Calder's neck, it left him free to touch Robby anywhere. His hand slid up under Robby's shirt, playing with the steel bars in his nipples as teeth tugged at his earlobe.

"Oh, fuck," Robby whispered, knowing it would get lost in the music.

He was happy the others on the dance floor couldn't see them, couldn't see how easily his body reacted to Calder's touch. He was already so hard, his cock

exasperating

straining against the zipper of Wyatt's borrowed jeans. At the rate he was going, he was going to owe Wyatt a new wardrobe. Could you return somebody's clothes after you'd come in them? What was the proper etiquette there?

Robby gasped as Calder's hand slipped into his jeans and closed around his erection. "Fuck, baby. Are you already hard? God, that's hot. Come on."

Robby whined as Calder's hand disappeared, but then he was being dragged into a darkened hallway that led to the restrooms. There were a few people lingering in the shadows, but it was too dark to see their faces. Robby frowned as Calder pushed him inside the restroom and into the large stall at the end.

As soon as the lock fell into place, Calder slammed him against the wall and kissed him, his hands cupping Robby's face. He could only hang on. Calder was usually frustratingly slow and patient, but this time he was frantic, his mouth biting kisses along Robby's jaw and throat that felt like they might leave bruises. Part of him hoped they did.

Calder's hands worked free the buttons on Robby's jeans. "What are you—"

"You have to be quiet, angel. Can you do that for me?"

As Calder went to his knees before him, Robby

could only think to say, "I don't know."

Calder grinned, tugging the tight jeans and underwear down to mid-thigh. Robby slapped his hand over his own mouth as lips closed around his cock. His eyes rolled in pleasure as Calder's mouth enveloped him in this perfect tight wet suction.

Robby gripped the metal bar on the wall with his free hand to keep himself up on his feet. He whined as Calder's tongue played with his foreskin. "Oh, my God. Oh, my God," he mumbled behind his own hand.

The door opened and somebody walked in to use the urinal. Robby squeezed his eyes shut. It took all his willpower to stay quiet until the toilet flushed and the door closed once more. Two more people came and went as Robby's ability to stay quiet waned.

It wasn't a blowjob. It was a full on assault on Robby's senses. The tile was cold against his ass and Calder's mouth was so warm and his hands were digging bruises into Robby's thighs, and he wanted to scream at the waves of pleasure sparking along his body. When Calder took him deep and swallowed, Robby dropped his hands to Calder's hair bundled on top of his head, gripping him tight, his hips thrusting almost against his will as he fucked into his mouth.

Robby finally pried his eyes open enough to look

exasperating

down and make sure he wasn't hurting Calder. That was all it took. The sight of Calder on his knees before him, Robby's cock disappearing between his lips. His orgasm slammed into him without warning. He didn't have time to say a thing before he was flooding Calder's mouth, his throat convulsing around Robby as he swallowed it all.

He heard the door open but couldn't stop himself from chanting, "Fuck. Fuck. Fuck."

When Calder finally stood, he kissed Robby, tongue thrusting into his mouth so he could taste himself. Why was that so hot? He didn't waste too much time on the thought, instead dropping to his knees before Calder, glancing up to whisper, "I don't really know what I'm doing."

He unbuttoned Calder's jeans, noting he hadn't bothered with underwear.

"Don't worry about it, angel. You're not going to get your first lesson in a dirty club bathroom. Let's go home."

"But I want to take care of you, too," Robby said firmly, cognizant of somebody washing their hands in the sink.

Robby watched as Calder seemed to war with himself. "Fuck," he finally muttered.

Then his hand tangled in Robby's hair, tilting his

head back. His other hand fisted his cock, jerking himself roughly. "Just open your mouth for me, angel." Robby did as he was told. Would probably always do what Calder said without question. "Oh, fuck. Good boy. Stick out your tongue."

Fuck. Robby would never, in his wildest dreams, have imagined a scenario where somebody like Calder would have him on his knees. He'd never been so turned on in his life. If he hadn't just come two seconds ago, this would have pushed him over the edge. Calder was beautiful in a raw and rugged way, but feeling his fist in Robby's hair and seeing the heated way he looked at Robby while he worked himself, there was nobody sexier in the world. Not to Robby.

"Oh, fuck. Fuck. Yeah," Calder panted, and then he was painting Robby's face, his lips, his tongue, even his lashes with his release.

It was the hottest thing that had ever happened to Robby, hands down. He was still reeling from it when Calder carefully helped him to his feet and gently cleaned him up with a paper towel. When he was finished, he kissed Robby's lips. "Are you okay, angel? I didn't hurt you, did I?"

The question caught Robby off guard. "Hurt me? No? How?"

"I was a little rough with you. I dragged you into a

bathroom. I just lost control for a second. I'm sorry."

Robby frowned. "I-I liked it. It was hot. Nobody ever loses control over somebody like me."

Calder shook his head in a way Robby didn't quite understand.

Robby yawned despite their four hour nap just hours earlier. "Can we go home and watch a movie?"

"Sure, angel."

"Oh, and can we stop at Del Taco? I'm starving."

Calder gave him a strange smile. "Sure, angel."

"You're being weirdly agreeable," Robby said, tone suspicious.

Calder guided him from the bathroom and out the side door immediately to their left, which dumped them out the side of the building. There was the sound of shouting, and then Robby was blinded by bright flashes of light.

"Robby, did you kill that man in self-defense?" a woman's voice asked, shoving a huge microphone in his face.

The lights made Robby disoriented, and he could only see tiny lights dancing before his eyes. "What?"

"Get back," Calder yelled. "All of you, back off. If you have questions, talk to his attorneys."

"Come on, Robby. Just a statement. Why did you lie about who your father was? Are you a member of his church? Do you bear the mark? Just answer the question."

Robby startled as an arm came around his shoulder before he realized it was Calder. The short trek to Calder's truck seemed to take an hour, and even once he was safely inside, cameras went off at his window, muted voices shouting questions he didn't understand.

Calder yanked his door open and hopped inside, shouting, "Back up or get run over," before slamming the door shut and turning over the engine. He hit a button on his steering wheel as he backed out of the spot, forcing the reporters to move to the side.

"Yeah?" came a gruff response through the truck's speakers.

"Hey, boss. I got a situation out back. There are a shit ton of vultures out here. I don't want them following us back to my place."

"Fuck. Alright. Give me five minutes before you take off."

"Roger that."

The five minute wait took five hours. Robby bit the inside of his cheek to stop himself from crying, crossing his arms over his chest to keep from sticking his fingers in his ears to drown out the incessant chatter as they lobbed questions at him, screaming

exasperating

over each other, and snapped photos.

But then, suddenly, they were running away from them. Calder was right, they were vultures. Vultures who'd just found another meal. Elijah was leaving out the same side entrance, hand in hand with Shepherd. He gave a friendly wave to the reporters, seeming to bask in the attention of the flashing lights. Robby had never been so grateful for Elijah's celebrity status. He knew there would be all kinds of stories tomorrow talking about him and Elijah dancing together, but he just couldn't care. He didn't put his seatbelt on. He just let himself slump over until his head rested on Calder's thigh, curling himself up in a ball and letting his eyes fall shut. Calder's fingers threaded in his hair, gently combing through the strands in a way that made Robby's chest hurt.

He'd just wanted one good night.

eighteen

CALDER

AFTER THEIR RUN IN WITH THE PRESS, CALDER HAD taken the long way home, looping around blocks to ensure nobody followed, before finally parking and getting Robby inside his apartment. They'd skipped the tacos. Calder had managed to coax a drained Robby into the shower before tucking him into bed.

"Where are you going?" Robby asked.

"I have some leads to run down. Get some sleep. I'll be right outside the door."

It wasn't a lie. Calder's apartment was painfully small. He could easily keep an ear out for Robby while trying to figure out what he was missing with this

exasperating

mysterious dead guy who'd stumbled into Robby's life.

Robby made a whiny noise and sat up. "I don't want to sleep alone. Stay with me."

It wasn't a request.

"Fine. But I need to work and you need to rest." Calder couldn't imagine giving in to anybody else so easily. This kid was a menace, a wrecking ball crashing through all his walls.

Robby smiled, flopping back and nestling beneath Calder's mismatched sheets and his oversized blue comforter. Robby looked good in Calder's bed. Too good. Calder shook the thought away, leaving long enough to grab his laptop. He hadn't bothered to dress after their shower, just sliding on a pair of navy blue boxer briefs. Robby hadn't even managed that, and knowing Robby was naked under those blankets all but ensured Calder would have a hard time concentrating on work.

Once Calder was in bed, he extinguished the light and set his laptop to night mode, shrouding the room in almost total darkness. Robby rolled onto his belly, his head turned away from Calder, and soon, his breathing became rhythmic. Calder lost himself in the chase. He emailed a list of information he needed from Webster, including any closed circuit camera footage from the locations Robby had been the day he went to jail. He did more research on Magnus Dei. There was a chat thread with horror stories from various members who'd escaped. Calder couldn't help but wonder what Robby's childhood was like. He finally gave up, closing his laptop and setting it on his side table.

Calder startled as Robby spoke. "Who is it you don't want to pick up at the funeral home?"

His heart raced. "Jesus, angel. I thought you were sleeping."

Robby rolled over, sneaking under Calder's arm and putting his head on his chest. "I can't sleep. We took a four hour nap. Who is it?" he prodded.

"How do you even know about that?" Calder asked, not mad, just curious.

Robby peeked up at him, his long lashes forming shadows along his cheeks in the thin sliver of moonlight. "I heard you listening to your voicemail the other day. Is it family?"

Calder's heartbeat thudded heavy in his chest. "It's a long story, angel."

"You know everything about me. You've seen me humiliate myself so many times. I just want to know something about you. Something real. Something personal."

Calder's chest tightened. He never spoke of Jennifer. Not to anybody. He'd never even told his mother about her. "It's not a nice story. I did something selfish, and somebody got hurt because of it."

Robby frowned, the scowl so out of place on his pretty face. "I can't believe that's true. That's not who you are."

Calder looked down at him. "You don't really know me, angel."

"Sure, I do. If you really think what you did was bad enough to change what I think of you then tell me and prove me wrong."

Calder sighed. "You are surprisingly relentless for somebody who is afraid of everything."

"That's 'cause I'm not afraid of you," Robby said.

Calder gave a humorless laugh. "Maybe you should be."

Robby giggled. "That was really dramatic."

Calder couldn't help but smile. Robby's laugh was infectious. "Okay, that was a little dramatic, but you're kind of asking me to rip open my old life."

"Technically, the funeral home already did that. Ignoring stuff doesn't make it go away. It just makes it worse."

Calder shook his head. He had a point. Besides, somewhere deep down, Calder knew he'd already made up his mind to tell Robby. The masochistic part of him hoped that it might chase him away so he didn't have to break his heart later.

"It started a long time ago. I was eight, and my older sister, Megan, was sixteen. I was a surprise to my parents who were already in their forties when I was born, but they weren't upset about my arrival. At least, they never implied as much. My dad taught middle school science, and my mom was a loan officer at a bank. We were a super average middle-class family." He took a deep breath. "Until my sister left work one night and never came home."

Robby sucked in a breath, taking Calder's hand, like they'd come to a scary part in a horror movie. It felt like one at the time. Calder tried to distance himself from the story. Just state the facts.

"It was almost eleven before my parents started to worry. She was usually home by then. The store closed at ten on weeknights, and it was a Wednesday. My mom worried my sister's car might have broken down somewhere between the store and the house. There were no cell phones back then, so dad got in the car to go look for her. But her beat up Camaro was still in the lot. All the lights were off in the store, and the doors were locked. My dad got our neighbor, Ed, and the two drove around for hours hoping to find her, but she was just gone.

"I slept through most of it until the police arrived.

exasperating

The lights woke me up. The officers assured us that she'd probably just gotten a ride from friends and they'd talked her into going out. My parents told them that wasn't something she'd do, but they just dismissed them. When she didn't come home, they implied she'd run away. It was clear to my parents the cops weren't going to look too hard for her.

"Things just sort of fell apart after that. My mom lost her job, my dad became obsessed with finding my sister and started to fall down a rabbit hole of conspiracy theories. They loved me but it was clear that there was a big hole in our lives. They sort of ignored me. I understood, though. I missed her, too. She was my sister. She used to read to me and do all the voices. Sometimes, she'd take me out after Mom and Dad had gone to sleep and we'd get milkshakes at the drive thru."

Calder fell silent, gathering his thoughts. It seemed strange to talk about her after a decade, like conjuring a spirit he'd expelled years ago. Guilt ate at him. What had she ever done to Calder to make him force her out of his memories? Nothing.

"Are the ashes your sister's?" Robby asked softly before placing a kiss on Calder's bare chest.

"No, angel." That would have been too easy. "I guess I was obsessed with the case, too, and I fixated on being a Texas Ranger. I wanted to help find missing people. Living in El Paso, they immediately tried to put me in a position working border patrol, but I didn't want to spend my life chasing after people who just wanted a better life. But that wasn't why I was there. They put me on a special task force dealing with human trafficking. It's a huge business in those parts, not just with Coyotes preying on vulnerable people trying to get into the U.S., but American girls and young children are also sold into the sex trade over the border.

"I realized pretty quickly there was a chance this is what happened to Megan. I didn't share my theories with anybody, but I kept my eyes open. I knew what happened to girls like my sister. Best case scenario, she was dead. Worst, she was a slave, drugged and beaten, bought and sold. Girls in that world didn't last very long. We didn't rescue nearly as many girls as we lost, and the ones we did save had years of recovery ahead of them. I convinced myself we were heroes. We were fighting the good fight. Doing everything in our power to get to the people at the top.

"We caught a break when one of the girls leveled up in the organization. Sometimes, when the girls aren't… profitable anymore, they'll turn them into recruiters. Her name was Jennifer, and she didn't want to recruit girls. She couldn't stomach the idea of having anybody go through what she went through. She wanted out. She came to us for help. She wanted us to get her out. Said she could give us names, dates, meeting spots, tunnels. The wheels move slowly on these kinds of deals, and in the meantime, Jenny had to do her job so the bosses didn't get suspicious. She hated it, but if she didn't meet her quota, the punishments were severe, so we were all forced to go on with our lives and pretend we weren't allowing girls to be raped and drugged and sold as property. A week after Jenny came to us, my parents died in a car accident. I threw myself into my job.

"Backpage launched a few months later. A sort of sleazier version of Craigslist, if you can believe that. Backpage allowed traffickers to place ads for girls, most of them underage. There were pictures, descriptions, all written in code. We checked ads daily, extracted girls when we could. But one day, while looking through these ads, one of the photos was a reflection of the girl holding the camera. A girl who looked just like Megan. An older version of her, but still her. I showed the ad to Jenny, and she swore she didn't know the girl in the photos or the girl taking the picture but that she did know Elizer, the boss, had started using the site for his girls. I asked Jenny to try to get information from him about the girl, but she said it was dangerous, that he'd know something was up. I begged her to just try, to just see if he'd give up anything, even if it was only to say she wasn't one of his girls."

Calder took a deep breath and let it out. "The next day, we found Jenny in the parking lot of an abandoned building, barely breathing, beaten to within an inch of her life. He'd branded her face. The branding wasn't new, she'd already had an E branded on her hip. Marking up her face was a message.

"We tried to find family members or even friends but there was nobody. She wasn't brain dead. She could breathe on her own. But she just wouldn't wake up. I used to visit her every day after work, but she never regained consciousness. I quit the Rangers. I couldn't keep fighting against the tide. For every girl we rescued, fifty more were taken. Trafficking is a huge business, and there are just too many of them to stem the flow. I moved out here. Linc and Jackson gave me a job. I kept paying Jenny's medical bills. It was the least I could do. Last month, she got a lung infection and they just couldn't control it. And then she died."

Robby sniffled, warm tears falling onto Calder's chest. "I'm sorry."

Calder glanced down. "Why are you sorry, angel?"

"Because you're sad. Because you lost your sister.

exasperating

Because you feel guilty about this girl who had a horrible life."

"She got hurt because I couldn't get the idea out of my head that a girl who I saw in a reflection was my long lost sister. I didn't even know if my sister was alive or if my sister had been trafficked. Statistically speaking, she was dead twenty-four hours after she went missing. I put my far-fetched hope over a real girl's life."

"You don't know that he beat her up for asking a question about a photograph. She was sucked into a super dangerous world whether she wanted to be or not. You didn't put her in that situation, whoever kidnapped her did. We've all done stupid things that have consequences."

Calder lifted Robby's hand to his lips and kissed his palm. "What stupid thing have you done, angel?"

"I abandoned my brothers and sisters to a monster. I saved myself and left them behind," Robby said softly.

"Do you have a lot of siblings?"

Robby nodded against Calder's chest. "I had seven when I left. Four of them were older than me. My mom was pregnant when I came out to them, so I suppose I have at least one more now."

"They have each other though, right?"

"My parents are very Old Testament with their

punishments. Kneeling on rice. Being beaten with a belt. Being dunked in ice water and made to stand outside for hours. Nobody is too young for punishment."

Calder's heart twisted in his chest. "You are barely twenty-one years old. What were you going to do? Sue your parents for custody?"

"I could have done something. Anything really. But I didn't. I saved myself and never looked back."

Calder tugged Robby's hair and kissed him gently. "You need to stop being so hard on yourself."

"You should learn to take your own advice," Robby told him.

"Maybe so, angel. Think you can sleep now?"

"Can I sleep right here?" Robby asked, throwing an arm and leg over Calder.

"Of course."

Calder wanted to tell him he could stay forever if he liked, but he didn't. He just closed his eyes and forced himself to try to sleep.

nineteen

ROBBY

ROBBY SAT UP WITH A START, GLANCING AROUND AT the shadows of the room, his heart hammering against his ribcage, his body coated in a fine sheen of sweat. He gulped down deep breaths as he willed his body to relax. It was just a nightmare. He wasn't even sure what he'd dreamed about. All he had was a lingering uneasy feeling and a body that didn't quite realize he wasn't actually in any danger.

At some point, he'd rolled away from Calder, but now he tucked himself in close, pressing his head to the older man's furry chest, letting Calder's heartbeat lull him. He tried to fall back asleep, but his brain was working overtime, playing the greatest hits of every embarrassing thing he'd done since birth. He hated nights like this when self-doubt and guilt gnawed at him like little bugs.

He distracted himself by letting his fingers trail along Calder's chest, mapping a line between his nipples that hardened to tight peaks at his touch, down over the muscled plains of Calder's abs to the happy trail that disappeared beneath the waistband of his boxer briefs. He bit his lip, glancing up at Calder's face, his lips slightly parted as he took deep rhythmic breaths.

He ran his hand over the top of Calder's underwear, squeezing his soft cock and sucking in a breath as it hardened at his touch. Was this okay? Should he wake Calder and ask his permission? Robby sighed, dropping kisses on Calder's chest before resting his head on his belly, gently stroking him through his underwear.

"Whacha doin' down there, angel?" Calder asked, voice gruff.

"Just playing," Robby said, pushing Calder's underwear down just enough to reveal the head of his cock before licking over it carefully. "Is this okay?" Calder groaned, and Robby froze. "Is that a yes or a no?"

Calder stretched, arching his hips upward. "Yes. It's

an enthusiastic yes."

Robby took advantage of Calder's lifted torso, shoving his underwear down to his thighs. He got on his knees, once more darting his tongue out, tasting Calder's skin with tiny kitten licks as he tried to figure out the proper mechanics of a blowjob. Calder's fingers curled around Robby's leg, his thumb skimming over the sensitive skin of his inner thigh. It wasn't like Robby didn't know what a blowjob entailed. Well, he at least had a general idea, but Calder's touch was definitely a distraction he hadn't planned for. But maybe he should have.

All Robby could do was try. He took Calder into his mouth, pressing down until his nose skimmed against the springy curls of Calder's pubic hair and his cock shoved past his tonsils, triggering his gag reflex. He pulled off, eyes tearing as he glared at Calder's erection.

Calder chuckled, his hand teasing at the skin on the back of Robby's neck. "Easy, angel. Not so much."

"I just want to make you feel good," Robby muttered, grateful it was too dark for Calder to see him blushing.

"You don't have to blow me to make me feel good. Your hand works, too. Hell, just you half-naked and squirming your hot little body on top of me has been more than enough." Robby knew Calder was trying to make him feel better but good wasn't good enough. He took Calder's spit-slick erection in his hand and jerked him a few times. Calder hissed, his hips coming up off the bed as he fucked himself into Robby's tightened grip. "Yeah, like that, angel."

Robby wanted Calder to enjoy their time in bed, but he wanted to know what he was doing, too. Calder's mouth had felt so good on him in that bathroom. Robby wanted to make Calder feel that good, too. He pressed his mouth back down over Calder, keeping his fist at the base so he didn't go too deep. He tried not to blush at the loud sucking noises he made as he bobbed his head.

Calder moaned. "Oh, fuck. That's it, baby. That's so good. Good boy."

Calder's praise emboldened him, and once he found a rhythm, he had Calder fisting the bed sheets and making the sexiest noises Robby had ever heard. He wanted to make Calder come. Wanted to taste it flooding his mouth, but before he could figure out how to take him deeper, Calder was tugging at his hair, pulling him back up to capture him in a kiss.

Robby found himself underneath the heavy weight of Calder's frame, his wrists captured by Calder's hands. "My turn," Calder growled, biting at Robby's jaw and throat.

Robby shivered as much over Calder's raw snarl as

his words. Robby yelped as teeth tugged at the bars through his nipples until it was just this side of painful before Calder was biting at his ribs, his hip bones.

"Roll over." It wasn't a request.

Robby did as Calder demanded, panic consuming him when Calder gripped his hips and yanked them into the air. Had this all suddenly escalated faster than he'd planned? He wanted to go all the way with Calder, more than anything, but weren't they skipping some steps? He forced himself to relax as Calder spread him open.

"Damn, even your hole is pretty," Calder muttered.

Before Robby could even respond, Calder's tongue teased across his entrance. Robby gave a strangled moan, arching his back, pushing himself closer. "Oh, my God. Oh, my God," Robby heard himself whispering as Calder's mouth did things to him that were probably still illegal in most states. How could that feel so fucking good yet feel like it wasn't enough at the same time?

Calder laved over Robby's hole with his tongue before pushing it against him. "You like that, baby?"

Pleasure caused goosebumps to erupt along his skin and his hips swayed closer to Calder against his will. "Yes. Yes. Yes."

Calder massaged Robby's hole with his thumb

before letting it slide down to massage behind his balls while his tongue went back to flicking over his entrance. When Calder's hand closed around his cock, jerking him in time with his tongue, that was it—Robby couldn't stop himself from falling over the edge with a surprised cry, streaks of cum landing on Calder's worn blue comforter.

When Robby felt Calder shift his weight, he flipped over, careful to avoid the wet spot he made. Calder settled himself between Robby's legs, kissing him thoroughly. "I guess you liked that, huh, angel?"

Robby could feel Calder's hard cock, wet at the tip, pressing against his inner thigh. It occurred to Robby then that this didn't have to be over for the night. Just because he'd come didn't mean there wasn't more they could do. He made a decision then. "Fuck me," Robby said, ignoring Calder's question.

Calder gave him a startled look. "What?"

He wanted to bury his face in Calder's shoulder as he spoke, couldn't bear the thought of looking him in the eye as he begged for what he wanted. But Calder needed to hear the words. He needed to know. "I want you inside me. I want you to take my virginity. I won't tell anybody. Nobody will ever have to know but us. Please? I want it to be you. It's supposed to be you. I've known it since the second I saw you."

exasperating

Calder stared at him, a thousand emotions seeming to flit across his face before he settled on a strained look. "I don't want you thinking that you're my dirty little secret. You deserve better than that."

Robby blinked rapidly as he teared up, his heart shriveling in his chest. "If you don't want to, I get it. I'm sure having sex with a virgin is probably boring and awkward."

Calder grabbed Robby's hand and brought it to his cock. "Does this feel like I'm bored? Every fucking thing you do turns me on. Three hours ago, I told you something I've never shared with another living soul. This isn't about me not wanting to be with you like that, it's about me not wanting to have to lie about what you are to me."

Robby was almost positive his heart stopped beating. "What…what am I to you?"

Calder brought his forehead to Robby's. "Fuck, angel. I don't know. Special? Important? Cared for? More than you should be but too much for me to push you away?"

Robby swallowed the lump in his throat. "I didn't mean to push you. I just want to be with you in all the ways before this goes away."

Calder dropped a soft kiss to his lips and then sat up. Robby's stomach sank. He bit down hard on his lip to keep himself from crying for the thousandth time. Then Calder was reaching for something on the side table. Robby frowned as Calder's phone lit up. Was he making a phone call? Now? Robby had never been so confused. He heard the gruff greeting, even with the phone pressed to Calder's ear.

Calder only uttered two words. "I quit." Then he pressed end and tossed the phone aside, catching Robby's mouth in a kiss. "If we're going to do this, we're going to do it my way. Understand?" Robby nodded eagerly. "I need you to trust me. Can you do that?"

"Yes. I trust you."

Calder stared down at him for a long minute. "Fuck, you're so sweet. I don't know where you came from, because I don't deserve you, but I'm glad you're here. I need you to believe that."

"I do."

twenty

CALDER

CALDER MAY HAVE JUST BLOWN UP HIS ENTIRE LIFE, but he found it hard to care with Robby gazing up at him with those huge green eyes, swearing his trust with the solemnity of somebody swearing a lifelong vow. He kissed Robby's forehead and then his eyelids, pushing a sweaty lock of hair off his face, before laying beside him. "Turn on your side. I want to look at you."

Robby did as Calder asked, doing that lip biting thing that was always Calder's undoing. His cock was already throbbing but there was no way he was rushing this. Calder rested his head on the pillow beside Robby's, just looking at him as he ran a single finger along the curve of Robby's hip and up the ridges of his spine, up along his cheek, and down again. With each pass, his fingers drifted slightly lower, coasting over the generous swell of Robby's ass, sliding up the cleft between his cheeks. Robby's lashes fluttered, and he gave a contented sigh.

"Fuck, you really are so fucking beautiful," Calder whispered, giving the boy an almost chaste kiss.

Robby smiled even as he looked at Calder with confusion. "What are we doing, exactly? Are you seducing me? 'Cause I already said yes."

Calder shook his head with a smirk. "I just want you relaxed."

Robby buried half his face in the pillow, peeking out at Calder. "I just came my brains out. If I was any more relaxed, I'd be unconscious."

Calder arched a brow before rolling away, kicking off his underwear that were still caught around his thighs before rifling through the bedside drawer, retrieving lube and a condom and setting them within reach. Even with only half his face revealed, Calder could see the moment the situation became real for Robby, his eyes going wide. "See, it's okay to be nervous, but I do sort of know what I'm doing."

Robby's tone was salty as he muttered, "You've had enough experience."

exasperating

Calder gave him a playful swat on the butt, noting the way Robby's pupils blew at the contact. He tucked that bit of information away to explore sometime later. "Listen here, sass mouth. You said you trusted me. Besides, isn't this why you were so hellbent on putting yourself in my way? 'Cause you thought I'd rob you of this pesky virginity?" Robby opened his mouth, his expression of denial almost comical. Calder shook his head. "Nope. Don't try to deny it. You and the wonder twins are about as subtle as a Mack truck."

"Maybe at first," Robby said.

Calder leaned in close, dragging his lips across Robby's in a barely-there kiss. "But not now?"

"No. Not now," Robby whispered, deepening the kiss.

Calder continued his caresses as they kissed, addicted to the way Robby gasped and sighed and moaned into his mouth whenever Calder found a spot Robby liked. As his hands mapped the plains and angles of Robby's body, Calder's mouth wandered to his jaw, his ear, his neck, whispering once more everything that made Robby sexy in Calder's eyes.

Robby's kisses became needier, his sighs turning to groans of frustration. Any other time, Calder would have grabbed him and thrown him down, burying himself deep inside, riding him rough and hard the way he'd fantasized about, but he wanted Robby's first time to be everything he'd imagined it would be. If that meant Calder had the world's worst case of blue balls, so be it.

But Robby was clearly losing patience as well. He was already hard again, and if he kept wiggling his hot little body like he was, it would be over before it started. Robby might have a twenty-one-year-old's rebound time, but Calder didn't.

Finally, Robby hooked his leg high on Calder's hip, whining as their cocks slotted together, rocking against him frantically.

"You ready for more, angel?" Calder asked between kisses.

"Yes," Robby moaned. "Please."

"Fuck. I love when you say please."

Calder picked up the lube, coating his fingers before tossing the bottle back onto the bed. He hitched Robby's leg a little higher to slip a hand between the boy's thighs. Calder kissed Robby once more as he slipped his fingers between his legs. Robby sucked in a startled breath as Calder massaged his hole. Robby whimpered into Calder's mouth.

"You sure you want this, angel?" Calder asked, playing at his entrance.

"Stop teasing me," Robby whispered, burying his

face in the crook of Calder's shoulder.

Teasing him? Calder was just doing his best to keep from blowing his load before he even made it inside. He groaned as he pressed his finger into the tight heat of Robby's body, working his way past the initial resistance. Robby clung to him, his blunt nails digging into Calder's shoulders, panting against his skin.

"You okay, baby?"

"Yes, it doesn't hurt." Calder crooked his finger, feeling for the spongy gland just inside. He knew he found it when Robby gave a long, low moan. "Oh, God."

Calder smiled against Robby's cheek. "Yeah? Does that feel good?"

"Do it again," Robby begged.

Calder did as Robby asked, loving the way he fell apart a little more with each stroke. He rocked himself back on Calder's finger, chasing his own pleasure. He looked so beautiful with his eyes closed, his head thrown back, his teeth clenching his bottom lip like he was trying to keep from crying out. Calder could look at him forever.

When Calder withdrew his finger, he pressed back in with two, bearing down on Robby's prostate and massaging it once again. His noises were killing Calder. He wanted to record every whine, whimper, and moan. It was the sexiest thing he'd ever heard. There was no artifice, no fake enthusiasm. Robby was just himself and he wasn't hiding a thing from Calder. When Robby wanted more, he tried to take it, fucking himself back on Calder's fingers wantonly.

"I want more. I want you now. I'm ready," Robby mumbled against Calder's throat.

"I'll decide when you're ready. You've never done this before. Just let me take care of you, okay?" Robby gave a petulant whine that made Calder smile. "You can pout all you want, angel. I think it's sexy." Robby blushed, ducking his head at Calder's words. "Think you can take another finger?"

"I could probably take a tractor trailer back there by now," Robby grumbled.

"That's the spirit," Calder said around a laugh.

His amusement died abruptly when Robby hissed in pain as Calder slipped a third finger inside. "Shh, just relax, baby. Just relax and let me inside."

Robby whimpered, his lips seeking Calder's as he worked his fingers in slowly, waiting for Robby to adjust to the invasion. He kissed Calder like it could take away his discomfort. Hell, maybe it did somehow. Soon, Robby was once again working himself back on Calder's three fingers. "Come on. I need more. Please, I'm ready already. Please, Calder. I want you inside me. I want you to fuck me. Please."

Calder's heart squeezed in his chest at Robby's cries. He'd had sex with so many people, but he couldn't remember ever feeling this overwhelmed, not even when he'd lost his own virginity. "Yeah. Yeah, okay, baby. I got you."

Calder gave Robby another quick kiss before he slipped his fingers free, wiping them on the already messy sheets.

Calder opened the condom and slipped it on, wondering if Robby could see his hands shaking in the dim lighting. Why did this feel like so much more than it was? He applied another heavy coat of lube to his cock, determined to make this as good for Robby as he could.

Once Calder had him back in his arms, he couldn't help but say, "Last chance to back out, angel."

Robby gave him a look that almost made Calder laugh.

"Just shut up and fuck me already," he groaned.

Calder couldn't help but smile. He hiked Robby's leg up higher, hooking the boy's knee over his arm before lining himself up with Robby's entrance and pressing forward. Robby hissed as Calder breached that first tight ring of muscle. "Just breathe, baby," Calder whispered.

Robby didn't answer out loud, just nodded and buried his face against Calder's chest.

Calder entered him at an almost glacial pace, rocking his way in one inch at a time, holding him close, until he was finally buried within him. They both breathed hard. Calder did his best to try to regain some control but he was submerged in the most perfect heat and even the slightest movement sent jolts of stimulation along his spine until his whole body felt like a live wire.

"You okay, angel?" Calder whispered against his ear.

"I think so, yeah," Robby said, voice muffled.

"Can you look at me?"

When Robby leaned back to glance up at him, his eyes were wet. "I'm okay. It's just…a lot."

Calder kissed him. It was a lot. For him, too. He couldn't recall ever wanting this level of intimacy with anybody he'd taken to bed before. Even this position, face to face, bodies entwined, was never something Calder would have done with anybody else.

"Are you okay?" Robby asked.

Calder smiled at him. "I think so. Yeah."

Robby kissed him once more, his tongue slipping inside as he rocked himself back on Calder's cock. Fuck. He was so tight. So perfect. Calder thrust his hips upward as Robby brought himself down, moaning

exasperating

into Calder's mouth. "I want more."

Calder laughed. He'd picked this position because it had allowed him to keep his thrusts shallow. He hadn't expected Robby to be so needy his first time. Calder rolled the boy onto his back, catching his other leg over his elbow, allowing him to thrust deeper into him. "Is this what you need?"

Robby's eyes rolled back as Calder worked his hips faster, thrusting deeper into the most perfect soft heat. "Yes. Oh, fuck. Harder."

Jesus. Calder may have just created a monster. He loved it. He gave him what he asked for, slinging his hips faster, canting Robby's hips so each thrust was brushing against that tiny bundle of nerves that had all kinds of curse words falling from the boy's lips. "Oh, fuck, Calder. Keep doing that. Oh, fucking fuck. How does that feel so good?"

Calder growled at the sound of his name on Robby's lips. All thoughts and worries disappeared, replaced by instinct and need. Calder wouldn't last much longer. Giving Robby what he begged for was driving Calder closer and closer to the edge of his own release. The boy's cock was hard again, trapped between their sweat slick bodies.

He captured his lips in a sloppy kiss, breathing the words into his open mouth. "You hard again, baby?

You wanna come?"

"Yes, yes, yes," Robby chanted, gripping the pillow behind his head.

"Touch yourself, get yourself off for me. I want to watch." Calder sat back on his haunches, dragging Robby closer, practically bending him in half to drive into him. Robby wrapped his hand around his uncut cock, jerking himself in rhythm with Calder's thrusts. "Oh, fuck. Yeah. That's it. God, you're so fucking sexy. Make yourself feel good, angel."

Robby came hard with a hoarse shout, painting his release across his belly and chest. That was really all it took. Two more thrusts and Calder was joining him, his whole body shaking as he fell over the edge.

Calder collapsed on top of him, both of them sweaty and breathing heavily. "Wow."

"Yeah," Robby panted.

Calder slipped free of Robby's body, tying off the condom and tossing it into the trash can beside the bed. He draped himself over the boy, dropping his head onto Robby's shoulder. "Are you okay?" he asked, still slightly winded.

Robby's fingers tangled in Calder's sweaty hair. "Yeah. Are you?"

"I don't know," Calder answered honestly. "I think so."

exasperating

After a minute, Robby took a deep breath, his chest rising and falling beneath Calder's cheek. "This didn't have to mean anything. If that's what you're worried about," he said, dejected.

Calder lifted his head to look at him. "What? That's… That's not what I meant. It meant something. You mean something to me. I just… I just don't know what to do with that information right now. I don't know how we fit into each other's lives, but I know I don't want you going anywhere. Can that be enough for now?"

Robby studied Calder like he wasn't sure he could believe him or not. "Yeah. It's enough. For now."

"Let's get cleaned up. I have cum drying in all the worst places."

They showered quickly, knowing they only had a good fifteen minutes of hot water before they both got an ice bath. Once they finished showering, Robby was as wired as an over-caffeinated Pomeranian so Calder threw on sweatpants and an old t-shirt and sat on the lid of the toilet, watching Robby blow dry his hair into the high swoopy hairstyle that would have made anybody else look like an exotic bird but on Robby looked hot. The boy made everything look sexy, even Calder's old black and white polka-dot boxers paired with Wyatt's red cropped hoodie. Maybe that was why Calder let Robby talk him into drying his long hair until it hung tousled around his shoulders like he was in a hair care commercial.

They stripped the sheets together, throwing on another mismatched pair. With Robby too restless to sleep, Calder pulled up another old movie. The boy made Calder sit on the floor while he sat cross-legged on the mattress to braid Calder's hair. It all felt so…domestic and intimate. Robby chatted about everything and nothing, and Calder found himself smiling as the boy sectioned out his hair and began to work each section into a plait.

"Where did you learn to do this?" Calder asked.

"I had to help my mom do the little ones' hair on the farm. I got really good at braiding because the women are never allowed to have their hair down." Calder dropped a kiss on Robby's knee, but he yanked Calder's head back with a giggle. "Stop wiggling, you're going to mess up all my hard work."

Calder grinned. He would never get tired of that laugh. "Do you ever miss it? The farm? Was it all bad?"

Robby's hands stopped. "I miss my siblings. I miss church. I really liked believing in something bigger than myself. Sometimes, I even miss my mom. But more than anything, I miss the idea of having a mom, like the kind of mom other people have where they care about your day and your happiness and they think nothing is good enough for you because you're their baby. My mom was never like that. Kids were for working the land. Kids had to know their place. They should be seen and not heard. My mom hated me 'cause I was always mouthy and asked too many questions."

Calder laughed, glancing up at him. "You? I can't believe it."

Robby imitated Calder's laugh mockingly before leaning down to lick his nose. "Haha. I wasn't always shy. But my parents are really good at driving home a point."

Calder's chest ached at the implication. He couldn't imagine the abuse Robby had likely endured in the name of his parents' distorted version of God. "Why didn't you ever go to church once you were out?"

Robby shrugged. "I don't know. Once I came out of the closet, it was hard to know which churches would accept me without calling me a sinner or a sodomite."

"They exist," Calder promised.

"Did you ever go to church?"

Calder laughed, putting on his thickest Texan drawl. "Shit, son. My daddy used to say, 'The Texas stadium has a hole in the roof so God could watch his favorite team play.' Church is required if you live in the Lone Star State."

"Did you like church?" Robby asked, setting down one section of hair and starting another.

"I mean, I liked it okay, I guess, but we stopped going after my sister disappeared. My dad got too weird for even our most fervent congregation members. He started talking about people kidnapping girls for satanic rituals as part of some conspiracy regarding the New World Order. After that, it all started to seem pretty ridiculous to me."

Calder's pulse jumped as Robby dropped a kiss on his head. "Calder?"

"Yeah, angel?"

"I think you should ask Linc to help you try to find your sister."

A shock wave of adrenaline spiked through Calder's body like he'd shoved a knife in the toaster. "I don't know if I can open that part of my life back up again."

"That's just it. You closed it up but that wound is still there underneath. It's infecting everything you do."

Part of Calder knew Robby was right, that he needed to close the chapter on that part of his life for good, but that meant facing the truth. "I guess I'm just afraid to know for sure. It's easier for me to believe that she somehow saved herself and has a new life and a new family than to face the much more likely scenario that

exasperating

she died from a drug overdose or at the hands of some thug."

"Well, I'm living proof that your past always comes back to get you eventually."

Calder snagged both of Robby's hands and pulled him down, tilting his head back to kiss him. "I know you're right. I do. I'll talk to Webster about it tomorrow."

"Whatever you find out, I'll be here. As long as you want me around."

The uncertainty in his voice killed Calder. But no matter how scared Robby was, he always said what he thought, consequences be damned. It was an insanely brave way to live. "Thanks, angel."

"Well, as long as I don't end up in prison," Robby added, his voice quivering despite his attempt to make it sound like a joke.

Calder turned, getting up on his knees, so he was eye to eye with Robby. He cupped his face with both hands. "Believe me when I say this. I will never let you see the inside of a jail cell again. Not ever. Tell me you believe me."

Robby's eyes welled with tears, and he nodded. "I believe you."

"Good. Let's go back to bed for a while."

twenty-one

ROBBY

THE SMELL OF COFFEE AND BACON FORCED ROBBY'S eyes open. For the first time in a few days, he didn't instantly wonder where he was. He rolled onto his back, stretching his limbs with a groan—muscles he never knew existed protesting and an unfamiliar ache in his backside reminding him of exactly what they'd done last night. He smiled to himself, grabbing Calder's pillow and pulling it against his face, inhaling the familiar scent. Last night had actually happened. Calder had taken Robby's virginity, and they'd talked until they'd fallen asleep, wrapped around each other. Robby wasn't sure it was possible to be happier than

exasperating

he was right then.

"Rise and shine, angel," Calder called. "Grubs on."

Robby dragged himself into a sitting position. Calder's phone blipped from the side table, indicating a text. "Somebody texted you," Robby managed, voice sleep soaked.

"What's it say?" Calder asked from the other room.

Robby's brows shot up. "You want me to look at your phone? What if it's one of your groupies?"

"You think I'd give them my private number, angel?" Calder asked, amusement evident in his voice.

"Haha," Robby said, refusing to let Calder's teasing ruin his good mood. "I don't know your code." Calder called a four digit number out to him without hesitation, and Robby's heart skipped a beat. It was stupid to read anything into that, he supposed, but it felt like it meant something, like it meant Calder had nothing to hide. Robby pulled up the message. "It's from Linc. He said, 'Resignation not accepted, asshole. Get your ass into the office and bring the kid.'"

Calder barked out a laugh. "Get in here and eat your breakfast. I've been slaving away for hours."

Robby stood with another stretch, adjusting Calder's boxers as best he could, before shuffling into the kitchen like a zombie, stopping short when he saw Calder dressed in his usual attire of ripped jeans and a ratty band t-shirt, hair already piled on his head. In his lap sat Cas, gazing up at Calder with his good eye, tongue lolling as Calder fed him tiny pieces of bacon. The dog really wasn't supposed to have bacon but they both looked so content, Robby didn't dare say anything. Cas was ancient and bacon was delicious. A little couldn't hurt.

Calder had set a place for Robby, piling more eggs and bacon and toast on his plate than Robby could ever hope to eat. Even if he wasn't filming now, he would be soon and his trainer would kill him. *But*, a voice nagged, there was a possibility he was going to prison, so maybe he should enjoy what he could while he could.

As he walked past, Calder snagged Robby by his hoodie, tugging him down for a kiss. "You look like a baby bird, angel. That hairstyle doesn't hold up to you sleeping on your face all night. How do you breathe like that?"

"Don't tease me before I've had my coffee," Robby grumbled, dropping into his seat and taking a sip of the hot liquid, letting it burn its way down with a sigh. "So, does Linc's text mean you're still going to be my bodyguard?"

"I'm not going anywhere, regardless of what Linc says or does. You're stuck with me until we figure this mess out."

And then what? Robby shook the thought away. He needed to just try to be happy for now. They could worry about the rest later.

While he ate, Calder cleaned the pans in the sink and put them away. He seemed to make more of an effort to straighten up with Robby there, but it was unnecessary. The place looked lived in but not dirty. Robby's apartment was sterile. There was nothing there that represented him because it never really felt like home. He and Cas were always just taking up space. Here, Cas's toys were scattered on the couch and rug and Robby's pants were still on the bedroom floor where he'd lost them last night. Calder's apartment felt more like home than anywhere Robby had ever been, and he wasn't quite sure what to do with that.

When he finished shoveling food into his mouth and had set his fork down, Calder leaned over him, sliding his hands up Robby's shirt to play with those steel bars in his nipples. He instantly melted back into the chair. Calder chuckled. "If it was up to me, I'd take you right back to bed, angel, but we gotta go. Go put some clothes on, and we'll walk Cas and then take him with us to the office."

Robby whined, dragging Calder down for a dirty kiss that had Calder plunging his hands into Robby's pilfered underwear. Before he could even appreciate Calder's groping, it was gone. "Now, who's the tease?" Robby grumbled.

Calder chuckled. "Don't pout. I promise, as soon as we get home tonight, I'll do whatever you want to this hot little body of yours."

Robby stood, wrapping his arms around Calder's neck, pressing himself close. Calder's arms went around him, grabbing two handfuls of Robby's ass. "Anything?" Robby pressed.

Calder ducked his head, growling against Robby's ear. "Mm, anything your kinky little heart desires. Spanking? Wanna be tied up? Want to sit on my face?" Robby whimpered at the last one, his hard cock already tenting his boxers at the words. "You like that one, huh? Well, be a good boy for me today and I'll make it happen."

"Fuck," Robby muttered, pulling Calder in tighter. "Why does that get me so hot?"

"I don't know, but I'm glad it does," Calder mused. Robby jumped as a hand slapped his ass hard. "Now, go get dressed before I bend you over this counter and fuck you silly."

Robby glowered at Calder before rubbing his smarting ass cheek as he walked away. "Yeah, big time tease."

exasperating

Robby dressed quickly, pulling on a pair of ripped black skinny jeans and reaching for one of Wyatt's shirts before his gaze snagged on Calder's closet. He wandered there instead, reaching up and snagging a black t-shirt with a white graphic for a tattoo studio emblazoned across the front and tiny paint splatters everywhere. Robby smiled. Everything Calder owned was covered in splotches of paint. He pulled it on and threw on his chucks before frowning at his hair. Calder was right. He did look like a baby bird. He grabbed a white beanie cap hanging half out of Calder's drawer and a gray cardigan of Wyatt's and considered himself presentable enough for friends.

Robby grabbed Cas's crate, but Calder scooped up the dog and opened the door. They still needed to walk him. When they were halfway down the apartment stairs, Calder grabbed Robby's hand, and he was almost positive his heart became light enough to fly away. He was finally getting to experience life like a normal person.

Calder dropped Robby's hand to push open the security gate and usher him through, and that was when he spotted them…and they spotted him. He didn't know how many of them there were—more than enough to converge on the two of them, surrounding them almost instantly with their cameras and microphones.

"Robby, have you and Elijah buried the hatchet?"

"Is this your new boyfriend?"

"How did it feel to kill a man?"

"Can you comment on your father's harassment complaint?"

"Are you in a cult?"

"Is it true you've been fired from your show?"

"What will you do now?"

The questions came at him from all sides until he was dizzy, his head swiveling this way and that, trying to find a clear path so he could flee. Cas growled and yipped, but it was lost in the fray. Suddenly, Calder's arm came around his shoulders as he bulldozed his way through the throng of media. Robby kept his head down, trusting Calder not to let him stumble and fall.

When somebody grabbed Robby's hand, he snatched it back, only then realizing they had slipped him a note. His head jerked up as he scanned furiously through the crowd, his eyes lighting on a familiar face, the shock of recognition spiking his heart rate. "Rebecca?" he whispered.

But she was already fleeing, giving him one last look over her shoulder before ducking around the corner. He shoved the paper in his pocket so he didn't lose it. What the fuck? Was that her? It had been so long

exasperating

since he'd seen her. Her hair was longer, and she was wearing jeans and a black hooded sweatshirt. He couldn't recall ever seeing her out of her long blue frock with the white ruffles. Was it really her? Had he just imagined it?

He didn't have time to really stop and ponder it. Calder was doing his best to get him to the truck. When Calder had finally gotten him inside with his seatbelt fastened, he just clenched his eyes shut until they were pulling out of the parking lot.

"You can open your eyes, now, angel. We're good."

Were they? "I'm sorry," Robby said.

Calder took his eyes off the road briefly to frown at Robby. "Sorry for what?"

"That. Back there. You didn't sign on for any of that. I-I don't know how they found me."

Calder scoffed. "That shit don't bother me. If I had a problem with being photographed by paparazzi, I wouldn't babysit celebrities for a living. You seem way more shaken up than I am. Are you okay?"

Robby closed his eyes for a long moment, trying to make sense of what just happened. "I think so. It's just that…"

"Just what, sweetness?"

Robby dug the piece of paper from his pocket, staring down at it with equal parts bewilderment and anxiety. "My sister."

Calder's brows knitted together. "What?"

"My sister…Rebecca. She was there. In the crowd. She handed me this note."

He waved the folded up paper as proof he wasn't making this up, that his sister was somehow there outside of Calder's apartment even though he hadn't seen her in years.

"What's the note say?"

Robby unfolded it with shaky hands. There, in neat script, were just two words.

Help me.

Below the words was a phone number with an LA county area code. Robby couldn't speak. He let Calder pluck the note from his fingers.

"Do you think this is for real?" Calder asked.

Robby shrugged, leaning his forehead against the cool glass of the passenger side window. "I don't know. I haven't seen my sister since we left her with Brother Samuel all those years ago."

"Brother Samuel?"

Robby shivered like somebody had walked over his grave. "Yeah. The original church founder. He and my father had a falling out years ago, and they agreed to separate the flock. The one condition was that my

exasperating

father give Rebecca to Samuel as a third wife."

"Third wife?"

"Samuel was already married to Regina and Malinese, but he'd wanted Rebecca for way longer than was legal. My father sold my sister in exchange for the church's name and the members who wished to follow him to Los Angeles. To be fair, she really wanted to go. She was obsessed with him."

"Your dad and this Brother Samuel sat down and divided up the members of the church, and then he took your sister and the group and left?"

Robby shook his head. "We left. We all left the farm and came here so my father could live out his dream of making Magnus Dei the next Church of Scientology. As far as I knew, my sister was back in Kentucky with Samuel and the others."

"So, what the hell is she doing here in California?"

"I really don't know."

For as horrible as his father was, nobody was worse than Samuel. He'd asked the children to treat him like their true father, but Robby had always found him… vacant. Empty. There was something about Brother Samuel that had unsettled Robby from as early as he could remember. The thought of him there…in LA… this close…chilled him down to the marrow of his bones.

"Could he have something to do with the man coming to your apartment?"

Robby shrugged. "I don't know. I don't know anything. He never liked me. He hated me and my sister, Ruthie. I don't know why he'd care about me or my life here. Maybe Rebecca finally saw him for the monster he was and escaped? Maybe he's still in Kentucky and she came here to find me?" He hated the hopefulness in his voice. He knew better than to hope for things. Not everybody got to have a family. Not everybody got to have a husband and kids and a picket fence and a house full of strays and siblings who griped about babysitting. That only existed for other people. Not him.

"I don't know either, angel. But we'll figure it out."

twenty-two

CALDER

CALDER LEFT ROBBY AND CAS IN THE OFFICE KITCHEN with Wyatt under strict orders not to give Robby any caffeine. Being ambushed by the press had left the kid so wired he was practically generating a frequency. Calder assumed Linc wanted Robby there so he could talk to them both together, but Calder wasn't sending Robby in there blind. He was too vulnerable and Linc's beef was with Calder, not the boy.

Calder rapped his knuckles against the slightly ajar door before pushing it open. Linc sat behind his huge mahogany desk . He heaved a sigh when he saw Calder and tossed his pen down. "Get in here and sit down, asshole."

Calder dropped into the seat on the other side of the desk. "I'd respectfully like to remind you that you're not the boss of me anymore."

Linc scoffed. "What the fuck, hoss? You were willing to quit a six-figure job to stick your dick in this kid?"

Calder shook his head, irritated with Linc's cavalier assessment. "It's not about that."

"Then explain it to me? What is this compulsion that leads you to fuck up every good thing you have? You up and quit the Rangers, you constantly fuck up this job. You like to act like you just roll along with nothing touching you, but somewhere deep down, there is something driving this."

Calder scrubbed his hands over his face. He hadn't expected this. He thought Linc would give him a lecture and send him on his way. He hadn't expected to be called out over his self-destructive behavior. Maybe Robby was right. Maybe he did need to look more into what happened to Megan. But, before he did that, he needed to make one thing clear. "You told me that I wasn't allowed to have sex with Robby and still be employed with Elite. I made a decision. I'd rather have him than this job. I'm not trying to fuck up my life. I have plenty of money saved. Shit, Linc, this might be the first time I'm trying to *save* my own life."

exasperating

Linc leaned forward in his seat. "Level with me, are you falling for this kid?"

Yes. "Yeah, I think I am."

"Christ," Linc muttered, pinching the bridge of his nose.

Calder frowned. "I mean, I know Elite is getting a bit of a matchmaking reputation, but I would have thought you of all people would be happy to see me falling for somebody. If I'm sticking my dick in him, then I'm not sticking my dick in the clients. Problem solved."

"Why'd you have to pick that kid?"

Calder looked towards the closed door. "How could I not? He's…perfect."

Linc slammed his fist on his desk. "You know what? Fine. But I want you to know that I now owe Wyatt a thousand fucking dollars and I'm taking it out of your yearly fucking bonus. You know how smug he's going to be about this? I hope this kid's worth it."

"He is," Calder said without a moment's hesitation.

"Well, mazel tov, I guess. But what are we going to do about his case? I can't have you guarding your boyfriend. It's bad for business."

"You and Shep both did it," Calder reminded him.

"Yeah, and both times, we made stupid mistakes that could have ended up with them getting hurt," Linc countered.

"I'm not walking away from this. Give me a leave of absence, fire me if you have to, but I'm sticking this out until the end."

Linc grunted. "Were you always this much of a pain in the ass?"

Calder shrugged. "Well, yeah. But I'm the only guard with a PI license. So, you tolerate me."

"Fine. But if this goes sideways, it's on you."

Calder winced. "Well, funny you should say that…"

"I'm going to rehire you just so I can fire your ass. What now?" Linc asked, exasperated.

"Somebody tipped off the press that Robby was at my place. They ambushed us on the way out this morning. We can't go back."

Linc nodded. "You can use one of the safehouses. I can send Connolly to collect some of your personal items from your apartment. Just make a list. Is that it?"

"Nope. Robby recognized somebody in the crowd this morning. His older sister. She slipped a note into his hand. It just said 'help me' and gave a phone number."

Linc jammed his finger down on a button. "Get the client in here, please," he growled into the intercom before releasing the button. After a moment, he jabbed it down again. "Keep the dog out there. It gives me the creeps."

exasperating

Calder's mouth fell open. "Hey, Cas can't help how he looks. It's not his fault he's ugly."

Linc snorted a laugh. "Jesus, this kid's really done a number on you."

Robby creaked the door open like he was trying not to wake them, closing it softly behind him before trudging forward, arms crossed like he was cold.

"It's okay, angel. You aren't in trouble. Linc's face always looks like that," Calder assured him, waving Robby to the empty seat beside him.

Linc flicked him off before turning his attention to Robby. "You still have the piece of paper the woman gave you?"

Robby nodded, fishing the paper from his pocket and handing it to Linc before sitting on the edge of the seat beside Calder, almost like he wanted to be prepared if he had to flee suddenly.

Linc pushed a single button on his phone. Webster's voice popped up on the other line. "'Sup, brother?"

Linc didn't bother to return the greeting. "I need you to trace a phone number for me."

"Uh, can it wait, like, two hours? I'm balls deep in the financials for the Delaney case and I'm just about to make them scream my name."

Linc rolled his eyes. Calder laughed but Robby flushed, his gaze dropping to his hands. Was he thinking of last night? Of Calder buried balls deep inside him? Of the noises he made or how hard he'd come? Did he want to do it again? Calder couldn't fucking wait to do it again. He mentally shook the thought away. Linc was willing to forgive only so much, and overlooking inappropriate office boners was a big ask, especially after everything else.

"No. Now."

All traces of humor were gone as Webster replied, "Roger that. Give me fifteen."

Linc ended the call. "Are you sure this was your sister?"

Robby licked his bottom lip, nodding. "I only saw her for a minute, but yeah, I'm pretty sure. Who else would ask for my help?"

"Do you trust your sister?" Linc asked.

Robby shrugged. "I don't really trust anybody… except you guys."

Linc scribbled notes as he lobbed questions at Robby. "Could your sister be working with your father? Could this be a trap? What's your sister's age? Birthdate?"

"My sister and my father aren't close. I don't think it's a trap but I don't know. She's about four years older than me, I guess. We never actually celebrated birthdays, so I don't really know."

exasperating

"You don't know your birthday, angel?" Calder asked, surprised.

"I mean, my father put September ninth on my birth certificate, but I don't know if that's my birthday or he just made something up for the birth certificate he ordered from the state. We were all born off the grid. The government didn't know most of us existed until my father needed them to know."

Calder shook his head. Jeb Shaw was a fucking monster in a thousand dollar suit. Everybody knew Magnus Dei was a cult of loons but nobody understood just how horrible conditions could be in places like that, how fast things could go from a dream to a nightmare. As a Texan, Calder remembered watching Waco unfold practically in his backyard. Even as a teenager, the horror of it was evident. Seventy-six people willing to die for a man who spouted nonsense. Would Jeb Shaw's people die for him? Would they kill for him? How about this Brother Samuel? Which of these men were after Robby and why? Hopefully, Rebecca might have the answers.

"Tell me what you know about the church," Linc said.

Robby once more wrapped his arms around himself. "They call themselves Christians. They preach the gospel with an emphasis on Old Testament. They teach that God is jealous, petty, vengeful. They are quick to punish, slow to praise. Most of the women looked to Samuel as some kind of messiah figure. They often shared his bed, even my mother. I think that's when my father decided that what he wanted didn't align with Samuel's goals. Whatever those might be. My dad wanted money. He wanted the spotlight. He wanted fame. He saw religion as a way to justify his fury and indignation about growing up poor and staying poor. It's been years since I left. I don't really know what's happened since. That's why I think I need to talk to my sister."

"You can't meet your sister in public and you damn sure aren't meeting her wherever she's hiding out," Calder said, leaving no room for argument. "I won't have you putting yourself in harm's way."

"Ask her to meet you here, Robby," Linc said. "Neutral territory. Also, if she's on the run, then this is the safest place for her, right?"

Robby nodded.

Linc's phone rang. Once more, he left it on speaker. "Whacha got?"

"Burner phone. I can try to triangulate a signal but it's not really going to help. That's about the best I can do. Anything else? Or can I get back to the Delaney financials?"

exasperating

"I need you to do something for me," Calder said before he lost his nerve.

He thought he'd maintained his composure when he spoke, but given the stricken way both Linc and Robby were looking at him, maybe not. "What can I do for you?" Webster asked, sounding almost sympathetic.

"I—" Calder hesitated. Robby took his hand, threading their fingers together. Calder watched Linc make a note of it, but he had bigger things to worry about at the moment. "I need you to try to find my sister, Megan Michelle Seton. Date of birth four eleven sixty-eight. Brown hair, brown eyes, strawberry birthmark the shape of the Death Star on her left shoulder. She went missing in eighty-four. Disappeared outside Dugger's Grocery in El Paso, Texas. Nobody's seen her since."

The silence was deafening. It was like they were all staring at an invisible corpse and nobody wanted to disturb the dead. Maybe it was the quiet? Maybe it was the way Robby squeezed his hand or the fact that Linc looked poleaxed. "I know, okay? I know she's probably dead. I know she probably died hours after she disappeared. I've run the numbers. I know the statistics. I'd just like to know for certain. If possible, I'd like to bury her with my parents. I just need to know. Can you please help me do that?"

"Yeah, man. I can help you do that. It's not a quick ask, but I'll get on it as soon as I put the Delaney thing to bed. Okay?" Webster asked.

Calder nodded even though there was no way Webster could see him. "Yeah. Yeah, okay." Once Webster hung up, Calder looked to Linc. "Anything else?"

"The keys to the safehouse," Linc said, opening his middle desk drawer and tossing a set of keys in his direction. "The keys to the Land Rover are on there, too. Ditch your truck in the garage and take that. The press knows what you're driving and they have your license number. Have Robby make the call to his sister from one of the office lines before you leave. Just to be safe."

"We'll use the one in the conference room. I'll be in touch."

Calder and Robby were almost to the door when Linc called out, "Watch your six, hoss. I really hate religious zealots."

Calder gave one last nod. "Will do."

twenty-three

ROBBY

REBECCA DIDN'T ANSWER. ROBBY LEFT HER A MESSAGE telling her she could meet him at the Elite headquarters tomorrow morning. His hands had shaken so badly Calder had taken the phone from him and hung it up, as if worried he might somehow damage the equipment. Robby was just done with this day. He wanted to go home. Except, they weren't going home. They were going to a safehouse.

They rode in silence, Southern rock playing softly from the speakers of the Land Rover, which was new enough for Robby to still smell the leather. His stomach churned, dread heavy like a stone in his belly. What did it say about his family that he didn't know if he could trust his own sister? What did Linc's not accepting Calder's resignation mean to their relationship? If one could even call it a relationship.

"Are we over?" Robby blurted.

He wanted to suck the words back into his mouth before they'd even left his tongue, but it was too late. Calder glanced over at him, his eyes hidden by his sunglasses, his mouth gaping slightly. "What? Why would you even think that? Have I given you any reason to think this is done?"

Robby shook his head, embarrassed. His misery coursed through him, a living creature with claws and fangs, shredding his insides and his sense of what was real and true. He felt raw and needy, everything in his life uncertain except Calder, and yet, he worried he couldn't trust that either. They were temporary. That was the unspoken agreement they'd had since this began. But then Calder had said that he cared about Robby. That he was too important to him. He'd quit his job to be with Robby in every way and not be a liar.

Calder took Robby's hand, lacing their fingers together, just as Robby had done to him in Linc's office, squeezing tight. "I know you've had a rough couple of weeks, angel, but you're tilting at windmills. We're fine. We're better than fine. Okay?"

exasperating

Was he making problems where none existed? Imagining enemies that didn't exist? Was he only imagining his father as an enemy? Was his sister really just reaching out for help? These last few months, his life had spun out of control. He'd felt completely alone and hopelessly lost at sea without a shoreline in sight. And now, there was Calder and he made everything so good that it made the idea of losing it feel like it was the worst thing imaginable. He had no idea where any of this was coming from but he felt like it was choking him. He couldn't even answer.

Calder turned the truck into the parking lot of an old brick fire station. Robby frowned at Calder, his minor meltdown temporarily halted by his confusion. Calder clicked a button, and the red door of the garage rose, allowing them to drive in before it closed behind them. He got out, throwing a latch of some kind—maybe a lock—before opening Robby's door and helping him from the car.

Robby expected Calder to turn and lead the way inside, but he crowded Robby up against the side of the truck, cupping his face. "Tell me what's bugging you. Really."

"I can't."

"That's not like you, angel. You always tell the truth, even if it scares you."

Robby stared at a stain in the brick over Calder's shoulder, his heart pounding like he had just run a marathon. "I'm not afraid it will scare me. I'm afraid it will scare you," he muttered.

"Oh, I don't know. I'm pretty unflappable."

Robby met Calder's gaze, blinking tears from his eyes. He took a deep breath, feeling like there was only one way this conversation would end. "I think I'm in love with you."

Calder laughed, and to Robby's utter humiliation, he began to cry harder. Why was he like this? Then Calder's arms were around him. "I hate when you cry, sweetness. You're breaking my heart. Why are you so upset?"

"Because this is all temporary. I'm either going to prison, or we'll figure out what really happened to that guy in my apartment and I won't need your protection anymore, and then you'll just be gone and I'll be alone again," Robby wailed into Calder's t-shirt.

"Angel, I love you, too, but I have to tell you, you have a flair for being dramatic."

It took too long for Calder's words to penetrate, but when they did, Robby was in the middle of a big hiccuping sob. He wiped his face on Calder's shirt before looking up at him with wet eyes. "You do?"

Calder tilted his head, looking at Robby like he was

exasperating

crazy. "I quit a six-figure job for you. I mean, don't get me wrong, that ass is fantastic, but I wouldn't quit just to have sex with you. I could have lied to Linc, but I knew the minute he saw us together he'd see what everybody probably sees when I'm with you, and that's that you own me, sweetness. I'd do anything for you."

Robby's head spun at Calder's words. "Really?" he managed, dragging the back of his hand across his runny nose like a five-year-old.

"Yes, really. Now, please, please, stop crying. Let's go inside and take a shower."

"I'm sorry."

Calder pressed his lips to Robby's forehead. "Don't be sorry, angel."

He stepped away from him, pushing him towards the door that Robby assumed led into the interior of the fire house. Calder punched in a door code and swiped a key fob over the pad. The door gave loudly. Robby didn't know what it was made of but it was heavy and cold, so he assumed it had to be heavy-duty material. Steel, maybe?

Past that door was a staircase leading upstairs. It was definitely no longer a fire station. Floor to ceiling windows allowed sunlight to stream inside the large living space and kitchen. The place had an ultra-modern feel, which was to say it felt stark and barren like a hotel room. There was no warmth. No energy. It was nothing like Calder's well-loved couch or the bed that smelled like him. It was just another place to hide. Like Robby's sterile apartment. A place where people stayed, not a place where they lived.

He found Calder in the bedroom, gun in hand. Had he had it with him the entire time? Sometimes, Robby forgot that Calder had the skills necessary to kill if he had to. He supposed the thought shouldn't turn him on but it did. He watched silently as Calder checked the chamber, clicked something on the side of the pistol, and set it inside the top drawer of the side table beside the king-size bed.

Calder wrapped his arms around Robby from behind in a bear-hug, walking him into the bathroom. He flipped on the tap, undressing first Robby then himself as the water heated to an acceptable temperature. Calder washed Robby thoroughly, paying almost too much attention to his ass, teasing his soapy fingers between Robby's cheeks, grazing his hole just enough to make him whine in frustration. By the time Calder declared them both clean, Robby was already hard and Calder wasn't far behind.

They dried each other off and wandered back into the bedroom where Robby flopped onto the fancy, overstuffed chaise with a sigh, starfishing himself so

exasperating

his arms and legs hung off the side. Calder grinned at him, straddling Robby and leaning down to hover over him. "What's the matter, sweetness?"

"I hate this place," Robby said.

Calder laughed. "This place was designed to be both incredibly safe and ridiculously luxurious. We've guarded princes in this house. Diplomats, pop stars, even a magician once. You miss your fancy pants apartment?"

"I miss your apartment. Can't we just go through the back entrance or something? Every complex has one."

Calder shook his head. "Do you think those vultures haven't thought of that already?"

"This place feels like a museum. Your house feels cozy. Warm. Like a home."

Calder's grin slipped off his face as he brushed his lips across Robby's once, then again. "Places aren't home, angel. People are."

Was that true? Did that make Calder Robby's home? "Well, this place doesn't smell like home. It smells like lavender and vanilla."

"Well, now that you are squeaky clean why don't we go dirty up those sheets until it smells like you and me in here."

Robby's heart skipped in his chest. His tongue

flicked out to wet his lower lip. "Okay."

Calder rocked his hips against Robby's, their cocks slotting together like puzzle pieces. "Mm, somebody's already excited," he noted with a low rumble. Robby ducked his head, all kinds of dirty thoughts flooding his brain. Calder, of course, noticed immediately. "You blushing because I noticed you're hard already? It's a little late for modesty now, don't you think?"

Robby shook his head. "I was just thinking about what you said earlier."

Calder frowned. "You're gonna have to be more specific than that. I've said a lot of things."

Robby forced his face into the crook of Calder's shoulder, his words muffled. "You said if I was good we could do…things."

Robby could feel Calder laughing. "Did I say that, angel?"

"Yes," Robby said, clutching Calder closer so he didn't have to look at him.

"What'd I say exactly?" Robby groaned, knowing Calder was enjoying making him squirm. "It's okay. Don't be shy," Calder drawled. "You know how much it turns me on when that sweet, innocent little mouth of yours says filthy things. You can whisper it in my ear if you want."

Robby pressed his lips to the spot just below Calder's

ear. "You said we could try things like…spanking and that other thing."

Calder wasn't laughing now. "What other thing, angel? Just say it. I want to hear you ask for it."

Maybe Calder was teasing him, but there was no missing the heavy length of his cock now pressing against Robby's hip. It emboldened him. He dropped his head back to the mattress, gazing up at Calder's chocolate brown eyes. "I want to sit on your face."

Calder snarled, his hips surging down to grind against Robby's as he kissed him, plunging his tongue into his mouth before breaking off to give Robby a look that made his cock throb. "Do you think you earned it, sweetness? Have you been good for me?" Robby nodded. "Say it."

Robby swallowed hard. "Yes."

"Good boy," Calder practically purred.

Robby whimpered, rocking his pelvis against Calder's, desperate for any kind of friction. Would he ever get tired of this? Would everything Calder said and did always have this effect on him?

Calder stood, tugging Robby up with him. He moved to the bed, lying down in the center with his head on the pillows, gesturing to Robby. "Come here, angel." Robby climbed onto the bed. "Face the mirror," Calder said, helping Robby swing his leg over so his calves sat on either side of Calder's head. The mirror image was obscene in the best possible way. Calder hadn't so much as touched him and his cock was already throbbing.

Robby shivered as hands ran along the outside of his thighs, blunt nails scraping his skin until Calder gripped his hips and drew him down onto his mouth. At the first touch of Calder's tongue, Robby moaned like a porn star. He couldn't help it. How had he never known that could feel so good? He tried to keep his weight balanced on his knees, but Calder was having none of it. He pulled Robby back until Calder's beard was scraping the delicate skin as he buried his face between Robby's cheeks, licking and sucking at his entrance with a delicious pressure that had Robby crying out, "Oh, God. Oh, fucking fuck."

He couldn't tear his eyes off the mirror, off the picture they created. Calder's naked body was beautiful, his muscles straining, his perfect cock standing at attention, and Robby felt beautiful, too. Calder made him feel beautiful. Calder loved him. Calder thought he was worthy of love. Calder thought Robby was sexy and that made him feel sexy. He ran his hands along his thighs, his stomach, he tugged at his own nipples, the stimulation even better as he watched himself ride Calder's face with abandon, body gyrating as he took himself in hand, chasing his own pleasure.

"Turn around, angel."

It took a moment for the words to penetrate but he jumped to comply. Once he straddled Calder's chest, his mouth closed around Robby's cock, taking him deep, sucking him like he was trying to extract Robby's soul through his dick. Robby couldn't help the way he yelped or the way his hands fisted in Calder's hair as he fucked into his mouth and the tight, wet heat. "Oh, God. You're going to make me come," Robby warned.

If he thought Calder would pull off, he was wrong. Instead, Calder sucked harder, took Robby deeper until his balls were drawn up tight to his body and his every nerve hummed with pleasure. "Oh, fuck. I'm-I'm gonna…" He didn't even finish his sentence before he was coming hard down Calder's throat, his whole body going rigid at the waves of sensation pulsing through him.

When Robby could form a cohesive thought again, he slid off Calder, rolling onto his belly, his whole body feeling like it was made of Jell-O. Calder's fingers trailed along Robby's spine and down the cleft of his ass, his fingers teasing at his hole, still slick with spit. Robby lifted his hips, whining a bit as Calder's finger penetrated him just the slightest bit. He was still a little sore from the night before but not so much that he didn't want to do it again. "Fuck me," he begged, his voice just above a whisper.

"Are you sure?" Calder asked, his lips dragging along Robby's shoulder.

Robby nodded into the pillow. "Yeah, I'm positive. I want you inside me again."

Robby didn't open his eyes as Calder's weight disappeared. He had no doubt that Calder would return. When he did, his fingers were slick with what felt like lube. He sucked in a breath as Calder's finger pushed inside.

"You okay?" Calder asked.

Robby turned his face towards him. "Yeah, just sensitive." It wasn't a lie. Every time Calder's finger grazed against Robby's prostate, it sent a jolt through him in a way that was almost uncomfortable.

Calder worked him open slowly, his mouth exploring whatever skin was within reach while he whispered things nobody had ever said to Robby before. That he was beautiful, sweet, perfect…loved. It felt like a dream. The most perfect dream. By the time the blunt tip of Calder's cock pressed against his hole, he wasn't sensitive anymore, he was desperate. He didn't think his body would rally so he could come again, but he wanted to feel Calder filling him up. He needed to feel that connection.

Calder breached him slowly, letting gravity do the work until he was fully seated inside. He wrapped his arms around Robby, lacing their fingers together, his lips pressing kisses to the back of Robby's throat, his shoulder, his ear. "Fuck, you're so tight," he whispered as he fucked into Robby with slow, even strokes. "You feel so good, angel."

Robby wanted to tell him he felt good, too, but he couldn't. He couldn't get the words out. With Calder's weight on top of him, his arms around him, his cock inside him, he was drowning in Calder's touch, his scent. It was all just too much—overwhelming in the best possible way. As Calder's pace increased, so did the sensation. Robby canted his hips, arching his back for Calder who growled, gripping him even tighter. The change in angle sent every thrust brushing against that spot inside Robby that made him feel like a live wire. "Oh, fuck. Oh, do that again. Harder. Please."

Calder groaned, his legs forcing Robby's wide so he could drive into him with the force Robby demanded. "Is this what you want, baby?"

"Yes. Yes. Please. Please. Please," Robby sobbed, burying his face in the pillow as Calder fucked him with a ferocity Robby had never thought anybody could ever feel for him.

"Christ, I'm gonna come. Fuck."

Suddenly, Calder's weight seemed to disappear. "No," Robby cried. "I want you inside me. I want to feel it."

Calder froze above him. "Are-Are you sure, angel?"

"Do it. Please."

Calder's fingers threaded into Robby's hair, twisting his head back for a kiss, thrusting his tongue into his mouth in time with his cock driving into Robby's body. Robby was certain his heart was expanding until it was too big for his chest. Would it always feel like this?

Calder thrust hard two more times before his hips stuttered and he gave a guttural shout. He bit down on Robby's shoulder as he emptied himself into him. Neither of them moved right away. Calder was softening inside him and they were both sweaty, but Robby didn't care. "Wow," he managed breathlessly.

Calder nodded against his shoulder. "Yeah. Wow. I think we're probably going to need another shower."

"I feel like we're going to need a crime scene clean up crew," Robby teased.

"'Cause I murdered that ass?" Calder teased.

Robby groaned. "Ugh. Why are you like this?"

"I don't know, but you fell for me, so what does that say about you?" Calder challenged.

"You fell for me, too," Robby countered before

exasperating

realizing what he said. His heart seized in his chest as he waited for Calder to deny it, even though he'd just said it not an hour ago.

"Yeah, well, falling for you was easy, angel."

Robby flushed, burying his grin in the pillow. He didn't think he'd ever been this happy before in his entire life, and for once, it didn't feel like he was waiting for the other shoe to drop. At least, not yet.

twenty-four

CALDER

"SIT DOWN, ANGEL. YOU'RE GOING TO WEAR A PATH ON the carpet."

Robby spared a glance at Calder before resuming his circular pacing around the conference room table, chewing on his thumbnail as he walked. Rebecca was late—by a whole forty minutes—and Robby seemed to have convinced himself that the girl wouldn't show. That he'd managed to spook her with a simple voice message. Calder wasn't so sure. The girl had been desperate enough to contact Robby, even knowing all eyes were on him right now. While a cult in the middle of Nowheresville, Kentucky probably

exasperating

didn't pay the news much mind, Robby's father had spies everywhere, and Calder had to believe that the man wouldn't be happy to know his daughter had abandoned her husband.

When Robby wandered close enough, Calder snatched the back of his hoodie and tugged him into his lap, wrapping his arms around the boy's narrow waist. He wiggled uselessly for a minute, attempting to free himself from Calder's grasp before finally giving up, sagging against him, defeated. "What if she doesn't come? What if she's scared to come here? What if something happened to her because of me?"

Calder shook his head. "How could this be your fault, angel? You're just caught up in something we haven't quite managed to unravel. But we will."

The elevator dinged, announcing another arrival. Robby jerked his head in the direction of the door, deflating as he saw Connelly leave the elevator and head to Linc's office. He dropped his head in defeat, but Calder watched as a girl followed him off the elevator. Her dark blonde hair peeked out from under a Dodgers baseball cap that did nothing to hide her hollow eyes and sunken cheekbones. She also wore a Dodgers hoodie with her ill-fitting jeans, like she'd had to shop at a kiosk outside the stadium. That had to be her. He nudged Robby. "Look who's here."

Robby's head shot up just as the girl looked towards the glass conference room and spotted Robby sitting in Calder's lap. Robby rocketed to his feet, hurrying to where she stood. "Rebecca."

"Obi?" she cried, running into his arms. They hugged each other tightly in the middle of the office.

The siblings clung to each other, unaware of the curious looks they received from the others in the office. Calder stood, aiming to lead them into the conference room where there was slightly more privacy. When Robby saw him standing beside him, he gave him a wet smile. "Rebecca, this is my… This is Calder."

"Are you his boyfriend?" she asked, her green eyes wide with interest.

Robby's gaze cut to Calder like he waited for him to deny their relationship. As if he would do such a thing. "Yes. I suppose you could say that."

"Nice to meet you," she said, throwing her arms around him in a tight hug. He hugged her back, even as his stomach clenched.

"Why don't we go into the conference room and speak?" Calder asked. "I'd like to have an associate sit in on this, if you don't mind. It helps to have somebody else in the loop."

"Sure, that's fine," she said, her spunky Kentucky

exasperating

accent the antithesis of Calder's slow drawl.

Had Robby once had the same accent? He couldn't picture it. Calder guided Rebecca to a seat and sat opposite her. He'd expected Robby to take the chair beside his sister, but instead, he sat beside him, rolling his chair until it bumped up against Calder's, like Robby needed him as close as possible.

Calder hit a button on the boomerang shaped device in the center of the conference room table. Linc's voice filled the space. "Is she here?"

"Yeah, we're ready for you."

When Linc entered the room, Rebecca seemed to shrink in on herself, and Calder realized how young the girl really was. Not that much older than Robby really. Maybe meeting here wasn't such a great idea, after all. If she was intimidated, she might not talk.

"I got your note, obviously. So, how can I help you?" Robby asked, sounding slightly stonier than he had just a moment ago, as if he'd remembered some long forgotten feud.

Rebecca wrapped her arms around herself just like Robby did when he was nervous. "I-I'm scared about what's happenin' at the farm."

It was such a vague statement, but Robby's leg started to jitter under the table. "What about it?" he asked.

A single tear slid down Rebecca's cheek, but she wiped it away, sniffling, and then sat up slightly straighter. "I think I made a mistake. I think maybe you were right about the place all along."

"Rebecca, how about you start by telling us what's got you spooked enough to come all this way just to hand Robby a note," Calder said, hoping to steer her towards any helpful information.

"He's got guns," she blurted. "A lot of them. And I think he's got some of the kids makin' bombs."

"What?" Robby gasped.

Rebecca shook her head like she didn't even believe the things she was saying. "I know. I know it sounds crazy, Obi, but he—Samuel—he's gone crazy, like *really* crazy."

"Like guns and bombs crazy?" Robby asked, incredulous.

"It wasn't like it just happened overnight. It was sort of slow like. At first, he started talkin' 'bout how he was the anointed one and how he'd been chosen to raise God's army, which near as I could tell was just more noise so he could justify why he was sleepin' with everybody's wives. But then he started separatin' everybody, isolating the parents from their kids. Then the women from their husbands. He claimed that they all belonged to him now and he needed to be creatin' as

exasperating

many babies as he could to raise them up to be soldiers." She shook her head, clasping her hands together on the table, her fingers twitching. "Then he kicked me out of my own house. Said I was damaged goods 'cause I still hadn't gotten pregnant after all these years." She flushed, her cheeks pinking just like Robby's.

"Why didn't you just leave?" Robby asked.

"Where was I gonna go? I don't know nothin' else. Besides, once he wasn't climbin' on top of me all the time, he started lettin' me do supply runs, which is when I started going to the library and readin' up on you and Daddy and whatever else I could find." She smiled to herself, but then it just slipped away. "Then I found out about Dinah. He'd moved her into our house. She was sat beside him at dinner and she was dolin' out punishments like a good little helper. Then she showed up to church with a band on her finger and declared herself Samuel's true wife."

"I mean, it's not legal, but I imagine none of the marriages performed there are, if that's your concern," Linc said.

Rebecca cut her gaze to him. "My concern is that Dinah is twelve years old."

"Jesus," Linc muttered.

"Yeah. He's gone insane. He keeps talkin' 'bout the end times and how he's bein' persecuted by the government and how Satan is usin' them to create a new world order. About six months ago, the guns started showin' up. Crates full. I don't even know where he's gettin' them or how. It's not like we have money. We're self-sustainin'. Then, last month, bags and bags of fertilizer started comin' in and gettin' stacked in the barn. His talks of doomsday and the apocalypse are getting worse, too, and he's sayin' that God is talkin' to him and tellin' him that sacrifices must be made and not all of them will survive and how it's better to die in service to the lord than to live to be old and do nothin'. He's crazy. They all are."

Calder scrubbed his hands over his face. Christ. What was it with these crazy fuckers? Did they truly believe their own bullshit or was this just about power? "Have you tried going to the police?"

"I can't. They're on his side. It's why he moved us away from Kentucky and out here to California. The cops are in on it."

Robby frowned, his hand reaching for Calder's under the table, squeezing tightly. "How do you know that?"

"Because I tried to leave a few weeks ago. I wanted to get help, to get to you. But the local police came and got me and drove me back. They said it was in my best interest to not try to leave again."

exasperating

"So, you've been in California this whole time?" Robby asked.

She nodded. "Samuel said the state of Kentucky was conspirin' against him and said we had to get out. We just up and left everythin' behind and ended up on a property in Northern California about two hours from here, but that was before he started to go all weird."

"How many people would you say are living at the compound right now?" Linc asked.

Rebecca answered without hesitation. "Eighty-six. Thirty of them are children, thirty-one if you count Dinah, but she's not in the children's quarters anymore, obviously. I tried to get them out, but he caught me and I was punished."

Robby's hand clenched down on Calder's hard enough to cut off the blood supply. "Punished?" he managed, like he had to force the words past his lips. "Did…did he hit you?"

Tears spilled down her cheeks as she laughed bitterly. "Oh, he's gotten way more creative than that. The odd beatin', cold baths, and kneeling on rice, that's for the little ones… No, he's way more imaginative with us adults."

She shoved up the sleeve of her shirt and showed the rectangular burns across her palms. They appeared mostly healed but were still the bright pink of new flesh, not the shiny pink of a long forgotten scar.

"Oh, my God," Robby said, blinking back tears of his own. "Why didn't you—" He cut himself off. "I'm sorry I wasn't there."

She shrugged a shoulder. "I've been through worse. But I gotta get to the kids. The others, they've made their beds, but those babies did nothing wrong."

Linc shook his head. "We're going to get everybody out. Safely. I have a friend who works with the ATF back in Florida. I'm sure he'll be able to hook me up with a contact here."

"ATF?" Rebecca asked.

"Alcohol, tobacco, and firearms. That's who handles these types of cases," Linc said.

"Or mishandles," Calder muttered. At Linc's quizzical expression, Calder said, "We all know what happened in Texas. Almost everybody died. Even the kids."

Linc shook his head. "That was thirty something years ago and they made massive organization-wide changes to make sure these types of things don't happen again." Turning his gaze to Rebecca, he added, "We need to do this by the book or Samuel could just walk free, and how much damage do you think he'll do once your wannabe messiah thinks he's untouchable?"

exasperating

Rebecca shoved her thumb into her mouth, worrying her nail between her teeth. Robby looked to Calder. "Do you think this is the right call?"

Calder sighed then nodded. "All things considered, yeah, angel. Taking down a cult of this magnitude requires a very precise strategy. One none of us are equipped to pull off."

There was a rap of knuckles against the doorframe, and then Webster was sticking his head in. "Sorry to interrupt, but can I see you when you're done? Alone. It's about that thing you asked me to look up."

Calder's stomach plummeted to his boots. He gave a stilted nod. No matter how bad it was, Calder had spent the last three plus decades preparing himself for this moment. If Webster found anything, it likely wasn't good, but at least it was closure.

"Do you want me to come with you?" Robby asked.

"No, angel. Stay here and spend time with your sister." To Rebecca, he added, "You're welcome to come back to the safehouse with us."

She shook her head. "No, but thanks. I need to keep moving. Samuel already has his dogs after me, for sure. That's why I have cash and a non-traceable phone this time. I looked it up in the library."

Calder stood, dropping a kiss on Robby's head. "You got everything you need, boss?" he asked Linc.

"Yeah, we're good. For now. Go talk to Webster."

During the walk to Webster's office, Calder felt like he was walking through quicksand, each step pulling him farther down, making it harder to breathe. Webster's office gave Calder anxiety on a good day. He had four screens on the wall, each displaying different numbers scrolling rapidly downward like something out of The Matrix. On his desk, papers sat piled high and a PC shared space with a chunky looking laptop. Behind it all, Webster sat in khaki shorts and a pink polo shirt, looking like he was ready for a day of yachting, not hacking into uncrackable systems.

Calder took a seat in the chair across from him. "Whacha got?"

"It could be something or it could be nothing. Sixteen years ago, a body showed up in an alley just over the border in Juarez. No teeth, no fingers, just an E burned into her right breast and a strawberry birthmark on her back shaped like the Death Star."

Calder grunted, feeling like he'd taken a sledgehammer to his solar plexus. He'd known. He'd known it wouldn't be good. "What'd they do with her?" he asked, clearing his throat to keep his voice from breaking.

Webster leaned forward. "She was sent to Arizona University as part of a project to identify hundreds of unidentified bodies found along the border. Because her teeth and fingers were removed, they catalogued her remains, took a blood sample to test later if needed, and then had the body cremated and stored in the facility with others who were unidentifiable. I have a picture of her birthmark. If you think you can handle looking, I can ask the university to compare her DNA to yours to get a confirmation. It could take months, but at least then you'll know for sure."

Calder blinked, trying to process Webster's words, as he nodded in some attempt to prove he was listening. He was. He'd comprehended what the other man said, even as he tried to fight the urge to vomit. Somebody had taken his sister's teeth and fingers and then thrown her away like garbage. It seemed incomprehensible, even after his years working with human trafficking. He'd been right. Elizer had made his sister one of his girls. The E branded into her skin proved it. But, if this was his sister, she could have never been the girl in the picture. She was dead long before Calder had even made it onto the task force.

He took the photo from Webster, his hands shaking. The photo was blown up so only the girl's pale pink birthmark was visible. The mark sat higher now than he'd remembered, but that was what happened when people grew. He couldn't speak, he just nodded and handed the picture back. Finally, he said, "Have them run the tests, please."

"Yeah, you got it. I'll let you know whenever the results are back."

Calder stood and walked back to the main part of the office where Robby was hugging his sister goodbye. When he saw Calder, he gave him a smile, but it died at whatever expression he saw on Calder's face.

"Hey, what's wrong? Are you okay?" Robby whispered as the elevator doors closed on his sister.

"Can we just go home, angel?"

Robby nodded, his brows drawing together as he took Calder's hand. "Yeah, we can go anywhere you want."

twenty-five

ROBBY

ROBBY HELD HIS TONGUE THE WHOLE WAY BACK TO the safehouse. It wasn't that he was afraid to speak but more that he didn't want to give Calder a reason to have to answer. Whatever Webster had told him had shaken him badly. His white-knuckled grip on the steering wheel and the way the muscle in his jaw ticked told Robby that Calder was barely keeping it together.

Once they returned to their temporary home, Calder remained quiet. Robby made them both sandwiches, but Calder fed most of his to Cas then disappeared into the dining room. Cas followed along behind him and Robby did, too, though it seemed pathetic and weird to just follow Calder around. He worried his bottom lip between his teeth as he watched Calder move about, pulling paints from plastic drawers and tossing them onto the scarred wooden block table.

Should he leave? Did Calder want to paint alone? He had no idea what the protocol was for something like this. While Robby didn't know exactly what Webster had said, there was only one type of news that could impact a person so hard. Megan was dead. It seemed crazy that Calder would hold out hope she'd somehow survived, but Robby knew, deep down, that some part of him had needed to believe she was still out there somewhere, no matter how impossible it seemed.

Robby ached for him.

Cas jumped up onto the table like his legs were made of springs. Calder gave him a small pat on the head, moving the oils and such out of the way so the dog could curl up and watch. Robby wanted to watch too. Calder pulled a fresh canvas from underneath the table and set it on the easel, then he turned and walked directly to where Robby lurked in the corner. "I can—"

Calder gripped the hem of Robby's shirt, tugging it up until it bunched under his arms and he was left with no choice but to lift them. He had no idea what Calder was trying to do, but he was already half hard

exasperating

from the near feral look on Calder's face. Robby stared at Calder quizzically as he pulled him to the stool catty-corner to the easel and had him sit-stand against it. He shoved his hands in Robby's hair, deliberately undoing the little styling Robby had managed that morning. He was afraid to speak. He didn't want to interrupt the strange, almost electric tension in the air.

He bit his bottom lip as he tried to understand what was happening. Calder cupped his face, tugging his lip free, before slanting his mouth over Robby's in a bruising kiss that left Robby tenting his joggers and wanting much more than whatever this was. But Calder seemed satisfied with what he'd accomplished. He walked to the canvas, picked up his brush, and started to make broad sweeping strokes with an umber paint. Every few moments, Calder would flick his gaze to Robby and then back to the painting. That was when Robby realized…Calder was painting him.

Robby did his best to hold still, but it was hard when Calder was standing there with half his hair pulled up and off his perfect face and his fingers were covered in paint and each flick of the brush made the muscles in his arms and back flex. Robby loved watching Calder, loved being able to actually see Calder's vision materialize. The way he squinted at the canvas, the boldness and surety of his brushstrokes. It was fascinating. It was sexy. Robby stifled a groan. It was ridiculous that he was this turned on just from this, especially when he knew that Calder was painting to escape from his pain, to turn his focus away from Megan and whatever he'd learned.

Random curves and lines began to take on his likeness, first as an abstract and then as a much more beautiful version of himself. Not just beautiful but debauched, with a major case of bedhead and kiss-bitten lips and a look in his eye that made him feel exposed, like anybody who looked at that painting would know exactly how Robby felt about Calder. Was that really how Calder saw him? It didn't make any sense. Robby's self esteem wasn't so low that he thought he was ugly. He was just wholly… unremarkable.

Robby suddenly felt like he was choking. He cleared his throat. "I-I'll be right back. I have to…do something."

He scurried away from Calder like he was some scared little mouse, knowing deep down he was a fraud. Calder looked at him but maybe only saw Robby the way he wanted to. He couldn't see what a huge mess Robby truly was inside where it mattered. He didn't want to make this about him and his issues, not when Calder was obviously hurting. All he could

exasperating

do was just find a place to hide until the feeling passed.

He walked to the bathroom and turned on the cold water, splashing it across his face. What was wrong with him? Wasn't it a good thing if the person you loved thought of you as more than you actually were? Wasn't that the best possible outcome? Robby opened his eyes to see Calder standing in the doorway, something in his hand.

Robby turned. "I didn't mean to run off. I hope I didn't ruin—"

Suddenly, Calder's mouth was on his, the weight of his body shoving Robby into the counter with a force that might have hurt if Robby's brain hadn't fallen offline at Calder's first touch. Robby had no idea what was happening, but Calder was kissing him like they might never see each other again. His hands were rough and bruising, and he was pushing Robby's clothing down and out of the way. Calder spun him around as he dropped to his knees, spreading Robby open. He cried out in surprise as Calder speared his tongue into his hole.

Robby gripped the counter until his fingers ached. He couldn't think; he couldn't even fucking breathe. Calder's tongue felt so good that all his brain could manage was now and yes and please and more, more, more.

Robby's cock had been hard almost since Calder had kissed him in the dining room, but now, he was aching, his throbbing cock trapped against the counter. Calder buried his face in Robby's heat, fucking him with his tongue. He prayed his knees wouldn't buckle as Calder did things to Robby's body that made his eyes water.

Calder's hand snaked up onto the counter, snagging whatever it was he'd had in his hand when he'd first entered the bathroom. Robby's whine of frustration turned into a low moan as Calder's tongue disappeared and was replaced by two slick fingers. There was no finesse, no gentleness. He worked his fingers in and out of Robby's hole with purpose, and the thought of Calder's carelessness, his need to just get past this part so he could get inside Robby left him feeling overwhelmed in the best possible way.

Calder stood as he pulled his fingers free, tearing at his jeans to free his erection. Robby canted his hips backward without thought, suddenly desperate to feel the familiar ache of Calder's thick cock inside him. He hissed as Calder pushed his way inside, Robby's insides rearranging themselves to allow Calder's entrance. Once he was buried to the hilt, he gripped Robby's hips, his beard scraping Robby's cheek as he whispered, "Tell me you're okay."

exasperating

It wasn't said like a question but Robby answered it anyway. "I'm so beyond okay. Fuck me. Please."

Calder made a noise that Robby felt all the way down to his toes, this feral snarl that was sexy as fuck and dangerous as hell but still made Robby feel like there was nowhere safer than there with Calder. He still wasn't ready to be gentle. He fucked Robby hard and fast, each stroke driving him up onto his toes, his eyes rolling back as Calder somehow managed to hit that magical spot that had sparks shooting behind his eyelids. When he finally managed to open his eyes, his mouth fell open.

The picture they made was lurid but so incredibly hot. Calder fucked him like he was on a mission, like he couldn't keep his hands off Robby, like he needed to claim him, own him, make him submit. Calder's fist buried in Robby's hair, bending him back to capture his mouth in a sloppy kiss as he pounded into him even harder.

Robby wasn't forming words but he couldn't keep silent. Every thrust dragged a cry or a moan or just a breathless panting 'uh uh' that felt ripped from his toes. When Calder's hand finally closed around Robby's aching neglected cock, he sobbed in relief. It hadn't even occurred to him to try to take care of himself. For once, he was there for Calder's pleasure.

This was the one thing he could give him after Calder had given him everything, had been there for him, had taken care of him without question since day one.

He leaned back, trusting Calder to keep him on his feet, his lids at half mast as Calder jerked him in time with his thrusts, the dry friction just this side of painful. It didn't take long for Robby to feel that familiar sensation, that spark of heat at the base of his spine, his balls drawing up tight to his body. "I'm gonna come. I-I—"

Robby's whole body seized as his orgasm slammed into him, Calder catching the cum in his hand and using it to ring every last bit of pleasure from Robby until he cried out at the sudden sensitivity. Calder's arms slid under Robby's, his hands catching Robby's shoulders as he fucked into him again and again until Robby wasn't sure he could take anymore. Calder gave one last thrust, his hips stuttering as his teeth sank into Robby's shoulder and he made an animalistic sound.

Calder leaned back against the wall, bringing Robby with him. They both stood panting, sucking much needed air back into their lungs. They were both covered in cum and sweat and even bits of oil paint. After a few minutes, Calder peppered kisses along Robby's temple to his ear. "I'm sorry. I'm so sorry. That was too much. You're… I should have been more

exasperating

careful with you."

"Stop apologizing. I'm not made of glass. I liked it. I still can't believe somebody like you would ever even look at somebody like me."

Calder blew air out of his nose. "Stop saying that. How can you not see how fucking special you are? I've wanted you since the minute I laid eyes on you and not because you were forbidden fruit and not because you were some innocent little virgin. You are the most beautiful person I've ever met, inside and out. You live in the most shallow place in the world, yet you somehow manage to stay sweet and gentle. You adopt unadoptable dogs, and you stay friends with a person even after they hurt you, and you say what's on your mind even when you're terrified. People like you never really existed in my world, and I have no idea how we got here but this is where I want to be. You are who I want. Just you. Only you."

Robby's mouth was suddenly bone dry. "I just want you, too."

Calder kissed his head and gently pushed him away, his spent cock slipping free of Robby uncomfortably. "Let's get cleaned up."

Calder removed his jeans which were still caught around his thighs before helping Robby step free of his clothes. Once they were under the water, the steam in the shower all but choking Robby, Calder's mood shifted. He rested his forearms against the tile, his forehead pressed against his hands. Robby silently took the washcloth and began to clean Calder, careful not to linger for too long anywhere. When he finished with that task, he washed himself quickly before grabbing the shampoo and lathering Calder's hair. Calder didn't speak, just allowed Robby to shift him under the spray to rinse his head. When they were clean, the water began to turn cool and then frigid. Robby attempted to turn the water off, but Calder snagged his wrists, gently pushing him towards the shower door. Robby frowned but didn't argue. He just dried himself off, giving Calder one last look before he walked out.

Robby pulled on a pair of blue and white striped boxer briefs and sat on the bed facing the bathroom door. He didn't know what else to do. He wanted to give Calder his space but he wanted to be there if he needed him.

Calder finally emerged twenty minutes later with a towel around his narrow hips, his long hair free and still wet enough for huge fat droplets to slide down his chest and belly before disappearing into the white cotton fabric of the towel. He stopped short when he saw Robby, and for a split second, he felt like the earth stopped spinning. Would he ask Robby to go? Then

exasperating

Calder stumbled forward, dropping to his knees on the floor in front of Robby, burying his head in his lap. Robby's arms came around him automatically, his heart squeezing.

"You're freezing, baby," he whispered, grabbing the blanket from the end of the bed and wrapping it around Calder's shoulders.

Calder didn't speak, just snaked his arms around Robby's waist. Freezing water seeped through the thin material of Robby's underwear, but he didn't care. He didn't care about anything but Calder who clung to Robby like he was a life raft. He folded himself over Calder like a shield, wanting to hide him from all of this but knowing that he couldn't. All he could do was offer him a safe place to grieve. "You can fall apart, you know. I'm okay. You don't have to stay strong for me or whatever."

For a second, Robby thought maybe Calder would choose to ignore him, but then his shoulders started to shake and a jagged howl escaped, almost like a wounded animal, shattering Robby's heart into a million pieces. Tears slid down his cheeks as he did his best to just hang onto Calder as huge wracking sobs shook his body.

He didn't know how long they stayed like that, long enough for Calder to run out of tears.

"What was she like?" Robby asked when they finally moved from the floor to the bed and he was snuggled close under Calder's chin.

Calder gave a sad smile, shaking his head. "I thought she was my mother until I was four. She was always carrying me around and wouldn't let me do a thing for myself. My mom said I was slow to walk or talk 'cause Megan did it all for me. She was super bossy, and she always had to be right. When I would have nightmares, she wouldn't let me sleep with her 'cause she said I needed to learn to be brave. Instead, I'd just wait 'til she fell asleep and then go to sleep under her bed. But when Jamie Ryan shoved me off the school bus and broke my front tooth, Megan threatened to kick his big brother's ass in retaliation since she couldn't beat up a little kid. She read to me a lot. She would take me out in her car and we'd go driving up and down desolate roads, listening to Bon Jovi and Poison. She was a really good sister."

"She loved you. None of what happened to her was your fault. You know that, right?" Robby told him.

It seemed like such an obvious thing to say, but Calder hugged him closer, dropping a kiss on his head. "Logically, I know that. But when my head gets quiet, my brain takes over and I think of all the ways she must have suffered at the hands of those monsters, the things they made her do. If I had just stayed with the Rangers, maybe I could have done something to at least take that fucker Elizer down. How many other girls were taken after I left? How many girls could I have helped?"

"Calder…" Robby pressed his lips against Calder's jaw. "You are pretty amazing, but you can't single-handedly stop human trafficking. Like most evil things, when you chop off one monster's head, another three grow back in its place. You couldn't help Megan but you help people who are alive every day. People like me."

Calder nodded. "I know, angel. I just need to wallow in it for a bit."

"You can wallow as much as you want. I'll stay right here and wallow, too," Robby said.

Once more, Calder squeezed him tightly. "Thanks, angel."

twenty-six

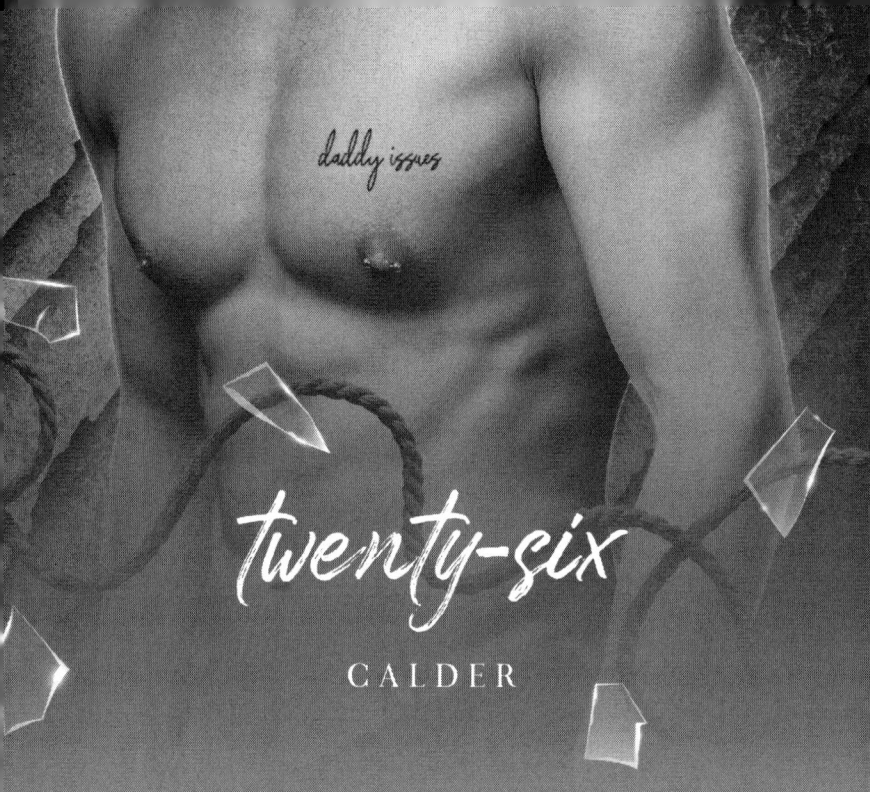

CALDER

CALDER WOKE TO A TONGUE LICKING HIS CHIN AND A warm body sleeping with an arm and leg thrown over him and a pool of drool on his chest. He forced his eyes open, raising his arm to pat Cas's scraggly tufted head, before gazing down at Robby. Sometimes, just looking at the boy overwhelmed him. He had no idea how he'd somehow earned Robby's affection. Calder had no illusions about who he was and the things he'd done in his life. He was wholly unworthy of Robby's heart, and there was probably somebody better out there for the boy, somebody without baggage, somebody his own age. But Calder was just selfish

exasperating

enough to not care. He wasn't letting Robby go, not as long as he wanted to be there.

Cas whined and Calder shushed him, gently untangling himself from Robby before scooping up their ragamuffin dog. Throwing on black sweatpants and a t-shirt, he carried him into the kitchen under his arm like a football. After starting some coffee, he then went to grab his leash, taking the dog downstairs to the little patch of grass behind the building to let him do his business.

At the top of the stair landing, he heard Tupac blasting from the bedroom and then Robby's sleep soaked voice muttered, "'ello?"

Calder dropped Cas's food in his dish and then wandered back into the bedroom. Robby sat cross-legged on the bed, nodding along with whatever the person on the other end was saying. When he saw Calder, his eyes went wide like he was receiving life altering news. Calder dropped down beside him, and Robby leaned closer, maybe so Calder could hear the voice on the phone or maybe just because he needed to hang onto something.

Calder carefully took the phone away, noting it was Robby's lawyer before he hit the speaker button, catching the man mid-sentence. "—told me this before you went to the Feds. We could have used this for leverage."

"It's Calder. Leverage for what? What's happening?"

"I was just telling Robby that he should have brought his sister to me first, not the ATF. We could have used her information as a bargaining chip to get them to drop the charges against Robby."

How did Stanton know about that? "We didn't take her to the ATF. We haven't even spoken to the ATF. How do you even know about that?"

"I get paid to know these things," the older man said vaguely. "Luckily for you, it seems you have all kinds of powerful friends. I didn't think the Edgeworth family had any clout left after what Montgomery pulled, but they clearly still know some pretty powerful people. Your friend's grandmother plays bridge with the District Attorney's Aunt Margo."

Calder cut his eyes to Robby who shrugged as if he had no idea what any of this meant.

Calder squeezed Robby's hand. "Bottom line it for us. Are they charging him or not?"

"Not. The DA suddenly doesn't think there's enough to charge Robby. Honestly, I don't think there was ever really a chance, but they didn't want to look like they were giving special favors to a celebrity. Appearances and all that. LA County does have a reputation."

exasperating

Robby clapped a hand over his mouth, collapsing back onto the bed and kicking his feet. Calder smiled. It was a relief to see Robby excited about something. How long had it been since the boy had looked genuinely happy?

"Thank you so much," Calder said.

"Thank me by paying my bill."

Then he was gone. As soon as the man disconnected, Robby rocketed to his feet, jumping up and down on the mattress in his blue boxer briefs with the red stars. Calder leaned back, putting himself in danger just to enjoy the view of an elated Robby. He'd missed the laughing, giggling, smiling boy he had seen in news articles and magazine spreads. Suddenly, Robby was standing over him. Calder caught him behind the knees, yanking until he collapsed, straddling Calder's torso. Robby caught his hands, leaning down to kiss Calder deeply.

"Did you hear that?" Robby asked, knowing full well Calder did. "It's over. It's all over. Finally."

Calder didn't want to burst his bubble but it wasn't entirely over. They still had no idea who the man was who broke into Robby's apartment. They still had no idea why he was there and whether somebody else might come after him later. They still didn't know if his father was involved. Was Robby safe? Would he ever be truly safe?

Before he could get into it, his own phone began to vibrate on the dresser. He reached back behind him, floundering blindly until he managed to snag it and bring it to his face. Linc. "What's up, brother? I hear we have you to thank for our early morning call from Robby's lawyer."

Linc snorted. "Not me. Wyatt. That boy cannot help but meddle and his grandmother is no better. There's nothing Violet likes better than throwing her weight around and proving she can still provoke fear in us mere mortals. I'm surprised it honestly took this long for them to drop the charges. But that's not why I'm calling."

A trickle of unease crept along Calder's spine, and he must have frowned because Robby's smile faded and he caught his bottom lip between his teeth, biting down hard enough to leave indentations in his lip. "So, why are you calling?" Calder forced himself to ask.

"Is Robby there with you?"

"Yeah," Calder said.

Linc sighed. "Put me on speaker phone."

Calder could feel his good mood fading by the moment. He did what Linc asked, putting the phone on speaker. "Go ahead."

"I spoke with my contact at the ATF. They've

exasperating

apparently had the farm under surveillance since they fled Kentucky, but they haven't been able to move on them because they don't have enough to execute a warrant."

Calder frowned. "What does this have to do with us?"

"They want Robby's sister. They need Rebecca to sign an affidavit. They'll probably need her to testify if this goes to trial."

"Against Samuel?" Robby asked, voice quivering just slightly at the man's name. "No. No way. He'll kill her."

"It's not that simple, kid," Linc said. "Your sister is married to Samuel. She's on legal documents. The farm property is in her name. If she doesn't agree to help out and give an affidavit, she could be named as a co-conspirator for any crimes committed by the farm. They are throwing her a lifeline."

Goddammit. He was really done with all this drama. He was getting too old for this shit. "So, she gives a sworn affidavit, they execute a warrant, and then she gets immunity?"

Linc grunted. "I mean, you'll need an attorney to nail down all those details, but that seems to be the gist of where they were going with this. Again, Rebecca needs a lawyer. She shouldn't say a word without one. We've got time. There's no rush. They are playing the long game with this. They can't risk him slipping through their fingers. Talk to your sister. Make sure she knows she has the upper hand."

"Yeah, okay. Tell Wyatt thanks for us."

There was a rustling and then Wyatt's voice appeared against the speaker, mumbling a sleepy, "Welcome."

Linc disconnected, and once more, it was just Calder and Robby. He hugged Calder close, head dropping to his shoulder. "I'm so tired of all of this. I just want to leave LA and never come back. I don't want to hear another word about cults or churches or cheese knives or paparazzi. Can we just run away?"

"Sure. Where should we go?" Calder asked.

Robby sighed. "I don't even know. Somewhere with lots of land for animals…and babies?"

Calder's pulse skipped, his heart racing. "Babies? You're so young."

"I've always known what I wanted," Robby said. "Do you? Want kids, I mean? Is that wrong to ask?"

Calder felt like his brain had stalled. Did he want kids? Some part of him had, yes. Always. But another part of him chilled at the thought of what a baby meant.

Robby leaned back, cupping Calder's hand. "I'm sorry I asked. It's way too early for that conversation,

exasperating

especially with all you're going through with Megan and… I'm…I'm sorry."

Calder shook his head. "I want to have kids. I want to have kids with you. Our kids. But some part of my brain tells me that we're just bringing another potential victim into the world. I don't think I could bear to lose somebody I loved that much ever again. I—fuck—yes. Yes. I do. I'm just scared."

Robby dropped his head, looking at Calder through long, dark lashes. "I'm scared, too. Of everything. But I'm less scared when I'm with you."

Calder leaned his forehead against Robby's. "I'm less scared with you, too, angel."

They just sat there for a long while, not speaking, just holding each other. When Cas came and sprung up onto the bed, Robby finally said, "I should probably call Rebecca, huh?"

"Yeah, that would probably be a good idea. Invite her over here to talk. Tell her to watch her six."

Robby frowned. "What?"

Calder chuckled. "Her back. Tell her to watch her back and make sure she's not followed."

"Yeah, okay."

"I'm going to go make breakfast. I'll make enough for all of us."

He stood, dumping Robby on the bed before leaning

down and giving him a quick, almost chaste kiss on the mouth. In the kitchen, he worked on autopilot, preparing breakfast while his brain tried to sort through a million complicated emotions. He mourned Megan. He did. He mourned for the sister he never got to have and the life she never got to live. The life they both could have had with parents who were both checked in and madly in love. He ached for the husband Megan never met and the kids they might have had. It wasn't one single man who had deprived Calder's family of the life they should've had, but one man's name always came back again and again. Elizer. That fucking monster had an entire network of broken people constantly recruiting young girls and boys, feeding them drugs and lies and pain to service a network of other soulless monsters. Monsters that couldn't be beaten, couldn't be satiated, stealing the innocence from victim after victim until they were just shells of people or until they were dead.

Calder flinched as a hand touched his shoulder, rounding on Robby before stopping abruptly. "Sorry, angel. I was just deep in thought."

"Thought about what?" Robby asked, hopping up onto the counter beside Calder, looking at him with enough empathy to make his throat tight.

"Megan. All the others just like her."

exasperating

Robby stole a grape off the counter. "Like Jennifer?"

Calder nodded, moving to stand between Robby's knees, dropping his head to Robby's chest. He wrapped his arms around Calder.

"Go get her."

Calder jerked his head up. "What?"

"Jennifer. You can't help the others right this second, but you can go get Jennifer's ashes. You can get her, and we'll find some place really beautiful to put her. Okay?"

"I don't know, angel. There's too much going on here right now."

Robby gently shook Calder's shoulders. "No. Stop procrastinating. Go get her today. She doesn't deserve to spend her afterlife in a cardboard box. That's not fair. You keep putting it off, but you'll feel better once she's here, with us."

"I can't leave you here alone."

"Why? The man who came after me is dead. Are you never going to leave me alone for the rest of our lives? That's going to get awkward, real quick. I'm here in an actual safehouse. I'm sure this place has every bell and whistle. There's really no safer place than here. Besides, I'll have Rebecca to keep me company."

Calder sighed. He really did owe it to Jennifer to go get her, but he hated the idea of leaving Robby alone.

Maybe he could ask Linc to just have one of the probie agents just do a driveby every hour or so. The funeral home was an hour outside of LA. He could be back in less than three hours.

Calder lifted his head, pressing his lips to Robby's. "Alright, angel. I'll go get Jennifer. But if anything—and I mean anything—happens, you call my cell phone immediately and I'll send help."

Robby nodded. "Yeah, okay."

"Promise me," Calder insisted. "I need to hear you say it."

"Okay, yeah, I promise. I will call you if the sky is falling."

Calder nodded. Robby was right. He couldn't spend every minute with him forever no matter how much the idea appealed to him, but there was just this feeling Calder couldn't shake. He couldn't quite put a finger on it but it made him want to keep a death grip on Robby.

twenty-seven

ROBBY

REBECCA ARRIVED ABOUT AN HOUR AFTER ROBBY called. Breakfast was a mix of rapid-fire bursts of meaningless chatting followed by awkward bouts of silence. Robby didn't know what to say to a sister he'd barely known, even though they'd spent years living in a small cabin where they practically slept on top of each other. Part of him still wasn't sure he could trust Rebecca. He didn't think she was out to hurt him, but he wasn't comfortable sharing too many private things with her either.

Calder was uneasy also, but Robby thought it had more to do with having to leave Robby behind to pick up Jennifer's remains than it did with being uncomfortable in Rebecca's presence. Calder always seemed at home no matter who surrounded him, especially women. Robby made a face at the thought before trying to shake it away. Calder had chosen him, had said he loved him, wanted children with him. He couldn't hold Calder's past over his head if they were going to have a life together. Robby's heart stuttered in his chest as the magnitude of the idea settled under his ribcage. Calder wanted a life together…with Robby. Holy shit.

He covered his mouth with his hand to cover his stupid grin but Calder caught him. His brows knitted together as he gave Robby a half smile. "What's on your mind, angel?"

Robby shook his head. "Nothing. You should probably get going so you can get back."

Rebecca looked between them, confused. "You're leavin'?"

Robby nodded. "Only for a few hours. He has to run a quick errand. We'll be fine here alone."

Rebecca shrugged. "Oh, I ain't worried about that. I can take care of myself. You too, if needed."

Calder smiled. "Good, then I'll leave you in charge of keeping your little brother safe until I return."

It took a good ten minutes of goodbyes before Calder

truly left. Once he was gone, a strange emptiness filled Robby. Being without Calder felt unnatural. They'd spent so much time together over the past month that it was like missing a limb.

"You really love him, huh?" Rebecca asked.

Once more, Robby tried to hide his smile. "Yeah. I really do. I know that's probably not really okay with—"

"Don't you dare even finish that sentence, Obidiah Joseph. I know I was some insufferable nitwit when I was in high school but I'm way more cultured now."

Robby's mouth dropped open. "Really?"

She dropped her voice low like there was somebody else who might hear them. "Yeah, when my dirtbag husband decided he needed to take a child bride, he essentially turned me into the help, which meant I got to go into town and pick up supplies. He was so absorbed in his plottin' and struttin' around like some king that he didn't even notice that I'd stay gone for hours… Or maybe he just didn't care, you know? So, I started goin' to the library and I met somebody there. A librarian. His name is Beau, and he showed me all kinds of things."

She blushed but then squared her shoulders like she was reminding herself of something. Robby raised his brows. "Oh, yeah. Like what?" he asked, letting his accent sneak back into the last word as he leaned forward.

"Nothin' dirty. Samuel may not take our vows seriously but I have to. At least until I can divorce the son of a bitch. But Beau taught me all kinds of things. How to use the internet, how to order a copy of my birth certificate. How to open my own bank account. I know so much about the world now, Obi. I didn't know there was so much out there. Like I love the java chip frappuccino from Starbucks and the show *Riverdale* and K-pop and—did you know that people can just dye their hair like any ol' color? Like green and pink, and I even saw one girl whose hair was blue," she finished in a rush.

Robby smiled. He'd forgotten what it was like his first six months in LA, when he was still trying to learn about secular life. It had seemed like some hedonistic playground. Every single thing had fascinated him and scared him. Most of it still scared him.

"This must all seem ridiculous to you. Like, you're a big star now and live in a fancy house, and you're on tv so you must know big celebrities and go to rich people parties. I bet the farm seems so silly to you."

Robby was shaking his head before she'd even finished. "Believe me, I'm not that kind of celebrity. Honestly, sometimes I miss the farm in Kentucky." At her horrified look, he explained, "Not the child labor or the beatings but the big family dinners, the always having kids to play with, never feeling alone. I loved reading the bible stories and feeling like there was something bigger. I just wish Samuel and Father had really, truly listened to the message."

"Well, maybe you should teach it to them."

Robby laughed. "Who? Father and Samuel? I'm thinking they're too far gone. Besides, nobody really ever listened to me."

Rebecca frowned. "Not them. Others. And you're wrong, Obi. Samuel and Father were so hard on you because people did listen to you. You made the congregation question the message. They couldn't have that. They needed everybody to keep bein' afraid or their whole charade fell apart."

Robby bit his bottom lip. Was that true? It couldn't be. Rebecca was just trying to be nice. He shook the thought away. "What do you wanna do 'til Calder comes home?"

"Um, can we watch your show? I've never seen it."

Robby wrinkled his nose. "Really? That's what you wanna do? It's really dumb. It's a kid's show."

"Stop that. You're my brother, and I'm super proud of you. You got out. You escaped and got to live the life you wanted. I want to see your work."

"I've never actually watched it," Robby confessed.

"You've never watched your own show?"

He could already feel his face flushing. "I can't. I tried once, but I was too embarrassed."

"Well, we're goin' to watch it, and you don't get to be embarrassed," she told him, her tone leaving no room for argument.

That was the Rebecca he remembered. "Okay, fine."

It took two whole episodes for Robby to stop hiding his face behind a couch cushion. Rebecca genuinely seemed to enjoy the show.

She kept saying, "I'm so proud of you."

Robby even started to believe it. He had missed this. It was strange to miss something he'd never really had. He and Rebecca had never even gotten along. She was always so caught up in impressing Samuel, a task that was much easier for any too young girl to accomplish as far as Robby was concerned. But she had been a child, too, just like him, even though she'd seemed so grown up to him. So wise. So…smug. It all seemed like forever ago. He needed to learn to just let it go somehow. He had so many siblings, but she might be the only one he'd ever see again.

A strange heaviness settled over Robby a split second before the phone started to ring from somewhere inside Rebecca's backpack-like purse. He

exasperating

wasn't alone. Rebecca frowned before jumping to her feet to dig for her phone. She stabbed at the answer button. "Ezra? What's wrong?"

Who was Ezra? Awareness crept along his spine as he tried to place why the name seemed so familiar. But it didn't matter anyway. The caller wasn't Ezra, it seemed.

"Dinah? How did you get this number? Where's Ezra? What… Calm down. Stop cryin'. I can't understand what you're sayin'. Samuel did what? What? No. That's crazy. You can't be serious? No. Don't do anythin'. I'm comin' home. If he tries to do this before I get there, take the children to the tunnel. Ezra knows where it is. I'll find you."

Rebecca picked up her bag, making for the door, a blind panic sending her spinning in circles and crying in frustration as she tried to dig for something in her bag.

Robby reached out and grabbed his sister by the shoulder, shaking her enough to get her attention. "Rebecca, stop. Stop. What is happening?"

Her face was red to the tips of her ears. "That was Dinah. Samuel knows he's under surveillance. I don't know *how* he knows but he knows. He's tellin' everybody that it's time to ascend and that his Father is callin' them all home. She said he asked her to prepare the children's drinks with some kind of bottle filled with a weird brown liquid. He told her not to worry, that everybody would just fall asleep. I have to go."

"No. You can't just go. What are you going to do? It's not safe."

Rebecca pulled a gun from her bag and chambered a round like she was in some kind of action movie. "I have my safety right here. I'm not lettin' him kill a bunch of innocent people. I'm certainly not lettin' him kill a bunch of helpless children, especially our brother."

Recognition ignited a fire in Robby's bloodstream. Ezra… His baby brother. The one born after Robby had left for Hollywood. He'd known the name was familiar. His mother had said it was her favorite name and she'd saved the best for last. Her last baby. "Why would Ezra be with you and Samuel?"

"Because Father found out the baby wasn't his. Apparently sharin' Mama with Samuel was one thing but let his spawn be a part of Father's creepy church was another altogether. So, he ditched Ezra with us. I've raised him since he was a week old. He doesn't know nobody but me. Even though Samuel doesn't let us see the kids too much. He said it makes them weak, that it makes us weak, too." A tear slipped down her cheek as she stuffed her gun back in her backpack. "It'll be fine. We'll be fine. I'll call you."

exasperating

"What? No. You aren't going to confront him alone." Robby's insides churned. "I'm coming with you."

Rebecca shook her head. "No. No way. You have enough troubles, you don't need ours, too."

"I'm not letting you go face Samuel alone. We'll call Calder on the way, and he can get help and send them to us. It'll be okay. Where's your car?"

Rebecca shook her head like she didn't want him to go but that she understood it was a fight she would lose. "I parked down the block around the corner. This is a terrible idea, just so you know."

Robby nodded. "Yeah, of course, I know."

As they took the stairs to the garage exit, Robby punched Calder's number on his cell phone, making a noise of frustration as it went straight to voicemail. He didn't know what else to say so he just started rambling. "Oh, my God. Seriously? You turned your phone off *now*? Listen, Rebecca and I are on our way to the farm to get the kids. Samuel has gone full Kool-Aid drinking Jonestown crazy and may actually be making everybody drink literal Kool-Aid. Rebecca has a gun and a car, and if you get this, please come save me because I don't want to die the same day I find out I'm not going to jail. Bring your A-Team or the X-Men, whoever, and please find us. My phone is on. You can trace it, right? Oh, God, please tell me you can trace it. Oh…and I love you. I really love you. Just in case you don't get this in time."

twenty-eight

CALDER

CALDER SAT IN HIS TRUCK, JUST STARING AT THE FRONT of the funeral home for longer than he'd ever admit. He didn't know why this was so hard. Jennifer was gone. She'd been gone for years, and no amount of wishing or prayers had been able to wake her up. He wished she would haunt him, haunt him or scratch him or shriek like a banshee in his nightmares. Something. Anything. He deserved that. He'd sent her back into hell on a hunch, knowing what might happen to her. Hell, knowing what already had happened to her. He'd put the mission in front of a single girl's life. He'd chosen Megan over Jennifer and Megan was already long dead.

If he'd known... If he'd known, he probably would have made the same choice anyway, and that was it, that was what really tore at his heart. He betrayed Jennifer again and again every time he played it back. He deserved some kind of punishment for that. He didn't deserve Robby. He didn't deserve happiness, but he would take it, which was so much worse in Calder's mind. It was the selfish thing to do. He should be willing to suffer, at least a little bit, for the one he couldn't save. The one he *chose* not to save.

He scrubbed his hands over his face as he noticed the parking lot beginning to fill, people leaving their vehicles and entering through thick wooden double doors. A funeral? A viewing? Fuck. He sat waiting and watching. People came and went, kids played, running between cars in the parking lot, dresses wrinkled and suit jackets carelessly tossed onto the hoods of cars to allow for ease of movement as they chased each other, laughing. Grief was a fleeting thing as a child. They often had no concept of death until it tucked itself in close enough for them to really feel its icy breath, for it to pluck a parent or a sibling or a friend. It was good. Children shouldn't be burdened by grief. There would be enough time for sadness and pain in their lives. Eventually, death came for everybody.

exasperating

"Christ, Calder. Stop being a moody son of a bitch and just go get it done," he muttered, his voice stolen by the rumble of his diesel engine.

He looked down at his tattered jeans and faded t-shirt, wishing now he'd thought better of how he was dressed. He was relieved to see there was another entrance to the building, one that read 'office.' Once he stepped inside, that relief vanished. He stood in a small wood-paneled lobby that smelled like butterscotch where there was a small pale green couch with tiny pink flowers and a row of chairs. On the small table sat a lamp, some pamphlets, and a flickering candle that Calder suspected had to be the source of the overly sweet scent.

There was a man with a receding hairline and a black suit sitting at a desk with a couple on the other side. They seemed far too young to be there. The woman held a tissue in her clenched fist, her hands balled at her knees. The man was pale and stared blankly ahead as the man behind the desk pointed at a book with his pen. Calder felt like he was intruding. When the man in the suit noticed him, he appeared to excuse himself. He came to the door.

"Somebody will be with you shortly, sir."

"Yes, that's fine," Calder managed, just as his phone buzzed in his pocket. Calder fumbled for it, knowing any minute it would start ringing loudly. He pressed down on the volume button with too much force, silencing the call, before sticking it back into his pocket in time to see the man close the door on him. Calder walked to the couch and sat, shoulders collapsing, as he sat counting the knotholes in the fake wooden panels.

Calder wondered how Robby was getting along with Rebecca. He knew how much Robby had missed his siblings, had missed having a family. Calder wanted Rebecca to be everything she seemed, for Robby's sake. He'd had so much pain and disappointment in his life. He deserved a little comfort and happiness, and even though Calder wished he was enough, he knew Robby needed his family.

Calder was reaching into his pocket when the door opened and a girl with green hair and black lipstick entered, wearing a black dress with a white Peter Pan collar and the biggest shoes Calder had ever seen. They looked like baby shoes but for babies who wanted to be four inches taller. The girl's face fell when she saw him sitting there, her eyes taking him in from head to toe as she sucked on the straw of her black Starbucks cup. She clearly was going for a look.

She glanced at the closed door and sighed. "Can I help you?"

Calder stood, shifting nervously from one foot to

exasperating

the other. "I'm here to pick up some remains."

"Cremains."

"Uh, what?" Calder asked.

"If the body has been cremated, they're called cremains," she clarified, tone bored.

"Oh. Okay, then. Cremains. Her name was Jennifer."

"Last name?"

"Seton. Jennifer Seton."

"Oh, it's you," she said. "We wondered what you looked like. Who you were. We even had a bet going that you wouldn't ever come pick her up. She your dead wife or something?"

Calder gaped at the girl before shaking his head. "What? Do you talk like this to all of your customers? Clients? Whatever?"

"I'm the makeup artist here. Daddy doesn't really let me talk to the customers-clients-whatevers. He says I lack...people skills. Luckily, I don't need them for my job. My clients don't tend to be super chatty. Usually," she added with a smirk.

Calder felt like he'd entered the twilight zone. "Who are you?"

"Evermore Rollins. Who are you?"

"That is *not* your real name," Calder said.

"No, it totes is. My parents run a funeral home and crematorium. Big fans of Poe. Most people just call me Ever. You didn't answer my question," she said, taking another sip of her drink.

"Calder Seton," he said.

The girl nodded, her green hair falling into her overly-lined eyes. "So, was she? Your dead wife, I mean."

"No. She's my…" He hesitated. She'd never been anything to him before Elizer had found her—his informant, his snitch? But he'd given her his last name when none could be found for her. "She was my sister," he finally said. It felt right, even if it wasn't true.

"Did you guys have a fight or something? Before she kicked it, I mean."

Calder laughed in spite of himself. "You are very direct."

"So they tell me. Aspergers, what are you going to do? It's why my parents don't like me up front."

"Yet, here you are," Calder mused. "Can I get my sister's ashes, please? I'm on a bit of a time crunch."

She rolled her eyes. "You wait, like, months to pick her up and now, suddenly, it's an emergency. Typical."

He laughed. "Please?"

Megan would have found this entire exchange hilarious. She was always blunt, kind of like Robby. Calder suddenly felt like he'd been mule-kicked, the pain pulling the air from his lungs and causing him to

exasperating

drop into his seat. He'd give anything to see his sister again, to hear her voice, to listen to her do impressions of the Muppets as she read to him. Why was he losing it again? He'd cried all his tears the other night.

"It's normal, you know," Ever said before clarifying, "To be all over the place, emotionally. Like, sometimes, even if you didn't like the person, you cry because you'll never have the opportunity to fix it. You cry because maybe you had the opportunity and you didn't do anything, or maybe somebody stole that opportunity from you. But none of that matters to the dead, you know. No matter what you believe, their troubles are over. Whether it's because they are just gone or whether you think they're chilling on some white fluffy cloud in Heaven, the only one whose feelings matter are yours."

He hadn't thought about God or Heaven or any of that bible school stuff since his family had stopped going to church all those years ago, but he believed that his parents had found peace, that they'd found Megan, and maybe, somehow, they'd even stumbled upon Jennifer up there somewhere. The thought brought him some measure of comfort. He nodded at the girl. "I suppose you're right."

"Yeah, I know. I gotta go downstairs to where we keep the…leftovers. I'll bring them right out since you're in such a hurry and all."

Calder shook his head. Would anybody believe this story if he told it? He doubted it. Jennifer's remains were in fact in a cardboard box. It was heavier than Calder had thought and it was stamped 'temporary.' It would be nice if that were true. He signed the papers and paid the bill before tucking the box under his arm.

As he was leaving, Ever took another sip of her drink. "See ya, Calder Seton."

"Maybe so, Evermore Rollins."

Once in his truck, he seatbelted the remains into the passenger seat, shaking his head at the thought of possibly being pulled over. He tugged his phone from his pocket to text Robby that he was on his way back when he saw he had ten missed calls and half a dozen voicemails, all from Robby.

Calder's heart dropped into his shoes as he dialed his voicemail. His blood whirred in his ears, deafening him to the recording prompts, but somehow, he managed to get the message to play, stomach lurching at Robby's frantic voice.

"Oh, my God. Seriously? You turned your phone off *now*? Listen, Rebecca and I are on our way to the farm to get the kids. Samuel has gone full Kool-Aid drinking Jonestown crazy and may actually be making everybody drink literal Kool-Aid. Rebecca has a gun and a car, and if you get this, please come save me because I don't want to die the same day I find out I'm not going to jail. Bring your A-Team or the X-Men, whoever, and please find us. My phone is on. You can trace it, right? Oh, God, please tell me you can trace it. Oh…and I love you. I really love you. Just in case you don't get this in time."

Adrenaline sent a shock of panic along his spine. He didn't bother listening to the other messages. He found Webster's number and dialed.

"Sup."

"I need you to trace Robby's phone."

"Trouble in para—"

"Now, Webster. I don't have time for this shit. I also need a location on this place called 'the farm.' The one Linc talked to the ATF about. Drop everything and get me that fucking address. Tell Linc and Connolly to meet me there. This gets critical priority. I'm serious. Don't fuck this up."

"Yeah…okay. Yeah. What do we need to know?"

"Samuel is accelerating some kind of end of days Jonestown timeline. Robby and his sister are en route and the sister's armed. They said they're going to save 'the kids.' I can only assume he means the kids at the compound. There are weapons and bombs on this property. Everybody needs to keep their head on a swivel. Linc should probably let the ATF know, too, but I'm not waiting."

"Calder—"

Calder disconnected, tossing his phone onto the seat and turning over the truck's engine. He didn't even know which way to go. Until Webster got him a location, he was stuck there, doing nothing, while Robby was driving towards a man who had no fucks left to give. He pounded his fist on the steering wheel once and then again.

"Fuck. Fuck. Fuck!" he shouted. He tilted his head back and closed his eyes. "Shit. I don't even know how to do this anymore, but please, please, please, God, please don't take him away from me. Not now. Fuck, please. Please, let him be okay."

His phone began to light up with Webster's name on the screen. "Yeah."

"I'm sending you the coordinates now. We're seventy minutes from the location. We've got backup en route. We'll meet you there."

"I'm not waiting for you," Calder said, already tearing out of the parking lot, leaving the small group of kids still playing staring.

"We never thought you would. Stay alive, brother."

That's the plan, Calder thought as he hung up. For all of them to get out alive.

twenty-nine

ROBBY

ROBBY'S BODY FELT NUMB. HE'D NEVER IMAGINED A scenario where he'd be forced to attempt to break into the farm, much less in broad daylight, but there they were, ducked down low in a crouch, creeping through the trees along the fenceline. Since he'd never been to the new farm, he had to rely on Rebecca to lead, which wouldn't have worried him so much if she wasn't clenching a gun in her right hand as she crept along in front of him.

To their left, just beyond the fence, there were nothing but rocks and pebbles, bleached white from the sun. Robby shivered. He remembered those stupid fucking rocks. Having to pick up handfuls at a time, having to dig the larger ones from the earth until his fingers bled, just to carry them to another pit. Then, once the one pit was empty, they'd go to the pit they'd filled and do it all over again. It was painful. It was demoralizing. It had made him feel helpless.

But there was nobody out there now, and that was almost worse. Samuel would never let the children stop working before the sun went down, and it was hours before sunset. Had he taken them all into the great hall? Was he currently encouraging each of his loyal followers to drink poison? If so, they were too late. The thought of a small boy, barely six, with his mother's hair and eyes, drinking poison, had his stomach clenching. Would he get to meet his brother? "We need to hurry."

Rebecca gave him an exasperated look. "We need to be careful. We got no idea what we're walkin' into. If Dinah didn't manage to get the kids to the barn, we're screwed. I have no idea how we'll get them out without usin' the tunnels, and if they're already in the hall with the adults…" She broke off, her voice catching. "Then I don't know what we'll do."

"Don't panic. We'll find them. We will. Calder will come for me. He'll bring his team, and we'll be fine. All of us." He wished he believed his own pep talk.

exasperating

Calder had never called him back. It wasn't like he wouldn't try to save Robby. Of course, he would. But there just might not be enough time, and Robby had to make peace with the fact that this was probably a suicide mission.

They stopped outside what looked like an old miner's shaft with a board leaning across it. Rebecca pulled a necklace out of her shirt and yanked it off. There was a key dangling from the end. It was no key Robby had seen before.

"Here, help me," she said, gripping one side of the board and dragging it out of the way.

That was when Robby saw the grate with a large padlock holding it closed. Rebecca unlocked the iron grate, swinging it open, before plunging into the darkness. Robby followed blindly, his shoes splashing into ankle deep water. He really hoped this wasn't a sewer. Robby fumbled for his phone, flipping on the flashlight, swinging it around wildly as he took in the concrete walls and the dirty water at his feet. It smelled like rot and mold, a fungal smell that made Robby feel like just breathing in there might actually kill him. It would suck to save the kids for all of them to die from toxic black mold or some kind of weird disease carried by rodents.

At the other end of the tunnel was another grate.

Rebecca unlocked it and carefully swung it open. She gave Robby one last look and stepped into a small closet sized room before climbing up a steel ladder and pushing up the door at the top. When she disappeared, Robby scrambled after her. He stumbled as he lost his balance. He would have fallen if there had been any room to do so. The whole area was stocked floor to ceiling with crates with only a narrow path between them. Both Robby and Rebecca had to turn sideways to squeeze by, stopping just short of an opening that led to what Robby assumed was the actual barn.

Rebecca held her hand up, listening carefully, repositioning her grip on the gun in her hand. It was eerily silent. If there were thirty children in there, at least one of them would be crying, moving, whispering. Robby's heart sank as Rebecca's shoulders sagged. Still, she kept her pistol in hand as they crept into the two story barn, open but for the hayloft above the two large entryway doors.

At first, he thought they were alone, but then he saw a small girl sitting on a hay bale in a dirty shift dress, her bare foot drawing patterns in the dirt below. She couldn't be more than twelve or thirteen.

"Dinah?" Rebecca said. "Where are the others? Where are the children?"

Dinah's head jerked up, her gaze darting towards

something behind them. A trickle of unease shivered along his spine as he slowly turned to see what the girl looked at.

Robby's mouth fell open at the sight before him. Samuel held a small boy against his chest, an enormous knife leveled against the child's throat. Ezra. He would have known him anywhere. They looked just alike.

"Hello, sweet Rebecca. Welcome back," Samuel said. "I see you've mended fences with your brother." He looked to Robby. "I don't suppose you've come back to us for good, Obidiah?"

Robby wasn't looking at Samuel but at Ezra who mouthed "Obi," as if he knew who Robby was. Had Rebecca talked about him?

Robby forced himself to stay calm, even as his blood rushed in his ears. "Yeah, no. I'm afraid not."

Samuel had sweat through his white shirt, the thin fabric clinging to his lanky body, his hair and skin damp. His muscles twitched as if against his will, and his gaze darted around, skating over things but never landing on any one person or thing for long. It gave Robby the creeps and reminded him of the tweakers on the boulevard. When he talked, his Kentucky twang was as sharp as the knife he wielded. "That's right. You've forsaken the almighty for a life of hedonism, just like your daddy."

Robby didn't bother to correct him. It was clear Samuel was on something. There was no point in egging him on. If anything, he just needed to keep him calm until Calder could get there. Unless, Calder hadn't gotten his messages. The thought stopped him cold. What if Calder wasn't coming? At least Robby had told him he loved him. That was something.

"Ezra!"

A cry from Rebecca pulled Robby from his thoughts, his pulse skittering as he saw the blade in Samuel's hand had nicked his brother's throat, causing blood to trickle along his neck. The boy trembled visibly, tears running down his dirt-stained cheeks, but he didn't dare move or cry out. God, Robby remembered those days of punishment, where every sound only prolonged the agony.

Samuel laughed, the sound jagged and cutting like broken glass. But he wasn't looking at Robby; he was looking at Rebecca who had leveled her gun at him. "Oh, sweet Rebecca. You forget, I'm the one who tried to teach you to shoot. How many shots would it take before you managed to hit me? You think you could get one off without hitting the boy here?"

One look at his sister and Robby knew Samuel wasn't bluffing. Her hands wobbled and tears sprang to her eyes. "He's your son," she whispered, looking at Ezra.

exasperating

Samuel grinned, wiping sweat from his eyes with the hand that held the knife. "Yeah, but I got tons of these critters runnin' round. But not you. It just kills you that this one wasn't yours. That your mama managed to pop out, what? Eight? Nine? Yet, you couldn't manage even one, barren as that rock pit out there."

Rebecca trembled but not with fear, with rage. "You're a monster. A crazy, delusional monster."

Samuel wrenched Ezra's hair back until the boy cried out, forcing the blade tighter to his neck. "Shall I show you what a monster I am? I've got nothing left to lose. Can you say the same?"

Rebecca made a noise of frustration. Robby made a decision. "Rebecca, give me the gun."

"What?" she mumbled, her brows knitting together, even as she kept her gaze on Ezra.

"You can't shoot, but I can."

It was true. Robby hated everything about guns. The noise. The violence. The smell. But he was a crack shot, always had been. It was the only thing that had ever made his father proud.

"Oh, I wouldn't do that if I were you. I'll slit this boy from ear to ear before you can even blink. Drop the gun on the ground and kick it to me." A sob escaped from his sister's lips, her confusion giving way to hopelessness. "Do it," Samuel spit. "You know this mortal skin suit means nothing to me. Our people are ascending even as we speak. Soon, I'll follow and so will you. But give me the gun and I'll let your brother here take the boy and go."

"What do you mean, they've started ascending?" Robby asked.

"Just what I said. I know the government's been watching and I know this one"—he pointed to Rebecca with the knife—"went and ran her mouth about things that were none of her business. That's why we had to move up our timeline. We were preparing to fight the army of demons outside. We had everything we needed. Now, we have to start over. Fight the demons as angels from Heaven."

Robby's body grew cold as he realized Samuel believed all of this. Some part of him had always thought Samuel was a charlatan, a narcissistic pedophile following from some cultish playbook. He'd never really let himself believe that his end game was to kill a bunch of innocent people. Robby had imagined this was just a trap. Dinah, the distress call, everything. And it was, he supposed, but he hadn't thought they'd lose everybody on the compound.

Rebecca dropped the gun, but she didn't kick it away. "Now, give him to me."

"Nah, not yet." He pulled something from his back

pocket. It was a flask. He tossed it in her direction. "Drink up, sweet Rebecca. Drink and I'll give the boy to your brother."

"No!"

They all turned to see Dinah standing there. Robby had forgotten her the second Samuel had emerged from the shadows. Now, she held the gun in her hands.

"Dinah. You put that gun down or so help me, I'll flay the skin from your bones," Samuel snapped, like he was used to intimidating the girl.

She sniffled. "You said it was a trick. You said I just needed to make Ezra tell me the phone number so that you could get them back here, so they could be with us again. You said there was no ascension."

Samuel shoved Ezra, forcing him to stumble into a hay bale in the corner. As soon as the boy was on his feet, Robby snagged him by the arm and pulled the boy behind him, all of them now watching Dinah closely.

A drug-addled Samuel was nothing compared to a distraught twelve-year-old waving a gun around. A gun she clearly didn't know how to use.

"Dinah," Samuel crooned, clearly changing tactics. "I just didn't want to scare you. Everything is going to be just fine. There's no cause for worry. Just give me the gun and all's forgiven. You know you're my special girl. My true wife."

Robby forced the bile in his throat back down at Samuel's words and what that likely meant. Jesus. Dinah's pupils were blown wide, and she was crying far too hard to make any rational decisions. If Samuel got that gun from her, it was all over.

They all watched, helpless, as Samuel took one agonizingly slow step after another, closing the distance between himself and Dinah. When he was close enough, he reached out, and that was when the world seemed to explode. Dinah screamed, and Robby's ears rang as he watched red bloom across Samuel's white shirt, just beneath his belly button. Dinah dropped the gun, and Robby hurried to pick it up and stuff it in the back of his pants.

Samuel stood there, just staring at the girl. Robby pulled Dinah away, shoving her beside Ezra, before Samuel could make another move. He looked down at his wound and laughed. "It will take a lot more than that to get me out of your life, Dinah. You little bi—"

The second bang was louder and far more jarring than the last. For a moment, he thought a bomb had detonated, but then he looked to Samuel, stomach lurching as he noted a neat hole between the man's eyes and the back of his skull sprayed across the concrete floor a split second before the man crumpled

exasperating

to the ground.

There was a blissful moment of relief where Robby thought, for just a second, it was over. Calder had finally come for him and everything would be okay. But the man emerging from the front of the barn wasn't Calder at all. It was his father.

"Hello, children."

thirty

CALDER

CALDER PARKED HIS TRUCK JUST BEFORE THE PRIVATE property sign. His truck was too loud to risk taking it any farther. He holstered his weapon before pulling an extra clip and his knife from the lock box in the truck's bed. He scanned for anything—sensors, tripwires, sentries. But there was nothing. Nobody. He carefully hopped the rusty gate that provided little protection should anybody choose to enter the property without permission. It was all too easy.

Calder didn't like the eerie silence. A place with this many people would be humming with activity with the sun still high in the cloudless blue sky. He

exasperating

followed the makeshift dirt road, always aware of the treeline on either side, listening and watching for any signs of life, but there was only the occasional rustling of the leaves when the wind blew.

As Calder rounded the bend in the road, the trees opened up to a large clearing with several brick buildings. He drew his weapon, releasing the safety and chambering a round. It didn't look so much like a farm as it did a compound or a makeshift military installation. That sent a shock of adrenaline through his system. Where was Robby? Was he okay? Was he still alive? The idea of finding Robby's limp and lifeless body made Calder stumble, but he shook the thought away, swallowing the lump in his throat. No. He'd already lost too much. He wouldn't lose Robby, too.

He made his way from building to building, looking inside and finding nothing. It was practically a ghost town. Jonestown. Calder scanned, looking for the biggest building. The one where a crazed cult leader might gather his flock for a final sacrament. He zeroed in on the large rudimentary building in the center of the compound, hoofing it double time to the side of it, grateful there were small windows along the edge that allowed him to peer inside.

Calder shivered as he noted the people on the other side of the glass. A hundred at least, all of them huddled together, some clutching toddlers and infants, as they all looked at each other with uncertainty. On the stage was a large yellow cooler the size of a beer keg, and two people filling paper cups and lining them along a table. Jesus. He really did want to kill all of these people. Shit. Where was Robby? He studied each face, but none of them were him or Rebecca. Had Samuel moved them somewhere else? Had he killed them already?

A hand settled on his arm, and he turned, jamming his gun into their ribcage, coming nose to nose with Connolly.

"At ease, killer. I'm assuming you didn't check your phone," Connolly said, nonplussed at the barrel poking against his massive frame. Connolly had a black eye and a busted lip but still grinned like, somehow, he was the one who'd come out on top. He wore camo pants tucked into military issue boots and a black t-shirt, his gun holstered under his left arm.

Calder caught Linc and Webster creeping towards them from the left. Calder relaxed a bit at their presence. "I have to find Robby and Rebecca."

"The only place we haven't searched is the barn," Linc said. "But you need to be aware of something."

"Yeah?" Calder prompted impatiently, eyes trained on the barn in the distance.

Linc rubbed the back of his neck with his free hand.

exasperating

"We're not the only visitors today. There's a dark blue sedan registered to Magnus Dei parked down the road, not too far from where we arrived."

"Robby's father? What the fuck is he doing here? Didn't he and Samuel part ways?" Calder asked.

It was Webster who answered. "Maybe not. I kept asking myself, 'Where would a hippy cult get the money to buy black market weapons?' They don't sell anything. They don't import or export anything. There had to be some kind of financial backer. That backer is Magnus Dei."

Calder shook his head. "What? But why?"

Webster shrugged. "The only people who know that are Jeb Shaw and our phony messiah over there." He pointed to the barn.

Calder sighed. "Can you de-escalate the situation in there?" he asked, pointing towards the group inside the building.

Connolly peered through the nearest window and snorted. "Yeah, I don't foresee a lot of pushback from this lot."

"I'm coming with you," Linc said, his tone leaving no room for argument.

Calder gave a stilted nod before jogging across the open field to the barn doors, which were sitting slightly ajar. He peered inside, his eyes attempting to adjust to the shadows after spending so much time in the sunlight. They could faintly hear voices coming from deep within. Linc gestured for them to breach the barn and separate so they could flank the group and use the hay bales for cover. Calder gave a single nod, then they both slipped inside. Calder was grateful for cement floors instead of aged wood, which might have given away their position.

His heart tripped when he finally got eyes on a living, breathing Robby. He stood with two young children crowded behind his back, fear etched along his face as he stared at something just out of range. Calder took two more steps, then stopped short when he saw Samuel's body on the ground, blood staining the dirt and hay that littered the flooring. There was a bullet hole in his forehead and a blood stain on his shirt that indicated he'd been shot twice or had sustained another injury. All thoughts of Samuel left him when he saw Jeb Shaw with a forty-four magnum Ruger Blackhawk trained on his son.

Calder almost would have laughed at the ridiculous weapon if he didn't know the damage a single shot could do. If Jeb Shaw pulled that trigger, Robby was dead in an instant. The look on his face told Calder that Robby was very much aware of the peril he was in.

"What are you even doing here?" Robby asked.

exasperating

It wasn't Jeb who answered, but Rebecca. "This is all my fault," she cried. "Before I came to you, I went to him. I'm the reason he showed back up in your life. I knew Samuel was losin' it, and I thought Father might be willin' to help, but he just sent me back to him."

Jeb shrugged. "A woman belongs to her husband, Rebecca. You know that. If a man can't trust his wife, he has nothing."

"So, you showed up at the police station that day, why?" Robby asked, voice wavering slightly.

Calder suspected he was trying to keep his father's attention off Rebecca. It seemed to work, at least for now.

"I was hoping to get you to come home before your sister found a way to escape again and managed to rope you into all of this. I did it to protect you. The church is your legacy."

Robby scoffed. "Then why did you send some man to my apartment to kill me?"

Jeb Shaw laughed. "Oh, that wasn't me either. Tell him, Rebecca. Tell him how you selfishly sent a dying man to break into your brother's home and sent him to his death."

Robby's gaze widened as he turned on his sister so Calder could no longer see his expression. "What? You sent that man after me? Why? What did I ever do to you?"

Rebecca started to cry, waving her hands as if she could erase it all. "It wasn't like that. I was trapped here. Samuel was starvin' me. He kept me tied up in here for two weeks. The only person I saw other than him was Dennis. He was new. He was dyin'. He came here hopin' for salvation, forgiveness for the things he'd done when he was leadin' a life of crime in Boston. He knew he'd made a mistake almost immediately. We talked when he'd bring me water twice a day and let me use the bathroom. After two weeks, he said he'd help. He's the one who got me the burner phone, and he's the one who agreed to get you a message. He tried to talk to you that night, the night you got arrested at the club, but he couldn't get anywhere near you and when he did, you just blew him off. He wasn't tryin' to kill you when he broke in…he was just tryin' to deliver a message…from me."

"I killed him," Robby mumbled. "I killed an innocent man."

"He was already dead," Rebecca cried. "He had pulmonary hypertension. It was fatal."

"Is that supposed to make it okay?" Robby snapped, back heaving.

She shook her head. "I'm sorry. I just needed help. Father's just tryin' to turn you against me. Ask him why he didn't seem at all shocked that Samuel was stockpiling weapons. Ask him. Where do you think he got the money?"

Robby whipped his head towards his father. "Why? Why would you help him after you worked so hard to distance yourself from him? Jesus, you gave him one of your children just to keep the church's precious name. Why would you bankroll his psychotic break?"

Jeb scoffed. "Why do you think? I only needed him to keep believing in this ridiculous notion of creating God's army long enough for him to amass enough evidence on the property to make sure he and this ridiculous hippie commune were taken out for good. Hell, why do you think the ATF already knew about this place? I'm the one who told them he was a danger. Once he was behind bars and this whole little band of sycophants disbanded, Magnus Dei would no longer live in the shadows and people would stop calling us a cult."

"So, you set him up? Did you know he planned to kill everybody?" Robby asked.

"Okay, I confess, that was not part of the plan, but it honestly couldn't have worked out any better. With no survivors left, this place will become nothing more than an urban legend, a footnote in the history books. Just another failed cult."

"What about all of us?" Robby asked, voice shaking. "You can't force us to drink poison, and nobody is going to believe Samuel blew his own head off with a different caliber gun after shooting himself in the stomach."

Robby put both hands on his hips, and that was when Calder saw it. A gun. Robby had a gun in his waistband. Calder's stomach lurched as a million scenarios played out in his head. Robby hated guns. He hated them. He'd said so. He hated violence and hitting people. If Robby went for the gun and his father shot him, that would be it. Game over. But Calder didn't have a clean shot. He locked eyes with Linc from across the barn, but he shook his head. Rebecca and Robby had inadvertently turned themselves into human shields. If he could only get one of them to step out of the way.

"Well since nobody will ever know I was here, I don't really care what they imagine the scenario is. I helped Samuel create this place. I know where every tunnel lies. I have been moving in and out of the compound unseen for months, and once I take care of you four, I'll use the tunnels to slip back out, and nobody will ever even know I was here."

Calder could feel the tension building, like a wire about to snap. He did the only thing he could think of. He stepped out of the darkness. "That's not entirely

exasperating

true," he said.

Jeb swung the gun at Calder. Robby's eyes went round, and he lunged for Calder, screaming, "No!"

Calder didn't even have time to say anything. He saw the flash of the muzzle, and then Robby was falling forward into Calder's arms, a look of surprise on his face that caused Calder's heart to stop. Two more rounds rang through the barn, and then Jeb fell to the floor, but Calder didn't care. He was only looking at Robby. Calder fell to the ground cradling Robby, holding his hand to the wound on the right side of his chest. "Don't you fucking die on me, angel. You hear me?"

Robby smiled, his pupils blown wide. "It's okay. It doesn't even really hurt much."

Those words sent ice water rushing through Calder's veins. He whipped his shirt off and stuffed it over the wound. "Call the paramedics!" he shouted. "I don't care if they have to get a fucking chopper out here!"

The two children were crying, and Rebecca was standing with her hands over her mouth, watching her brother bleed out. "Oh, God. Please help him."

From somewhere off in the distance, he heard Linc say, "Connolly, there's an emergency kit in my bag. Go get it and get back here immediately. Webster, get a medevac team and the cops out here *now*."

Calder just sat there, helpless, as Robby gazed up at him with this hazy sort of smile, like they were staring at each other on their wedding day instead of what was actually happening, which was Calder watching the life drain from Robby's eyes. "Stay with me, angel. You hear me? We've got plans. A whole life together. Don't you dare fucking close your eyes, just keep looking at me, okay?" Robby nodded, but his skin was chalk white, even his lips. "Don't die on me, angel. I love you. I'll give you anything you want. A ring. A kidney? A house full of kids and rescue animals. Anything." He looked over at Linc. "Where the fuck is the ambulance!" Connolly returned, and suddenly, they were trying to pull Robby from his arms. "No, stop."

"Get him!" Linc shouted, and Connolly grabbed Calder while Webster and Linc pulled Robby's shirt away. Calder almost vomited at the size of the wound in Robby's shoulder. The bullet had blown through muscle and tissue like paper.

Linc opened a small kit and grabbed something that looked like a syringe. He grimaced as he looked at Robby. "I'm not gonna lie, kid. This is gonna hurt like a bitch." He shoved something into the wound and Robby screamed like Linc was ripping his soul from his body. Calder fought to get free but Connolly was a tank compared to Calder. Connolly held him back as

exasperating

Linc slapped a dressing over the wound. "That should stop the bleeding until they can evacuate him to the hospital."

As soon as Linc stood, Connolly released Calder and he scooped Robby carefully into his lap. His eyes were wet and blood flecked his snowy white skin but he just smiled. "You promise?" he whispered.

"What?" Calder asked.

Robby gazed up at him, his breathing labored. "The kids, the animals…the ring. You promise?"

Calder nodded, sniffling, wiping at his tears as they fell onto Robby's cheeks. "Yes, angel. You just keep your eyes open and it's all yours. I swear it."

"Good," Robby managed, his laugh somewhat garbled. "You're so going to regret this bargain someday."

Calder shook his head. "Never. I'll never regret it."

"I love you," Robby said before giving a slow blink. "I'm so tired."

"Me too, angel, but you gotta stay awake."

"Don't be mad," Robby said just before his eyes slipped shut.

"No. Come on, angel." He shook Robby. "Wake up. Wake up."

Paramedics burst through the door, and suddenly, Calder was pushed to the side, forced to stand there and watch helplessly as Robby slipped away from him. All he could do was pray over and over again.

"Please don't take him from me."

epilogue

ROBBY

SUNDAYS AT THE FARM WERE, BY FAR, THEIR BUSIEST days. Down the hall, towards the kitchen, there was the sound of voices chatting and dishes clattering and footsteps bounding up and down the stairs. Robby smiled as he stood before the mirror, attempting to tie his tie. Even twelve months after his father shot him, Robby only had limited mobility in his right arm, which forced him to attempt to do almost everything left-handed, but he refused to be ungrateful. He was alive. He was *more* than alive.

He was alive and blissfully happy.

He felt the weight of Calder's stare a split second

before he looked up to catch his gaze in the mirror. He was already dressed for church, minus his suit jacket, which Robby imagined was somewhere thrown over a chair. He bit his lip, raking his gaze over Calder from head to toe. His husband was still the most beautiful man he'd ever seen. Calder came to stand behind him. "Here, let me," he said, gently batting Robby's hands away.

Robby leaned back into him, letting the warmth of Calder's body seep into his back as Calder took care of him, something it seemed he'd been doing pretty much since the moment they'd met. Robby liked to think he took care of Calder, too, at least in all the ways that mattered. "Thank you," he said, smiling at Calder in the reflection.

"Anything for you, angel. You know that." Calder finished, nodding at his handiwork, before turning Robby in his arms, pulling him back towards the bed and sitting on the mattress, tugging him down into his lap. "Are you nervous?" he asked.

His pulse skittered at Calder's question. "I'd be lying if I said no. But I suppose giving a sermon isn't all that different from learning my lines. Except, I never had to write my own lines before and I could ignore a bad review, but I can't ignore a bad grade."

Seminary school was far more difficult than Robby

exasperating

had ever imagined, but he felt called to it. The moment he'd made his decision, he'd felt at peace, and Calder had never questioned his decision. He'd only worried about the possibility of the school rejecting Robby's application due to him being an out gay man married to another man. But, it turned out, the Episcopal church allowed both women and gay married men as priests.

Calder cupped his face in his hands. "You're going to be amazing. You've got this. You've yet to get so much as an A minus in any class you've attempted."

Did he have it? This was the only part of his life where Robby found himself questioning his abilities. He'd used his savings to buy the farm from his father's estate. The only people surprised by his father being the farm's financial backer after everything that happened had been the media and possibly the ATF.

Transitioning from Hollywood to life at the farm wasn't as hard as Robby had imagined it might be. After the circus that had ensued following the death of his father and Samuel, the country seemed peaceful. It had been a nice place to recuperate from his gunshot wound.

"There's a first time for everything," Robby reminded him, wrapping his arms around Calder's neck and wincing.

"Shoulder bothering you today, angel?"

Robby nodded. "Ezra accidentally kicked me there yesterday."

Calder shook his head. "That boy is a menace."

Robby smiled ruefully. "Who taught him what a roundhouse kick was again?"

Calder snickered. "Yeah, yeah, yeah. But I also told him that we don't roundhouse kick people for fun."

There was a bang against the door frame, and then Ezra was standing before them. "But it wasn't for fun, Uncle Calder. It was a battle to the death. I had to defend my kingdom from the one-armed man."

"That would be me," Robby supplied helpfully.

Calder leveled a look at Ezra. Robby called it his Daddy look, though that word took on an entirely different context when Calder leveled that look at Robby. "Have you forgotten our talk about the difference between real and make believe?"

Ezra dropped his head. "No, sir."

"Good. Are Beau and your mama almost ready?" Calder asked.

"Yeah, but Mama's mad cause she's got luggage under her eyes and it's all Delilah's fault."

Robby and Calder laughed. "Are you sure she didn't say bags under her eyes?"

"How am I supposed to know?" he asked before darting off as quickly as he'd arrived.

exasperating

Once Calder and Robby bought the farm, they set about changing everything. They'd leveled the old buildings and built two rather enormous houses on the property. One for Rebecca and her librarian friend, Beau, who they learned was much more than just her friend when she'd shown up with tears in her eyes, a huge smile on her face, and a white stick with a pink plus sign in her hand. Delilah was born just in time to settle nicely into Beau and Rebecca's new house.

Rebecca breezed into the room, looking fresh as a daisy, without so much as a smudge beneath her eyes, Delilah on her hip. "How do I look?" she asked, spinning in a dress that wrapped around her middle and hid her slight postpartum bump.

"Gorgeous, as always," Calder said, giving her a huge grin.

She rolled her eyes. "You're ridiculous. Don't forget to trim your beard. We have that interview with the papers before church service, and nobody's goin' to trust any of us with their children if you look like some beatnik ragamuffin artist."

"But I am a beatnik ragamuffin artist," Calder said.

She gave a put-upon sigh. "I can't with you two today. Save all this lovey-dovey stuff for tonight when we don't have a million things to do. Everybody's at the breakfast table already, and we have to leave in forty-five minutes."

Calder captured Robby's mouth in a kiss. "Your sister is awfully bossy."

"She's always been bossy, but at least now, she's using her powers for good instead of evil."

Calder narrowed his gaze. "Is she, though?"

Robby slapped Calder's arm playfully. "Yes. Now, get up, sexy. We need to go eat breakfast."

Robby stood, but Calder snatched him once more, this time bringing him down to straddle his thighs. "How can I eat breakfast when the only thing I'm hungry for is right here?"

Robby flushed to the tips of his ears. How did this man still get to him over the simplest of compliments? He prayed he never tired of hearing Calder say things like that. He leaned in, nuzzling his nose against Calder's throat, kissing his way to his ear. "Didn't you get enough this morning? My sister isn't the only one with bags under her eyes. I could open my own luggage store with these babies." He pointed towards his eyes.

"I'm twice your age. I should be the tired one, trying to keep up with you and your twenty-two-year-old recovery time."

"Hey, I'm not the one who wanted to have sex in the shower this morning."

exasperating

Calder growled against Robby's cheek. "No, but you were the one begging me to fuck you up against the wall last night. Do you know how much effort that takes at my age?" Calder joked, gripping Robby's ass and dragging him closer so he could feel Calder's semi-hard length against him.

Robby whined but then forced himself to shake his head. "No. Nope. We are not doing this. You are not going to make me horny right before I have to give a graded sermon in front of an entire congregation."

"That's what the pulpit is for. Besides, you're the one who decided to become a preacher. It's not my fault I can't keep my hands off you. Besides, we're married. Even Jesus approves."

Robby scoffed. "My sister is right. You are ridiculous. Jesus does not approve of church boners."

Calder pouted. "You're no fun."

"Oh, my God, will you two get in here and eat your breakfast? You have the rest of your lives for whatever it is y'all are doin' in there," Rebecca shouted from the kitchen.

Robby sighed. "To be continued."

Calder stood with Robby still in his lap before gently setting him on his feet.

By the time they made it to the table, they had no choice but to scarf down breakfast as the camera crew had already arrived to begin setting up outside. Robby had butterflies in his stomach as he watched Calder and Rebecca go through hair and makeup, and Rebecca bitched the entire time about how Calder had not, in fact, trimmed his beard.

Once they were mic'd, the reporter began the interview. Robby didn't participate. That part of his life was over. Calder and Rebecca could be the public face of the foundation—Robby was content to put in the work behind the scenes. He had no interest in spotlights anymore.

Once the pleasantries were over, the reporter began questioning them about the real reason for the interview. "Tell us the purpose of the buildings behind us," she prompted.

Rebecca pointed to the white wooden signs with their tidy raised letters. "That's Jennifer's Place, and this one over here is Megan's Place."

"Jennifer's Place is a non-profit transitional housing program for children who've been rescued from human trafficking rings. They'll receive medical care and counseling and a safe and nurturing environment while they recover before returning to their parents or entering the adoption system," Calder said, delivering the information with that smooth Texas drawl that still did funny things to Robby's insides.

exasperating

Rebecca flawlessly picked up where Calder ended. "Megan's Place aims to provide similar programs for those over the age of eighteen who need to be able to support themselves and learn a job skill while receivin' the counseling and care they need."

"Now, Mr. Seton, we're told this is a very personal project for you. You've named these two buildings after two women who lost their lives before they could escape a trafficking ring, one of which was your own sister. How do you think your sister would feel about all this?" She gestured around her.

Calder swallowed hard, floundering. Robby's heart squeezed. Calder still had a hard time talking about Megan. Robby sighed in relief as Rebecca swooped in. "I think she'd be insanely proud of him and very honored."

"I'm certain she would," the reporter said with just the right amount of phony sympathy. "Your husband, Robby Shaw, excuse me, Robby Seton, has left Hollywood for seminary school. Is Magnus Dei affiliated with your program? Does he have plans to take over his father's church?"

Calder's voice took on a stern tone. "Magnus Dei is no longer a thing. It died when Jeb Shaw died. Robby is working on creating a relationship with his estranged mother and siblings but asks that you respect their privacy regarding these matters. On the matter of faith, my husband is going to seminary school because he believes that Jesus's message is very clear. Love everybody. Robby wants to remind people of that message. We're lucky that there's a church that not only embraces these doctrines but embraces this program. The only church affiliated with our foundation is Prince of Peace Episcopal Church." Calder looked pointedly at his watch. "Speaking of which, Robby is giving his first sermon in about thirty minutes and he cannot be late."

Robby swallowed the lump in his throat. Even now, Calder was still so protective of him.

"Thank you so much for your time," the reporter said, reaching out to shake their hands.

"Thank you," Calder and Rebecca said simultaneously.

"Sorry she ambushed you with the Magnus Dei crap," Robby said as they made their way towards the church in Calder's truck, Robby in the middle with his head resting on Calder's shoulder.

"It ain't no thing, angel face. None of those people matter. In a year, nobody will remember anything about cults or crazy suicidal megalomaniacs. They'll only know about the work we do here and the people we help, and we'll be too busy raising our own kids

exasperating

and taking in every stray you find of both the two and four-legged variety."

"Hard to believe all of this started with a shower," Robby mused.

"Nah, baby. All of this started the minute I saw you in that conference room chair, looking like the loneliest boy in the world."

Robby looked up. "I think I was, you know. The loneliest boy. Before you."

Calder took his eyes off the road to drop a kiss on Robby's forehead. "I think I was, too…before you. But this is one hell of an after we've made for ourselves."

It really, really was.

THE END

DEAR READER,

THANK YOU SO MUCH for reading *Exasperating*, Book 3 in my Elite Protection Services Series. I hope you loved reading this book as much as I loved writing it. The fourth book in the series, *Infuriating*, is available now on Amazon.

If you've read my books before, you have probably come to realize that I have an addiction to writing about the psyche and exactly how both nature and nurture often play a part in who a person becomes. I spent years working as an RN in a psychiatric hospital, most of those years I spent with children aged anywhere from five to eighteen. It took a big toll on me and my own mental health, which is why writing these characters has become my own form of therapy. While sociopathic bodyguards and megalomaniacal cult leaders are all works of fiction, my heroes and villains are all drawn from real people who I encountered in my time as a nurse.

Wyatt, Elijah, and Robby are all grown-up versions

of kids who I only met for a brief time, but to whom, for my own peace of mind, I needed to give a happy ending they may or may not have gotten in real life. As for the villains, I learned a long time ago, that sadly, it's the people closest to you who often do the most damage. This is all a rather maudlin way of saying thank you for reading my books and loving my characters and allowing me to use these stories as my own therapy sessions.

If you guys are really loving the books, please consider joining my Facebook reader group, ONLEY'S OUBLIETTE, and signing up for my newsletter on my website so you can stay up to date on freebies, release dates, teasers and more. You can also always hit me up on my social media. I love talking to readers.

Finally, if you did love this book (or even if you didn't. Eek!) it would be amazing if you could take a minute to review it. Reviews are like gold for authors.

Thank you again for reading.

ABOUT THE AUTHOR

ONLEY JAMES is the pen name of YA author, Martina McAtee, who lives in Central Florida with her children, her pitbull, her weiner dog, and an ever-growing collection of shady looking cats. She splits her time between writing YA LGBT paranormal romances and writing adult m/m romances.

When not at her desk, you can find her mainlining Starbucks refreshers, whining about how much she has to do, and avoiding the things she has to do by binge-watching unhealthy amounts of television in one sitting. She loves ghost stories, true crime documentaries, obsessively scrolling social media, and writing kinky, snarky books about men who fall in love with other men.

Find her online at:
WWW.ONLEYJAMES.COM

Printed in Great Britain
by Amazon